Seeking Whom He May Devour

Seeking Whom He May Devour

Translated from the French by
David Bellos

Fred Vargas

W F HOWES LTD

This large print edition published in 2005 by
W F Howes Ltd
Units 6/7, Victoria Mills, Fowke Street
Rothley, Leicester LE7 7PJ

1 3 5 7 9 10 8 6 4 2

First published in the United Kingdom in 2004
by The Harvill Press

A CIP catalogue record for this book is available
from the British Library

ISBN 1 84505 825 9

Typeset by Palimpsest Book Production Limited,
Polmont, Stirlingshire
Printed and bound in Great Britain
by Antony Rowe Ltd, Chippenham, Wilts.

TRANSLATOR'S NOTE

There are two principal organisations ensuring law enforcement in modern France. The *police nationale* operates in cities, whereas the *gendarmerie* is responsible for smaller towns and the countryside. Officers of the *police nationale* – such as Jean-Baptiste Adamsberg – are civil servants, answering ultimately to the Minister of the Interior; *gendarmes*, on the other hand, have military status and are garrisoned in places other than their home towns. *Flics* and *gendarmes* necessarily co-operate on many criminal cases, but do not always overcome mutual rivalry and mistrust.

CHAPTER 1

On Tuesday, four sheep were killed at Ventebrune in the French Alps. On Thursday, nine were lost at Pierrefort. 'It's the wolves,' a local said. 'They're coming down to eat us all up.'

The other man drained his glass, then raised his hand. '*A* wolf, Pierrot my lad. It's *a* wolf. A beast such as you have never clapped eyes on before. Coming down, as you say, to eat us all up.'

CHAPTER 2

Two men were lying prone in the under-growth.

'You don't reckon you're gonna teach me how to do my job, do you?' said one.

'Don't reckon anything,' said the other. Tall, with long, fair hair. Name of Johnstone. Lawrence Donald Johnstone.

They lay quite still, gripping their binoculars, observing a pair of wolves. It was ten in the morning. The sun was scorching their backs.

'That one is Marcus,' Johnstone said. 'He's come back.'

His companion shook his head. A short, swarthy, rather pig-headed local. He had been keeping watch over the wolves in the Mercantour National Park for six years. Name of Jean Mercier.

'That's Sibellius,' he muttered.

'Sibellius is much larger. Hasn't got that yellow tuft at the neck.'

Jean Mercier was needled, so he reset his binoculars, brought the viewfinder once more into focus, and looked closely at the male wolf prowling round his family lair and occasionally sniffing the wind, some three hundred metres to the east of their hide. They were near, much too near, it would be better to pull back, but Johnstone wanted to get one or two good shots at any cost. That's why he was there – to film wolves. Then he had to go back to Canada with his documentary in the can. But he had been putting off going back for six months, for reasons that were not entirely clear. To tell the truth, the Canadian was rooting in. Mercier knew why. Lawrence Donald Johnstone, celebrated connoisseur of Canadian grizzly bears, had fallen in love with a handful of European wolves. And he could not make up his mind to say so. In any case, the Canadian spoke as few words as he could get away with.

'Came back in the spring,' Johnstone muttered. 'Started a family. But I can't see who the she-wolf is.'

'That's Proserpine,' whispered Mercier. 'Out of Janus and Juno, third generation.'

'Alongside Marcus.'

'Alongside Marcus,' Mercier agreed, after a pause. 'And what's for sure is that there are brand-new cubs.'

'Good.'

'Excellent.'

'How many?'

'Too soon to say.'

Mercier jotted some notes on a pad attached to his belt, took a drink from his gourd, and got back into position without snapping a twig. Johnstone put down his binoculars, wiped the sweat off his face. He pulled over his camera, focused on Marcus and smiled as he switched it on. He had spent fifteen years among the grizzlies, the caribou and the wolves of Canada, wandering alone across the vast preserves to watch, record and film, occasionally stretching out a hand to the oldest of his untamed friends. Not creatures to be taken lightly. There'd been Joan, an old female grizzly, who'd come at him, her head down, to get a good scratch of her coat. And Johnstone had never imagined that Europe – so pinched, so wasted and tamed – could have anything of interest to offer him. He had not taken on this documentary job in the Mercantour Range very gladly. But what was he going to do?

And when it came to the crunch, he'd kept putting off going home, he was dragging out his stay in this neck of the mountain. He was dragging his feet, to be blunt. He was hanging around for the sake of these European wolves with their paltry grey coats, no more than poor panting cousins of those thick-coated, brightly coloured Arctic beasts that deserved all his affection, or so he reckoned. He was hanging around for the sake of the swarming insects, the rivulets of sweat, the charred undergrowth and the crackling heat of the Mediterranean lands. 'Just you stick around, you haven't seen the half of it,' Mercier would tell him rather pompously, with the proud manner of a hard-baked habitué and survivor of solar onslaught. 'This is only June.'

4

And he was hanging around, let's face it, for Camille.

Round here they called it 'rooting in'.

'I don't hold it against you', Mercier had said to him, quite seriously, 'but it's better you know: you're rooting in.'

'OK then, now I know,' Johnstone had replied.

He stopped the camera, put it down gently on his rucksack and shaded it with a white canvas sheet. Young Marcus had gone off out of sight, heading north.

'Gone to hunt before it gets really hot,' Mercier observed.

Johnstone sprinkled water on his face, dampened his hat, took a dozen sips. Good Lord, what a sun. Never known anything so hellish.

'Three cubs at least,' Mercier mumbled.

'I'm being fried alive,' Johnstone said, grimacing as he passed a hand over his shoulder.

'Just you wait. You haven't seen the half of it.'

CHAPTER 3

*C*ommissaire Jean-Baptiste Adamsberg poured the pasta from the pan into the colander, watched distractedly as the water drained off, then dumped the whole lot on a plate. With grated cheese and tomato sauce, that would do fine for tonight. He'd come home late after interrogating a cretin of a youth for hours on end, until eleven. Adamsberg was slow in any case. He did not like to rush things or people, however cretinous they might be. He especially did not like to rush himself. The television was on with the volume set low, nothing but wars, wars, and more wars. He ferreted about in the cutlery drawer, making all sorts of noise, found a fork, and stood in front of the set.

> *. . . wolves in the Mercantour National Park have once again gone on the attack in a locality in the department of the Alpes-Maritimes that had up to now been spared. This time, people are talking of an animal of unusual size. Truth or legend? To find out, our special . . .*

6

Adamsberg moved cautiously towards the TV, plate in hand, tiptoeing as if he did not want to frighten the announcer. One false movement from Adamsberg and the guy might fly from the screen without finishing the terrific wolf story he'd just begun. He turned up the sound and stepped back. Adamsberg was fond of wolves, the way you can be fond of your nightmares. His whole childhood in the Pyrenees had been shrouded in old folks' accounts of the saga of the last wild wolves in France. When he walked the mountain paths in the dark, at the age of nine, when his father sent him out to gather kindling – *no arguing, now* – he used to think he could see yellow eyes trained on him all along the way. *Them eyes, sonny boy, them wolves' eyes, they burn bright in the night, they do. Bright as a flaming brand.*

Nowadays when he went back down to those parts, to his mountain home, he retraced the same paths in the pitch dark. That's what makes human beings so hopeless, really. They cling to the worst things they've known.

He had heard it said – a few years back – that some wolves from the Abruzzi had crossed the Alps into France. Just a gang of tearaways, in a manner of speaking. Boozers on a night out. A friendly raid, a symbolic return, all hail and welcome to you three moth-eaten beasts from the Abruzzi. Ciao, fellas. Since when, he assumed, some guys had been pampering the predators on the sheltered marl of the Mercantour National Park, and the wolves had lunched on fresh lamb from time to time. But he had not seen such pictures before. So were those good lads from the Abruzzi suddenly getting violent? Adamsberg ate his pasta in silence as he watched sequences of dismembered sheep, bloodied soil, the gnarled face of a shepherd, and the stained carcass of one sheep that had been torn to pieces lying on meadow grass. The camera gave morbidly indulgent close-ups of the carnage, and the reporter plied the locals with leading questions, fanning the flames of anger among the country folk. They had edited into the news report shots of snarling wolves' snouts lifted from old documentaries, more probably about the Balkans than about the Alps. It was enough to make you think that the whole hinterland of Nice was reeling under the onslaught of packs of wild beasts while aged shepherds stood their ground with pride, looking the enemy in the eye. *They burn bright in the night, they do, bright as a flaming brand.*

But the facts were there. About thirty recorded wolves in the Mercantour, plus maybe a dozen lost cubs, along with feral dogs that were scarcely less threatening. Hundreds of sheep killed last season within a radius of ten kilometres around the Mercantour. These facts weren't aired in Paris because no-one in Paris gave a damn about stories of wolves and lambs, and Adamsberg was stupefied when he heard the figures. Today's two

8

savagings in the canton of Auniers had re-awakened the conflict.

A vet appeared on screen, pointing in a measured and professional manner at a gaping wound. No, there was not the slightest doubt about it, this is the bite of the upper jaw, fourth premolar on the right-hand side, see, and here, in front, this is the right-hand incisor, look here, and here, and on the underside, here. And do you see how far apart they are? These are the jaws of a very large canine.

'Would you say it was a wolf, doctor?'

'Either that or a very large dog.'

'Or a very big wolf?'

Then another close-up of a defiant shepherd. Since those filthy predators had begun stuffing their bellies four years ago with the blessing of the folk up in Paris he had never seen wounds like these. Never. Fangs as big as your hand. The hill farmer gestured towards the mountains on the far horizon. It's on the prowl, right up there. A monster such as you have never seen before. They can snigger all they like, them folk in Paris, but they'll stop laughing pretty sharpish when they set their eyes on it.

Adamsberg watched in fascination as he stood eating the last of his cold pasta. The news anchor moved on to the next report. Wars.

Commissaire Adamsberg sat down slowly and put his plate on the floor. Good lord, those Mercantour wolves. The innocent little pack they'd started with had done a fair bit of growing. It had expanded its hunting ground canton by canton. Now it had overstepped the borders of the department of Alpes-Maritimes. And of the forty or so wolves up there, how many were predators? Did they hunt in packs? Or in pairs? Or was there just one lone wolf doing the damage? Yes, that's the way it was in stories – a cruel and lonesome rogue, keeping his hindquarters low over his grey hind paws, slithering up to the village in the dark. A large beast. The Monster of Mercantour. And children asleep in the houses. Adamsberg closed his eyes. *They burn bright, my boy. Bright as a flaming brand.*

CHAPTER 4

Lawrence Donald Johnstone did not go back down to the village until half past eleven on Friday evening.

Between one and four in the afternoon the men of the Mercantour National Park took a long break, to read or to sleep, in the shade of one of the abandoned dry-stone dwellings dotted around the mountainside. Johnstone had taken possession of a disused sheepfold not far from the young Marcus's new territory. He'd had to clean out the droppings, but they were so old that they hardly had any smell left in them. But even so it had to be done, on principle. The tall Canadian was more accustomed to washing himself from the waist up with fistfuls of snow than to wallowing in sheep shit with his skin all gluey with stale sweat, and he found the French a thoroughly filthy lot. On his swift transit through Paris he had sniffed the heavy odours of piss and sweat overlaid with garlic and wine. But it was in Paris that he had met Camille, so Paris was forgiven. As was the overheated Mercantour and the village of Saint-Victor-du-Mont where he had provisionally shacked up with her. But they

11

were a filthy lot nonetheless, especially the men. He could not get used to black fingernails, matted hair, and shapeless, dirty grey T-shirts.

In his cleaned-up old sheepfold, Johnstone would settle himself every afternoon on a big canvas groundsheet laid on the bare, hard-dried earthen floor. He would sort his notes, go over the morning's shots, prepare for the evening watch. For the last few weeks an old wolf nearing the end of his life – a venerable loner of about fifteen called Augustus – had been hunting on Mont Mounier. He only ever came out of his lair in the cool evening air and Johnstone did not want to miss him. The old paterfamilias was not hunting really, more trying to survive. He was getting so weak he missed even easy prey. Johnstone wondered how much longer the old fellow would hold out, and how it would end. And how long he himself would hold out before he went to poach some meat for old Augustus, in defiance of Park law, which required beasts to cope and die on their own as at the dawn of time. But if Johnstone brought Augustus a hare to eat, that wouldn't upset the balance of the world – or would it? Whatever the rights and wrongs of it, he would have to do it without the slightest hint to his French colleagues. They were persuaded that giving a beast a helping hand softened it up and distorted the laws of Nature. Sure, but Augustus had already gone soft, and the laws of Nature had long been in shreds. So what difference would it make?

12

Then, after downing his water, bread and salami, Johnstone stretched out on the ground in the shade, with his hands clasped under his head, and thought of Camille, her body and her smile. Camille wore perfume, but what was quite special about her was an unbelievable grace that sent shock waves through your hands, your guts and your lips. Johnstone had never dreamed that he would quiver for a woman so dark, with straight black hair cut short at the back, who looked like Cleopatra. Funny thing, he thought, old Cleo's been dead two thousand years, but she's still the archetype for all clear-skinned, fine-necked, straight-nosed and dark-haired beauties. Quite a girl she must have been, old Cleo. But to tell the truth, he did not know much about Queen Cleopatra and hardly more about Camille, except that she wasn't a royal and earned her living alternately as a musician and as a plumber.

Then he had to drop these mental images that were stopping him from getting any rest, and he concentrated on the clatter of the insects. The little fellows were incredibly energetic. The other day, on the lower slopes, Mercier had shown Johnstone something he had never seen before – a cicada. The size of a fingernail, making lots of noise for no very good reason. Johnstone preferred to live in silence.

He'd annoyed Mercier this morning. But joking aside, it really had been Marcus. No doubt about it.

Marcus with the yellow tuft around his neck. He was a really promising wolf. Lean, persistent, and hungry. Johnstone suspected him of having eaten a fair flock of lambs last autumn in the area around Trévaux. That had been unabashed slaughter, with blood all over the grass and dozens of mangled carcasses – the kind of show that made the wildlife refuge staff despair. Though their financial losses were made good, the hill farmers got angry and brought in attack dogs, and in December there had almost been a mass hunt. But after the winter wolf packs had broken up at the end of February, things had calmed down. Peace.

Johnstone was on the side of the wolves. He reckoned that the bold beasts honoured the little land of France by crossing over the Alps like proud ghosts from the distant past. No way could you let them get shot by pint-sized, sun-baked humans. But like all nomadic hunters the Canadian was cautious by nature. Down in the village he never talked about the wolves. He kept quiet, obeying the lesson his father had taught him: 'If you want to stay free, keep your mouth shut.'

Johnstone had not been down to Saint-Victor-du-Mont for five days. He had warned Camille that he would be away until Thursday, using his night-vision camera to keep watch on noble Augustus desperately seeking prey in the dark. But as the old wolf had still failed to catch anything by Thursday Johnstone gave in and extended his vigil by one more night so as to find something

14

for the poor creature to eat. He had caught two rabbits in their burrow, slit their throats with his knife, and left the bodies on one of Augustus's tracks. He hid himself under bracken, wrapped in an oilcloth that was supposed to stop his human scent from escaping, and waited anxiously for the starving animal.

Now he was whistling as he walked through Saint-Victor, mightily relieved. The old fellow had come, and had eaten.

Camille was a night bird, so when Johnstone opened the door there she still was, with furrowed brow and her mouth half-open, hunched over the keyboard, concentrating on what she could hear through her headphones, with her fingers darting among the notes, hovering over them every now and again. Camille was never so beautiful as when she was concentrating on her work or on love. Johnstone put down his rucksack, sat at the table, and watched her for a while. Camille was shut away from the world and unaware of any noise because of her headphones, and she was now scribbling on manuscript paper. Johnstone knew she was making the music track for a romantic soap in twelve episodes with a deadline in November. The production was a dreadful mess, she'd said. And it was a big job, too. Johnstone did not like talking shop into the small hours. You got on with your work and that was that. That's what really mattered.

He crossed behind her, looked at the bare nape of her neck beneath her short-cut hair, gave it a quick kiss, mustn't disturb Camille when she was working, even if he'd been away for five days, he knew that better than anyone. She carried on at the keyboard for another twenty minutes then took off her headphones and came to sit with him at the table. Johnstone played back the shots of Augustus devouring the rabbits and passed her the viewfinder.

'It's the old fellow tucking in,' he explained.

'You can see he's still going,' Camille said as she squinted into the monitor.

'I slipped him the meat,' Johnstone said, pursing his lips.

Camille stroked the Canadian's fair hair, still looking into the camcorder.

'Johnstone,' she said, 'things are astir. Be prepared to defend them.'

Johnstone queried Camille in his usual way, an interrogative thrust of his jaw.

'On Tuesday they found four sheep savaged at Ventebrune, and yesterday morning nine more torn to shreds at Pierrefort.'

'Holy Moses,' Johnstone whispered. 'Jesus Christ.'

'They've never come so far down before.'

'There's more of them.'

'Julien told me. It got onto the news, it's becoming a national story. The hill farmers have said they'll give the Italian wolves such trouble as to make them wish they were vegetarians.'

'Jesus Christ,' Johnstone said again. 'Fuck that.'

He glanced at his watch, switched off the camcorder, and with a worried look switched on the portable TV which was on a tea chest in the corner.

'That's not the worst of it,' Camille added.

Johnstone turned to her with chin raised.

'They're saying that this time it's not an ordinary animal.'

'Not ordinary?'

'A different kind of beast. Bigger. A force of nature, with a monster's jaw. Abnormal, like. In a word, a ghoul.'

'Pull the other one.'

'That's what they're saying.'

Johnstone was stunned. He shook his blond locks.

'Your bloody backward country', he said after a pause, 'is populated by nothing but bird-brained yokels.'

He zapped from channel to channel looking for a newsflash. Camille bit her lip, sat cross-legged on the floor in her boots and huddled up to Johnstone. The wolves were all going to get it in the neck. Old Augustus included.

CHAPTER 5

Johnstone spent the weekend collecting the local newspapers, scouring the news, and going down to the café in the village.

'Don't go,' Camille pleaded. 'They'll tackle you.'

'Why would they do that?' Johnstone asked, with the sulky expression he always put on when he was worried. 'The wolves are theirs.'

'No, they're not. Folk round here reckon the wolves are urban mascots put among their flocks by people up in Paris.'

'I'm not from Paris.'

'But you look after the wolves.'

'I look after grizzly bears. That's what my job is. Grizzlies.'

'And what about Augustus?'

'Augustus is different. Respect the weak, honour thy elders. Nobody left to look out for him but me.'

Johnstone was not very good with words. He preferred to use gestures, grins and grimaces to express himself, like all hunters and divers skilled in making themselves understood without speaking. The hardest for him were the beginnings and ends

18

of sentences. Most often he uttered only the middle bits, more or less audibly, blatantly hoping that someone else would provide the missing parts and complete his labours for him. Perhaps he had sought his Arctic solitude to get away from human chatter; perhaps his long sojourn in the icy wastes had robbed him of a taste for words – absence of function unmaking the faculty; but whichever way it had come about, he spoke as little as he could, with his eyes to the ground, shielded by blond hair falling forward in a fringe.

Camille, who scattered words with cheerful abandon, had found it hard to get used to such sparse communication. Hard, but also comforting. She'd spoken far too much these past three years, all to no avail, and she had grown to be quite sick of it. The silently smiling Canadian thus afforded her an unexpected resting place where she could cleanse herself of bad habits – notably of her indulgence in argument and persuasion, by far the most obnoxious habits she had ever had. Camille could not altogether abandon the profoundly entertaining world of words, but she could at least cast off the great mental machinery that she'd formerly applied to convincing other people. Like some worn-out and disused leviathan it now lay rusting in a corner of her mind, with the wheels of its logic and the mirrors of its metaphors peeling off one by one like so many bits of scrap. Nowadays, with a man who was nothing but gestures and silence, who went on his way without asking anybody's advice and who wasn't at all looking for an explanation of life's mysteries, Camille could relax and clear out her head, as if she was sweeping piles of junk out of an attic.

She jotted a line of music on her manuscript book.

'If you don't give a damn for them, for the wolves that is', she asked, 'why did you bother to come here?'

Johnstone paced around the little room with its closed wooden shutters. Hands clasped behind his back he strode from one corner to the other, crushing a few loose floor-tiles beneath his weight, with the hair on his head brushing the main beam. These Alpine shacks had not been designed for full-sized Canadians. Camille's left hand was running over the keyboard trying to find the right tempo.

'To know which one it is,' he said. 'Which wolf.'

Camille turned from the keyboard to face him.

'Which *one* it is? So you agree with them? That there's only one?'

'Often hunt solo. Need to see the wounds.'

'Where are the sheep?'

'In cold store. The butcher's been keeping them.'

'Is he going to sell them?'

Johnstone smiled as he shook his head.

'No. "You don't eat dead meat", is what he said. It's for the post-mortem.'

Camille pondered with a finger on her lips. She had not thought about identifying the animal.

She did not believe the rumours about an outsize beast. It was wolves, that's all it was. But for Johnstone, obviously, the assailants might have their own faces, muzzles, and names.

'So which one is it? Do you know?'

Johnstone shrugged his massive shoulders and made a questioning movement with his hands.

'The injuries,' he repeated.

'What will they tell you?'

'Size. Sex. With lots of luck.'

'Which one are you expecting it to be?'

Johnstone put his hands over his face.

'Big Sibellius,' he spluttered through clenched teeth, as if he was informing on a friend. 'Lost his hunting ground. To Marcus, a young tearaway. Must be in a foul mood. Not seen the boy for weeks. Sibellius is a tough guy, real tough. Jesus. Could have established a new territory for himself.'

Camille got up and put her arms around him.

'And if it is Sibellius, what can you do about it?'

'Sedative dart, chuck him into the van, drive him back to the Abruzzi.'

'What about the Italians?'

'They're different. Proud of their wildlife.'

Camille stretched up to brush Johnstone's lips. He bent his knees, clasped Camille by the waist and lifted her. Why should he bother about a bloody wolf when he could stay his whole life long in this little room with Camille?

'I'm coming down,' he said.

★   ★   ★

At the café there was some pretty rough parlaying before they finally agreed to take Johnstone to the cold store. The 'trapper', as he was known around here – because they assumed that anyone who'd hung around Canadian forests could only be a trapper – was now seen as some kind of traitor. They did not say it outright. They did not dare. Because they were aware that they were going to need him, for his knowledge, and for his sheer strength. A hulk that size was not to be dismissed in so small a village. Especially a man who could stand up to grizzlies. Wolves would be child's play for a man like that, right? As a result it wasn't obvious on which side the trapper should be placed, whether you could talk to him or not. Not that it really made a great deal of difference, since the trapper himself never talked back.

Under the watchful eye of Sylvain the butcher and Gerrot the carpenter, Johnstone inspected the savaged carcasses, one missing a foot, another one minus a piece of shoulder.

'Not clear, these marks,' he muttered. 'They moved.'

He gestured to the carpenter that he needed a tape measure. Gerrot handed it to him without a word. Johnstone measured, pondered, measured again. Then he stood up, and at a wave of his hand the butcher took the carcasses back into the cold store, slammed shut the heavy white door and turned the handle.

'What's the answer?' Sylvain asked.

'Same culprit. I think.'

'A big animal?'

'A fine male. That much is for sure.'

In the evening there were still fifteen or so locals hanging around the square, in small knots around the central fountain. They were putting off going home to bed. In a way, and without admitting it, they had already started to stand guard. An armed vigil. Men like that. Johnstone went over to Gerrot, who was sitting on his own on a stone bench, staring at the toes of his heavy boots, as if lost in a dream. Unless he was just looking at his boots without dreaming. The carpenter was a sensible man, not much given to violence or to chatter, and Johnstone respected him.

'Tomorrow', Gerrot began, 'are you going back up into the Mercantour?'

Johnstone nodded.

'You going to identify the wolves?'

'Sure, with the team. The others must have started already.'

'Do you know which one it is? Any idea?'

Johnstone scowled. 'Could be a new one.'

'Why? What's bothering you?'

'The size.'

'Big?'

'Much too big. Very highly developed jaw.'

Gerrot leaned his elbows on his knees and squinted up at the Canadian. 'Bugger that,' he muttered. 'So it's true, is it? What people are saying? That it's not a normal beast?'

'Uncommon,' Johnstone replied in a similar mumble.

'Maybe you didn't measure it right, trapper. Measurements can hop around like anything.'

'Sure. The teeth dragged across the carcass. Skidded. Could have extended the bite-mark.'

'There you are, then.'

The two men sat in silence for a long moment.

'It's a big one, all the same,' Johnstone said.

'There could be some fun and games soon,' the carpenter said, as he scanned the square, watching the men with their fists in their pockets.

'Don't tell them.'

'They tell themselves, anyway. What do you want to do?'

'To catch the animal before they do.'

'I understand.'

On Monday at dawn Johnstone strapped up his kitbag, lashed it onto his motorbike and made ready to go back up to the Mercantour. To watch Marcus and Proserpine enjoying young love, to find Sibellius, to check the movements of the whole pack, to make a list of who's there and who's not, to feed the old fellow, and then to hunt for Electre, a small female who had not been seen for a week. He would track Sibellius towards the south-east, as near as he could get to Pierrefort, the village where the last attack had taken place.

CHAPTER 6

He tracked Sibellius for two days without sighting the beast, stopping to shelter from the sun by the side of a sheep pen only when the flaming orb was simply too hot to bear. In so doing he checked more than twenty-two square kilometres of hunting grounds for the chance remains of dismembered sheep. Johnstone would never have cheated on his one great love, the great bears of the north-west, but he was forced to admit that this straggly set of skinny European wolves had made pretty deep inroads over the last six months.

He was edging his way along a narrow path with a sheer drop to one side when he saw Electre lying injured at the bottom of a gully. Johnstone calculated his chances of getting to the bottom of the steep, scrubby slope down which the she-wolf had slipped, and he reckoned he could manage it without getting help. Anyway, as all the park rangers were out on patrol, he'd have had to wait far too long for back-up. It took Johnstone more than an hour to lower himself down the cliff, going from handhold to handhold under the mind-numbing

Saharan sun. The she-wolf was so weak he did not even need to strap her fangs before making an examination. Badly damaged paw, had not eaten for days. Johnstone laid her on a canvas sheet which then he tied up like a sling, so that he could carry it over his shoulder. The she-wolf may have lost a lot of weight, but she still wasn't an ounce under seventy pounds – a featherweight for a wolf, but a hell of a load for a man climbing back up a near-vertical slope. When he'd made it to the cliff-top path Johnstone allowed himself thirty minutes' rest lying flat on his back in the shade, with one hand on the she-wolf's coat so she should understand she wasn't going to die all alone up there as if at the dawn of time.

At eight in the evening he brought the she-wolf into the treatment hut.

'Any trouble below?' the vet asked Johnstone as he laid Electre on the examination table.

'Trouble about what?'

'About the savaged sheep.'

Johnstone shook his head. 'We'll have to get our hands on him before the locals come up here. And wreck everything.'

'You off?' the vet asked, as he noticed Johnstone grabbing a loaf, a salami and a bottle.

'Things to do.'

Yes, like hunting on behalf of the old man. Might take some time. He did not always get it right the first time. Like the ageing wolf himself.

Johnstone left word for Jean Mercier. They

wouldn't cross paths that night, he would sleep at his sheepfold.

The alarm was raised next morning, by Camille, on the mobile phone, around ten, while he was making his way to the north. Her breathless speech told Johnstone straight away that things were getting worse.

'They've been at it again,' Camille said. 'There's been a bloodbath at Les Écarts, at Suzanne Rosselin's place.'

'At Saint-Victor?' Johnstone exclaimed, almost shouting.

'At Suzanne Rosselin's place,' Camille repeated. 'In the village. The wolf killed five sheep and wounded three others.'

'Did he eat them there and then?'

'No, he just tore pieces out of them, the same as before. Doesn't look as though he's attacking for food. Have you seen Sibellius?'

'Not a sign.'

'You'll have to come down. Two *gendarme*s have turned up, but Gerrot says they haven't got a clue about how to examine the carcasses properly. And the vet's miles away on a foaling case. People are screaming and howling, Johnstone. Shit, man, you have to get down here.'

'Two hours' time, at Les Écarts.'

Suzanne Rosselin was the sole owner of the breeding station at Les Écarts, to the west of the village, and she ran it with an iron fist, people

27

said. A tall and corpulent woman, rough-mannered to the point of manliness, she was respected and feared throughout the canton, but she wasn't much sought after outside the lambing trade. People found her too abrasive and too crude. Furthermore she was ugly. It was said that thirty years back she had fallen for an Italian migrant and wanted to run off with him without her father's blessing. She had gone all the way with the man, so the story went. But life did not give her a chance to be a bad girl – the lover bolted back to the toe of Italy, and then, less than a year later, Suzanne's parents died. Betrayed, ashamed and without a partner, Suzanne grew hard of head and heart. So it was fate, they said, that had made her as masculine as she was. Other people said that was wrong, that she had always been butch. It was partly for these reasons that Camille rather liked Suzanne, who took verbal crudity to an incandescent intensity that could only inspire admiration – Camille's mother had taught her to consider vulgarity as a way of coping with life. She was also impressed by Suzanne's professional competence.

Camille went up to the sheep farm roughly once a week to collect the box of provisions that Suzanne made up for her. As soon as she entered the grounds of Les Écarts she left the snide remarks and insinuations of the village behind her. The five men and women who worked there would have gone to the stake for Suzanne Rosselin.

★　　★　　★

She strode along the pebble path switching back and forth along the terraces up to the high and narrow stone-built farmhouse, with its low door and small, asymmetric windows. Camille reckoned that the decrepit roof owed its continued existence only to the moral solidarity between tiles that had bonded together long ago. The place was empty, so Camille walked onto the elongated sheepfold five hundred metres further up the steep slope. She could hear Suzanne bawling in the distance. Camille screwed up her eyes against the sun and made out the blue shirts of two *gendarme*s as well as Sylvain, hopping around. Whenever meat was involved, the butcher had to be there.

Then she made out the priestly silhouette of Watchee, standing erect against the wall of the sheepfold. She had not yet had an opportunity of seeing Suzanne's shepherd close up, since this very old man was forever out in the fields guarding Suzanne's flock. People said that he slept in the old shack with his animals, but they did not seem to find that shocking. He was called 'Watchee', meaning 'watchman' or 'keeper', as far as Camille had been able to make out, but she did not know his real name. He was a slim, straight-backed old man with a head of longish white hair, and his two hands were resting firmly on the crook of a staff standing solidly in the ground, and with his haughty glance he cut a truly majestic figure, so much so that Camille wasn't sure whether she had the right to speak to him directly.

On Suzanne's other side stood Soliman, standing just as straight as Watchee, as if to match the old man. Seeing these two stationary guards to right and left of Suzanne, you could imagine them awaiting a signal from her to start using their staves to beat back an imaginary horde of marauders. But they weren't. Watchee was just standing the way he always did, and in these rather dramatic circumstances Soliman was only following suit. Suzanne was in discussion with the *gendarme*s and filling in the incident report form. The dead and wounded sheep had been taken into the cooler darkness of the pen.

Seeing Camille, Suzanne took her shoulder in her huge grasp and gave it a rough shake.

'So where's your trapper, eh? I could do with him right now. To tell us what's what. He's must have more between the ears than these two nitwits who'd be pushed even to wipe their own backsides.'

Sylvain the butcher raised an arm as if he was about to say something.

'Belt up, Sylvain,' Suzanne anticipated him. 'You're as dim as the others. No offence, you've got an excuse, and it's not your job.'

No-one took offence in any case. The two *gendarme*s seemed quite bored with it all and carried on filling in the forms, laboriously.

'I let him know,' Camille said. 'He's on his way down.'

'If you've got a minute, afterwards. There's a leak in my lavatory, I need you to mend it.'

30

'I haven't got my tools with me, Suzanne. I'll do it later.'

'Meanwhile, my lass, go take a peek at the mess in there,' said Suzanne, pointing a fat thumb towards the pen. 'Murder most wild, by mad brutes.'

Before stepping through the low doorway Camille gave a respectful and humble nod to Watchee, Soliman she shook by the hand. She knew Soliman quite well. He followed Suzanne like a shadow and gave her a helping hand in all her tasks. Camille also knew Soliman's story.

In fact it had been the very first story she'd been told after she arrived in the village, as if it was urgent for her to know it. Twenty-three years on, people still had not got over the shock of having a Black in the village. Just as in a fairy story, he'd been found as a baby in a fig basket on the church steps. Nobody had ever seen a Black at Saint-Victor or anywhere in the surrounding area, so they reckoned he must have been made in a town, maybe Nice, where anything can happen, even Black babies. But there he was at Notre-Dame de Saint-Victor, bawling his lungs out in the porch of the village church. As sun rose that day half the village stood around in complete bewilderment gazing at the basket and the utterly Black baby inside it. Then, bit by bit, initially hesitant female hands came forth to pick it up, then to rock it, then to comfort it. Lucie, who ran the café on the square, had been the first to dare to kiss its snot-stained cheek. But nothing seemed to calm the infant, who

31

was almost choking on his screams. 'The little darkie's hungry,' said one old lady. 'He's messed himself,' said another. Then truck-sized Suzanne burst onto the scene, pushed her way forward, picked up the babe and nestled it in the crook of her brawny arm. The kid stopped yelling straight away and laid its head on Suzanne's broad bosom. From that instant, everyone accepted as a plain fact of life – as if they lived in a fairy tale where princesses just happened to be wide-shouldered sheep breeders – that the little darkie would belong to the mistress of Les Écarts. Suzanne stuck her index finger into the infant's mouth and shouted out words that Lucie would not forget as long as she lived:

'Look in the basket, you tossers! There's bound to be a note!'

And there was. The priest went to the top of the church steps, ceremonially stretched forth an arm to call for quiet, and started to read the note aloud. '*Pliz luk ater im –*'

'Slower, you idiot!' Suzanne demanded, as she rocked the babe. 'Can't understand a word!'

Yes, Lucie would never forget that. Suzanne had no respect for anyone.

'*Pliz*', the priest repeated, '*luk ater im rit an proper. His name is Soliman Melchior Samba DIAWARA tell im is ma is good an is pa is crule as a swamp in hell. Luk ater im an luv im pliz.*'

Suzanne pushed herself right up to the priest so as to read over his shoulder. Then she grabbed the pee-stained scrap and stuck it in a pocket of her sack-like dress.

'Soliman Melchior Whatsisname?' said Germain, the roadman, with a giggle. 'And what came after? A load of nonsense if you ask me. Why can't he be Gérard, like a normal person? Where does his mother think he came from? A leg of lamb?'

There was a ripple of laughter, which quickly subsided. You had to admit, Lucie would add, that the folk of Saint-Victor weren't all bloody idiots, they could restrain themselves when push came to shove. Not like the Pierrefort lot, who held nothing sacred.

Meanwhile the baby's little black head was still nestling in the big woman's armpit. How old could he be? Four weeks at the most. And whom did he love? Suzanne. Life is like that.

'Right,' said Suzanne, looking the crowd up and down from the church steps. 'If anyone comes asking for him, he's up at Les Écarts.'

And that settled it.

No-one ever did come asking for wee Soliman Melchior Samba Diawara. But occasionally people wondered what would have happened if the boy's natural mother really had come back to claim him. Because from that crucial moment – 'the business on the steps', villagers called it – Suzanne Rosselin had grown fiercely attached to the child and it wasn't obvious she would have given him up without a fight. It took two years for the local notary to persuade her to get the official paperwork dealt with. Not to adopt the child, she wasn't allowed to do that, but to become his legal guardian.

And that's how baby Soliman became the Rosselin lad. Suzanne raised him like he was a local born and bred, but in her heart of hearts she treated him as if he were an African king, believing in a muddled sort of way that he was a bastard prince who'd been discarded by some powerful dynasty. Seeing how handsome he became – a real Adonis – he couldn't be anything less. At the age of twenty-three young Soliman Melchior was as conversant with grafting tomato plants, pressing olives, cultivating chickpeas and spreading muck as he was with the traditions and lore of sub-Saharan Africa. All that he knew about sheep had been taught him by Watchee. And all he knew about Africa, its glories and misfortunes, its stories and legends, had been taught him by the books that Suzanne scrupulously sought out and read to him, thereby making herself a highly knowledgeable Africanist too.

Even now Suzanne kept a weather eye open for serious television documentaries that would broaden the young man's education – on repairing a tanker-truck on a Ghanaian highway, on the green monkeys of Tanzania, on polygamy in Mali, on dictators, civil wars and coups d'état, or the origins and glories of the Kingdom of Benin.

'Sol!' she would cry out. 'Get in here! Your place is on TV!'

Suzanne had never been able to decide to her

34

complete satisfaction which African country Soliman came from, so she found it simpler to treat the whole of black Africa as 'his place'. And there was no question of the boy skiving a single one of these documentaries. Only once, when he was seventeen, had he attempted rebellion.

'I don't give two damns about these guys,' he moaned, as a report on hunting warthogs dragged out on screen.

And for the first and last time Suzanne responded by slapping his face.

'Don't you ever talk about your own folk that way!' she commanded.

But as Soliman was on the verge of tears, she tried to explain things in a kindlier way, clasping the boy's slim shoulder with her outsized mitt.

'Look, Sol, you don't have to give a tinker's fart for the country you're born in. You're born where you're born and that's that. But you have to stop short of rejecting your own folk, because that can land you in a load of shit. What's bad is the rejecting. Rejection, denial, contempt – that's for little big men with nasty minds, who think they made themselves all on their own and owe nothing to nobody what came before. Fuckwits, right? You've got Les Écarts behind you and you've also got the whole of Africa. Take both, two helpings is better than one.'

Soliman took Camille into the pen and pointed her towards the bloodied carcasses laid out on the

35

floor. Camille looked at them from a distance. 'What does Suzanne think?' she asked.

'Suzanne's against wolves. She says nothing good will come of them, and that this beast kills for sport.'

'She's in favour of hunting them down?'

'She's against hunting, too. She's says we won't nab it round here, it's already moved on.'

'And Watchee?'

'Watchee's not happy.'

'In favour of the hunt?'

'Don't know. Since he came across the savaged sheep he hasn't opened his mouth.'

'And what do you think, Soliman?'

At that moment Johnstone walked into the pen and rubbed his eyes to adjust them to the sudden gloom. The old shack stank to high heaven of lanolin and stale urine. The French really were revolting people, he thought. They might have cleaned the place up. Behind Johnstone came Suzanne, and she smelled bad too, he reckoned, and then the two *gendarmes*, at a respectful distance, together with the butcher whom Suzanne had failed to chase off. 'I'm the man with the cold store,' he had replied, 'and I'll be taking the carcasses away for you.'

'The hell you will!' Suzanne snapped back. 'They'll be buried right here at Les Écarts, and Watchee will do it with the proper ceremony for serving soldiers what die in action.'

That shut Sylvain up, no mistake, but he tagged along behind her nevertheless. Watchee stayed outside, by the door. Watching.

Johnstone nodded to Soliman and then knelt down next to the dismembered sheep. He turned them over, inspected the injuries, probed their dirty coats looking for the best-defined imprint of the teeth. He dragged over a very young ewe and looked hard at the bite mark on its neck.

'Sol, grab the torch and shine it over there,' Suzanne said.

Johnstone pored over the wound by the light of the yellow beam.

'The carnassial hardly scratched her,' he mumbled, 'but the canine dug right in.'

He picked up a long straw and poked it inside the bloody hole.

'What the hell are you doing?' Camille asked.

'Probing,' Johnstone answered, calmly.

The Canadian pulled the straw out and used his thumbnail to score off the limit of staining on the now crimson piece of straw. He handed it without a word to Camille, then took another straw to measure the distance between the wounds. He stood up and went out into the fresh air with his thumbnail still marking the straw. He needed to breathe.

'The sheep are all yours,' he said, as he went past Watchee, who responded with a nod.

'Sol,' he said, 'fetch me a ruler.'

Soliman bounded down to the house without breaking his stride, and came back in five minutes with the tape measure Suzanne used for sewing.

'Measure it,' Johnstone said, as he held the two straws out straight. 'Exactly.'

Soliman stretched the tape along the blood-marked straw.

'Thirty-five millimetres,' he announced.

Johnstone screwed up his face. Then he measured the other straw himself and handed the tape measure back to Soliman.

'And so?' one of the *gendarme*s asked.

'The canine tooth was almost four centimetres long.'

'And so?' the *gendarme* repeated. 'Is that awkward?'

Nobody said anything, pregnantly. They were beginning to see. They were beginning to understand.

'A large animal,' Johnstone concluded, summarising what everyone had grasped.

The group hesitated then began to break up. The *gendarme*s bade farewell with a salute. Sol went to the house again. Watchee went back into the pen. Johnstone went off to one side to wash his hands, then put on his motorcycle helmet and his gloves. Camille went up to him.

'Suzanne's invited us in to have a drink, to get this out of our minds. Come on.'

Johnstone pursed his lips.

'She stinks,' he said.

Camille stiffened.

'She does not,' she replied rather harshly, flouting all factual accuracy.

'She does,' Johnstone said.

'Don't be mean.'

Johnstone caught Camille's frowning stare and suddenly smiled.

'All right,' he said, and took off his helmet.

He followed her along the scorched grass track that wound down to the stone-built hovel. He had nothing against that other French habit of knocking yourself senseless with hooch from the stroke of noon. Canadians could compete in that event.

'All the same,' he said to Camille with his hand on her shoulder. 'She *does* stink.'

CHAPTER 7

That evening the national news featured the latest victims of the Mercantour wolves at some length.

'Shit,' said Johnstone. 'Why can't they just leave us in peace.'

Actually, the issue was no longer the wolves as a group, but *the* wolf of the Mercantour National Park. The lead item of the news was an overexcited report from the Alps, with rather more substance to it than in earlier stories. It prompted fear and loathing. It kneaded the related ingredients of fascination and horror into an unhealthy dough. The savagings were deplored with prurient gloating, the power of the beast was spelled out in detail: uncatchable, wild and, above all, huge. That was what really hooked the whole country and propelled its now passionate interest in the 'Monster of the Mercantour'. Its uncommon size raised it above the ordinary and placed it on a par with the cohorts of Satan. People had suddenly encountered a wolf out of hell, and no way were they going to let go of it.

★   ★   ★

'I'm astounded Suzanne let journalists inside,' Camille said.

'Went in without asking.'

'This time it'll be a whole lynch-mob. No stopping them.'

'They won't catch it in the Mercantour.'

'You reckon its lair is somewhere else?'

'Sure, it moves around. Maybe a sibling.'

Camille switched off the TV and looked at Johnstone.

'Who are you talking about?'

'Sibellius's brother. There were five of them in the litter: two she-cubs, Livie and Octavie, and three males, Sibellius, Porcus the Lame, and the last-born, Crassus the Bald.'

'Was *he* big?'

'Looked set to grow to a good size. Never seen him grown-up. Mercier reminded me.'

'Does he know where it is?'

'Can't pin it down. With mating season there's been lots of boundary shifts all over the place. Males can cover thirty kilometres in one night. Hang on, Mercier gave me a photograph. But only when it was a cub.'

Johnstone got up and looked for his rucksack. 'Shit,' he grumbled. 'I damn well left it with the old bag.'

'With Suzanne,' Camille corrected.

'With old bag Suzanne.'

Camille hovered, on the brink of starting a row. 'If you have to go down there,' she said in the end, 'I'll come with you. There's a leak in the toilet.'

'Filth,' said Johnstone. 'Filth just doesn't bother you.'

Camille shrugged as she went to gather her toolkit. 'It's true, it doesn't.'

At Les Écarts Camille asked for a bucket and scrubbing sheet and left Johnstone in the care of Suzanne and Soliman, who offered herb tea or a glass of spirits.

'Spirits,' he said.

Camille noticed how he shifted around so as to sit as far away from Suzanne as possible.

As she loosened the seized nuts on the sewer pipe Camille wondered if she could ever get Johnstone to utter a thank you, even a word of thanks. He wasn't objectionable, really, just barely cordial. Mixing with grizzlies had left his social skills undeveloped. And that weighed on Camille, even with someone as rough-mannered as Suzanne. But she did not go in for preaching. Drop it, she told herself, as she prised a perished rubber seal off with the tip of a screwdriver. Say nothing. Don't involve yourself, it's not your job.

She could hear the sounds of conversation coming up from the ground-floor living room, then doors slamming. Soliman ran along the corridor then up the stairs and stood to catch his breath at the door of the toilet. Camille was still on all fours. She looked up at him.

'Tomorrow,' Soliman declared. 'The hunt's on tomorrow.'

In Paris, *Commissaire* Adamsberg paid no attention to the programme flickering like a dream on the screen in front of him. He was uneasy about the hyped-up story he had watched on the news. If that ravenous wolf did not soon slack off a bit, Adamsberg thought, then there wouldn't be much hope for any of those unwary beasts of prey who had had the gall to drift like clouds over the Alps. This evening the reporters had taken care to get the pictures right, they'd zoomed in on the fine brown streaks on paws and spine that are characteristic of Italian wolves. The cameras were closing in on the culprits, the whole Mercantour affair could easily, very quickly, turn ugly. Tension was rising, and the size of the beast with it. He would be ten feet tall within a month. But that was nothing unusual. He had listened to dozens of crime victims describing their attacker – a real giant, sir, a monster to look at, and his hands were as wide as dinner plates. Then they'd catch the man, and the victim was often quite disappointed to see just how slight and ordinary his big bad wolf really was. Twenty-five years in the force had taught Adamsberg to be very wary of ordinary people, and to offer the hand of friendship to the oversize and to the mis-shapen who'd learned from early childhood how to take it easy so that people would leave them alone.

Ordinary people aren't so wise, they don't take it easy.

Adamsberg waited drowsily for the late-night news. Not to see the savaged sheep or to hear about the exploits of the monster-wolf again. But to catch that clip of the villagers at Saint-Victor milling around in the square at sundown. On the right of the image there was a girl who had caught his eye, turning three-quarters away and leaning against a large plane tree. She was tall and slim, she was dressed in a grey jacket, jeans and boots, she had dark shoulder-length hair, and her hands were in her pockets. That was all you could see. No face. Not a lot to make you think of Camille, but all the same it did make him think of her. Camille was the sort of girl who wouldn't have extracted her ankles from her cowboy boots just because it was 33°C in the shade. But there must be millions of other dark-haired, grey-jacketed girls who keep their boots on in the summer heat. And Camille had no reason to be standing in the village square at Saint-Victor. But maybe she did have a reason to be standing there, how the hell would he know, since he had not seen her in years, not a sign, nothing. He had not tried to contact her either, but that wasn't the same thing – he was easy to find, he hadn't budged from the station, he'd kept on grinding away at his caseload of murder, manslaughter and general mayhem. Whereas Camille had taken off as she always did without the slightest warning, leaving people lost in her wake. Sure, he'd left her, but why couldn't she send up a signal from time to time? She couldn't. Camille was a proud woman and answered to nobody. He'd come across her again just once, at least five years ago, on a train. They were lovers again for two hours and that was that, she just vanished, thank you and goodbye. OK, he could take it, he was fine, and who gives a damn? But all the same he would like to know if it really was her leaning against that plane tree at Saint-Victor.

The news bulletin was repeated at 11.45, sheep, farmer, sheep, then the village square. Adamsberg peered into the screen. Could be her. Could be Camille, the girl he couldn't care less about who often crossed his mind. Could be a million other girls too. He did not notice anything else, except for a big blond type standing next to her. A broad-shouldered, strapping young fellow with longish hair and an agile and seductive air, the sort of man who can put his hand on a girl's shoulder and expect the whole world to do his bidding. And Adamsberg was virtually certain that this one had his hand on boot-girl's shoulder.

Adamsberg slumped deeper into his armchair. He was not a strapping young fellow. He was not young. His shoulders weren't broad. His hair wasn't fair. He entertained not the faintest expectation of being obeyed. That fellow was a whole heap of things that he was not. Maybe his polar

45

opposite. OK, and then so what? Camille must have been having affairs for years with fair-haired men he had never heard of. He had been having other women of every shade for years, too, and it must be said that not one of them had Camille's peculiar disadvantage of remaining for ever shod in those bloody leather boots of hers. The other women had all worn women's shoes.

All right, nice knowing you, end of story. What worried Adamsberg wasn't the young man, it was whether Camille had finally settled at Saint-Victor. He thought of Camille as forever on the move, across cities, along highways, with a ruck-sack full of music and monkey wrenches, a woman never halting, never seated, and therefore funda-mentally unconquered. Seeing her in that village disturbed him. It made anything possible. For example, that she owned a house there, with a chair, a coffee mug, yes, why not a coffee mug, and a washbasin, and even so much as a bed, with a man in it, and maybe with this man she had a steady, static relationship, standing four-square like a farmhouse table, a simple, wholesome love scrubbed squeaky-clean every day. A stationary Camille, a consenting Camille, Camille at peace and welded to the fair-haired man. Which would mean two coffee mugs not one. And for that matter why not plates, cutlery, pots, lights and – in the worst case – a carpet. Two wholesome big plain squeaky-clean mugs.

Adamsberg felt himself nodding off. He got up,

switched off the TV and the light, took a shower. Two mugs brimful with plain healthy squeaky-clean coffee. Ah, but if things had come to such a pass, how do you account for the boots? What were those boots doing in the story if all Camille did was to walk from bed to table and from table to piano? And from the piano back to bed. With the squeaky-clean blond?

Adamsberg turned off the water and got dry. Where there's boots, there's hope. He rubbed his hair with a towel and caught his own eye in the bathroom mirror. He did think of that girl from time to time. He liked thinking of her, it was as simple as that. It was the same as going out, or going on a trip, seeing something or learning something new, thinking about something else, or putting up a new set for an evening's show. The 'Rambling Lady' show. And when the curtain went down on it he would go back to his usual daydreams, leaving Camille striding along some road or other. This evening's show about 'The woman who'd settled in Saint-Victor with a man with fair hair' had been much less fun. He wouldn't drop off to sleep tonight, dreaming of her being in bed with him, as he did from time to time, in gaps between affairs. Camille was his imaginary stand-by lover when reality failed to come up to snuff. But right now that blond fellow got in the way.

Adamsberg stretched out and closed his eyes. That girl in boots was not Camille, who had no business to be leaning against a plane tree in Saint-Victor.

The one on the television was certainly called Melanie. As a consequence of which the conquering hero had no right to interfere with *Commissaire* Adamsberg's inner life.

CHAPTER 8

Small groups began to gather in the village square at first light. Johnstone had hurried back to his hills the previous evening. So as to stay in full control of the wolf-pack and to fight with it if need be, to keep all the approach routes to the wildlife refuge under watch, and to protect the wolves from the slightest incursion on their territory. In theory the hunt would not stray far from the village of Saint-Victor; the huntsmen were not supposed to venture up into the Mercantour. In theory they were banking on an animal that had not been seen since last winter or on a brand-new arrival from the other side of the Alps. So theoretically the animals in the wildlife reserve's wolf-packs were not at risk. For now. But the expressions on people's faces, their narrowed eyes and their silent expectancy told a different story. They said: war. Men strutted around the fountain with hunting rifles hinged over their forearms or strapped to their shoulders. They were waiting for their marching orders, since several posses were supposed to leave different villages – Saint-Martin, Puygiron, Thorailles, Beauval and Pierrefort – at

49

the same time. The latest information was that the Saint-Victor party was to join up with the men of Saint-Martin.

The war was on.

Nine and half million sheep. Forty wolves.

Camille was sitting discreetly at a café table watching these martial drills through the window. Stern-faced men signalling their shared camaraderie among yapping dogs. Watchee had not responded to the call, nor had Soliman. Whether at the instruction of Suzanne Rosselin or from a personal decision, the village's sole regal shepherd was not joining the wolf hunt. That did not surprise Camille. Watchee was more likely to settle scores on his own. By contrast, the butcher was buzzing around one knot of men then another, seemingly incapable of staying in one place. After meat. Forever after meat. Germain, Tourneur, Frosset, Lefèbvre were all there, as well as other men Camille did not recognise.

Lucie watched the gathering from behind the bar.

'That fellow,' she said without moving her lips, 'that one's got a bloody cheek.'

'Which one?' asked Camille, as she moved next to Lucie.

Lucie waved a tea-towel towards a shape on the square.

'Massart, the slaughterhouse guy.'

'The fat one in the blue jacket?'

'No, the one behind him. Looks like he swallowed a gas cylinder.'

50

Camille had never seen Massart before. People said he never came down from his eyrie anyway. He worked in the municipal abattoir in Digne and lived on his own in a shack high up on Mont Vence, hauling up all his supplies from town. So he wasn't often seen, and people steered clear of him. He was supposed to be a bit odd. Camille thought he was just a loner, which comes to the same thing, for villagers. But he *was* rather odd, in fact. Physically odd. Big shoulders, a barrel-chest, short, bandy legs, simian arms. He wore his cap like a bottle-top and his hair in a fringe low over his eyes. Everybody from this part of the world had swarthy skin, save for Massart, whose pasty face made him look like a priest who had never set foot outside church. He was off to one side, leaning untidily against the side of a white van, with his rifle pointing down, and large spotted dog on a leash.

'Doesn't he ever go out?' asked Camille.

'Only to go to work at the slaughterhouse. The rest of the time he's shut up there doing who knows what.'

'And what's that?'

'Who knows? He hasn't got a woman. Never has had a woman.'

Lucie wiped the window with her tea-towel as if she needed time to find her words.

'Maybe he didn't manage to do it,' she said in a whisper. 'Maybe he wasn't capable.'

Camille said nothing.

'Some people tell a different story,' Lucie went on.

'Such as?'

'Different, that's all,' Lucie repeated with a shrug. After a pause: 'Anyway, ever since there's been wolves, he's never signed a petition against them. And there've been quite a few meetings and petitions, believe you me. But him, well, it's like he was in favour of the wolves. And what with living up there like an animal, with no woman, no nothing. Kids aren't allowed near his shack.'

'He doesn't look like an animal,' Camille said, noticing that his T-shirt had been ironed, his jacket kept clean, and his chin shaved.

'And today,' Lucie went on without hearing Camille, 'here he is with his gun and his pooch. Bloody cheek.'

'Doesn't anyone talk to him?' Camille asked.

'No point talking to him. He doesn't like people.'

Suddenly, at a sign from the mayor, the men stubbed out their cigarettes, piled into the cars, put the dogs in the back, started up the engines. Doors slammed, wheels spun, for a moment the whole square reeked of diesel fumes, and then it all faded away.

'But will they get near the beast?' Lucie wondered with her arms crossed on her counter.

Camille said nothing. Johnstone's position was clear-cut, but she wasn't so sure which side she was on. From afar, she would have defended the wolves, all and any wolves, but close up, things weren't so simple. Shepherds did not now dare to leave their flocks during seasonal migrations, the ewes weren't lambing properly, there were more and more savagings, more and more guard dogs, and children had stopped rambling over the peaks. But she also did not like war or extermination, and this hunt was the first step. Her thoughts went out to the wolf, to warn it of looming danger – run off, get going, so long, old chap. If only the wolves had not been so lazy, and had made do with the chamois in the wildlife reserve. But there you are, they went for the easier meal, and that's what the problem was. She had better get home, close the door and concentrate on work. Today, though, she did not feel at all inclined to compose.

So it would have to be plumbing. Her salvation.

She had several jobs in her planner: the tobacconist needed a central-heating pump changing, then there was a gas water-heater that came near to exploding each time it ignited (lots of equipment in these parts was in similar condition) and right here in the café was a soil pipe that was backing up.

'I'll deal with the soil pipe,' Camille said. 'I'll go and get my gear.'

Shortly before eight in the evening there was still no sign of returning hunters, which suggested that the animal had remained elusive. Camille was finishing off the last job on her list, putting the cowling back on the old boiler and adjusting the pressure. Only two hours left. Then night would fall and the search would have to be suspended until dawn.

From the outdoor washing trough that overlooked the whole village Camille kept watch for men coming back. She had laid her loaf and cheese on the ledge that was still warm from the day's sun, and she was nibbling at her food, making the meal stretch out as long as possible. Just before ten, cars flooded into the square, doors slammed, and guys now looking quite worn slithered out and unfolded their stiffened limbs. Their shuffling stride and glum tone, as well as the dogs' tired whelps, made it plain to Camille that they had drawn a blank. The beast had given them the slip. Camille flashed mental congratulations to the wolf. Be seeing you, old buddy.

Only then did Camille decide to go home. Before switching on the synthesiser, she called Johnstone. There had been no incursions by the hunters. Sibellius had not been seen, nor had Crassus the Bald. On Day One of the war, the combatants had stayed on side.

But the campaign wasn't over. The hunt would resume at dawn. And the day after next, on Saturday, there would be five times as many men available. Johnstone would stay in position, high up in the hills.

CHAPTER 9

The last two days of the week – before Sunday's rest day – witnessed the same departures, the same tensions, and then the same silence settling on the village like a lid. On Saturday afternoon Camille escaped with a long walk up to St Peter's Stone, a lump of rock that was supposed to cure impotence, sterility and disappointments in love, provided you sat on it correctly. Camille had never been able to learn exactly what that meant, apparently it was vaguely embarrassing. Anyway, she reckoned that if the stone could sort out so many troubles, then it really ought to relieve her grumpiness, her doubts, her low spirits and lack of musical inspiration, all of which were no more than secondary indications of impotence.

Camille took her metal-tipped walking stick and her copy of *The A to Z of Tools for Trade and Craft*. It was the sort of thing she most liked to leaf through at special moments – at breakfast, in her coffee break, or whenever she felt her heart sinking. Apart from that Camille had more or less ordinary tastes in reading.

Johnstone did not take kindly to Camille's liking for materials and crafts, and he'd thrown the *A to Z* out with the rubbish alongside other advertising bumf. It was quite enough for Camille to be a plumber, she did not have to drool over toolkits for every trade under the sun. Camille rescued the somewhat stained catalogue without making a fuss. Johnstone's overweening hopefulness about women paradoxically made him rather conservative. He saw women as belonging to a higher level of creation, he granted them mastery over instinctual reality, and believed that their task was to raise men above mere matter. He wanted them to be sublime and not vulgar, he aspired to their being almost immaterial, and not at all pragmatic. Such idealisation could hardly be squared with *The A to Z of Tools for Trade and Craft*. Camille did not dispute Johnstone's right to have his daydreams, but she considered herself equally entitled to like tools – same as any other fuckwit, as Suzanne would have said.

She shoved the *A to Z*, a loaf and some water into her backpack and left the village by the flight of steps that climbed steeply to the west. It took her nearly three hours of walking to get to the stone. You can't, after all, earn fertility just by snapping your fingers. Stones of that kind are never in your neighbour's back yard, that would be no better than cheating. They're always stuck in impossible places. When she got to the top of the rise where the worn old stone sat, Camille found herself staring at a fresh-painted sign politely warning ramblers to be wary of the guard dogs now used by local shepherds. The last paragraph ended optimistically: DO NOT SCREAM AND DO NOT THROW STONES AT THE DOGS. AFTER OBSERVING STRANGERS FOR A CERTAIN TIME, THEY WILL NORMALLY LEAVE OF THEIR OWN ACCORD. And abnormally, Camille added for symmetry, they'll jump at my throat. Instinctively, she altered her grip on her metal-tipped stick and looked around. What with wolves and dogs on the loose, the mountainside had become a wilderness once more.

She climbed onto the stone whence you could see down over the whole valley. She could make out the white streak of the line of cars belonging to the men of the hunting party. Distant halloos wafted up to her. So, basically, it wasn't much quieter up here, on her own. Basically, she was a bit scared.

She got out her bread and water and the tool catalogue. It was an exhaustive listing with sections on *compressed air*, *soldering*, *scaffolding*, *lifting gear*, and scores of similarly promising headings. Camille read every entry from start to finish, including detailed specifications like *jumbo weed hog, 1.1HP petrol engine, anti-recoil bar, low-vibration solid transmission with reverse thrust, electronic ignition, weight 5.6 kilograms.* Such descriptions – and catalogues were full of them – gave her profound intellectual satisfaction (understanding the object, how it fitted together, how it worked) as well as intense lyrical pleasure. On top of the underlying fantasy of solving all the world's problems with a *combined-cycle milling machine* or a *universal chuck tool,* the catalogue represented the hope of using a combination of power and ingenuity to overcome all of life's shitty obstacles. A false hope, to be sure, but a hope nonetheless. Thus did Camille draw her vital energy from two sources: musical composition and *The A to Z of Tools for Trade and Craft.* Ten years younger and she had also drawn on love, but she had really lost interest in that overused well. Love could give you wings, but it also knocked you off your feet, so it wasn't much of a bargain overall. Far less so than a *ten-ton hydraulic jack,* for instance. Broadly speaking, love meant that men stayed around when you didn't love them and ran off when you did. The system was simple, entirely predictable, and never failed to engender either massive boredom or catastrophe. To put up with all that just for twenty days' wonder, no, it really wasn't worth it. Lasting love, love on which you can build, love that brings strength, nobility, sanctity, purity and succour, in a word all the stuff you believe love can be before you really try the thing out, well, that was stuff and nonsense. That was where Camille was at, after years of try-outs, numerous mishaps and a really sore patch. A scam for the naïve and a godsend for narcissists, love was a rubbish idea. Which is to say that as far as the heart was concerned, Camille was halfway to becoming a complete cynic, and she felt neither contentment nor regret about that. The thick skin she had grown did not stop her loving Johnstone sincerely, after her own fashion. It allowed her to appreciate him, even admire him, and snuggle up to him. But not to entertain the smallest hope of anything. Camille had retained only immediate desires and short-range emotions, she had bricked up all ideals, hopes, and grandeur. She expected virtually nothing from anybody, or almost. That was the only way she could love nowadays: with greediness and goodwill verging on utter indifference.

Camille moved further into the shade, took off her jacket, and immersed herself for two good hours in close study of a *Water-cooled grinder with abrasive disk*, a *Turbo-charged double-protection sump pump*, and other clever contraptions that brought her both reassurance and instruction. But her eyes kept wandering from the page and peering into the far distance. She was not entirely at ease. She was holding her walking stick tight. Suddenly she heard something rustling, and then bushes being trampled. In a flash she was up on top of the stone, her heart racing and her stick on guard. A wild boar came out of the undergrowth ten metres away, saw her standing there, and then went back into the scrub. Camille took a deep breath, buckled up her bag, and went back down the path to Saint-Victor. It was not a good time for being on the mountain.

At dusk she perched on the rim of the trough in

the village square, with her legs crossed under her, and the bread and cheese laid out beside her. Awaiting the hunters' return, she could hear the muffled thuds of disappointment and defeat. From her lookout she also saw Johnstone coming back on his motorbike. Instead of parking it on its kickstand on the square, as he usually did, he drove on this evening, passed his weary companions, and rode straight up the steep incline to the house.

Camille found him sitting on the top step, lost in thought, his helmet still in his hand. She sat down next to him and he put an arm round her shoulders.

'Any change?'

Johnstone shook his head.

'Any trouble?'

Repeat gesture.

'Sibellius?'

'Found him. With his brother Porcus. Their territory is right down in the south-east. In a really nasty mood. Nasty but in clover. The hunters are going to try to get tranquillisers into them.'

'What for?'

'So as to get a cast of their jaws.'

Camille nodded to show she understood. 'And Crassus?' she asked.

Johnstone moved his head once again. 'Not a sign,' he said.

Camille finished her piece of cheese in silence. Dragging words out of the Canadian phrase by phrase could be tiresome.

'So nobody can find the beast,' she concluded. 'They can't, and you can't.'

'Can't be found,' Johnstone agreed. 'But he must leave a scent, the dogs ought to pick it up.'

'And so?'

'He must be one tough guy. Real tough.'

Camille pursed her lips. She wasn't convinced. It was true, of course, that they'd taken a hell of a long time to close in on the Beast of Gévaudan all that time ago. Assuming what they'd got really had been the right one. There had never been any definite proof. As a result of which, the Beast still preyed on people's minds after more than two hundred years.

'Well, well', she mumbled with her chin on her knees, 'I'm really surprised.'

Johnstone stroked her hair for a long moment.

'There's someone who's not surprised at all,' he said.

Camille turned to look at him. It was quite dark now, and she couldn't see his face properly. She waited. At night he had to say more because his sign language couldn't be seen. In the dark he could be almost fluent.

'Someone who doesn't believe in it,' he said.

'In the hunt?'

'In the beast.'

Another pause.

'Don't get it,' Camille said. She sometimes fell into involuntary imitation and compacted her own sentences by clipping the first word.

'Who doesn't believe there is a beast,' Johnstone explained, with effort. 'No beast. And who told me, confidentially.'

'I see,' Camille said. 'So what does this someone believe it is, then? A dream?'

'No.'

'A hallucination? A collective delusion?'

'No. Someone who does not believe there is a beast.'

'Nor sheep torn to bits?'

'No. Of course not. Sheep, yes. But no beast.'

Camille shrugged her shoulders in despair. 'So what does this someone believe it is, then?'

'A man.'

Camille sat up straight and shook her head. 'A man? Who kills sheep with his teeth? And what about those bite marks?'

Johnstone pulled a face in the dark. 'The person thinks it's a werewolf.'

Another pause. Then Camille put her hand on Johnstone's arm.

'A werewolf?' she whispered instinctively, as if the evil word could not be spoken out loud. 'A werewolf? You mean a nutter?'

'No, no, a werewolf. There's a person around here who thinks it really is a werewolf.'

Camille tried to make out Johnstone's face in the dark, to see whether he was having her on, or what. But the Canadian's expression remained stony and serious.

'Are you talking about the kind of guy who turns

into a monster at night with claws that grow and hair that sprouts all over and canines that stick out over his lower lip? The sort of guy who goes around eating people lost at night in the woods and then stuffs his hairy chest inside his suit jacket in the morning before going in to the office?'

'You got it,' said Johnstone, seriously. 'A werewolf.'

'And we're supposed to have one around here?'

'Yup.'

'And it's supposed to have eaten all those sheep since the end of winter?'

'Anyway the last twenty of them.'

'What about you?' Camille asked hesitantly. 'Do you believe in it?'

Johnstone smiled vaguely and shrugged his shoulders.

'Good Lord, no,' he said.

Camille stood up, smiled herself, and waved her arms as if she was chasing shadows away.

'So who's the oaf who told you all that?'

'Suzanne Rosselin.'

Camille, dumbfounded, stared hard at the Canadian still sitting on the step with his helmet in his hand, and still as calm.

'Is that true, Lawrence?'

'Yup. The other evening, when you were fixing the leak. She said it was a fucking idiot of a werewolf that was holding the whole region to ransom. That was why the tooth-prints weren't normal.'

'Suzanne said that? You really mean Suzanne?'

'Sure. The old bag.'

Camille stood there in dismay, her arms hanging loose by her side.

'What she said', Johnstone specified, 'was that the fucking idiot of a werewolf had been —' he hunted for the right word '— had been awoken by the return of the wolves and that now he was taking advantage of their raids, which allowed him to cloak his own crimes under their mantle.'

'Suzanne is not crazy,' Camille muttered.

'You know very well she's completely round the bend.'

Camille said nothing.

'If you were honest with yourself you'd admit it,' Johnstone said. 'And you haven't heard the worst of it yet,' he added.

'Don't you want to come inside?' Camille asked. 'I'm cold, really freezing.'

Johnstone looked up and then got to his feet in a start, as if he had only just noticed how much he had shocked Camille. Camille loved the old bag. He put his arms round her, rubbed her back. As for himself, he had heard so many never-ending folktales about old hags who turn into grizzly bears, which turn into ptarmigans which then became lost souls, that he had long since stopped being worried by barking mad animal superstitions. Humankind has never been entirely rational about the wild. But here, in this cramped little land of France, everyone had lost the habit of the wild. And the thing that mattered was that Camille loved the old bag.

'Come inside,' he said, kissing her hair.

Camille did not switch on the light, so she wouldn't have to extract words one by one from Johnstone. The moon was beginning to rise, that would be enough for seeing by. She nestled into an old straw-backed armchair, drew her knees up to her chin and crossed her arms. Johnstone opened a jar of preserved grapes, poured a dozen into a cup and handed it to Camille. He drained off a glassful of the preserving spirit for himself.

'We could drown our sorrows,' he suggested.

'There's not enough alcohol left in that jar to drown a fly.'

Camille swallowed the grapes and put the pips back into the cup. She'd have preferred to spit them into the fireplace but Johnstone did not approve of women spitting into fireplaces, since they were supposed to rise above the brutality of males, including their spitting habits.

'I'm sorry for what I said about Suzanne,' he said.

'Maybe she's read too many African folktales after all,' Camille speculated wearily.

'Perhaps.'

'Do they have werewolves in Africa?'

Johnstone spread his hands, palms upwards.

'They must do. Maybe they're not wolves, though, but man-jackals, hyena-men.'

'Let's have the rest,' Camille said.

'She knows who it is.'

'Who the werewolf is?'

65

'Yup.'

'Tell me.'

'Massart, the man at the slaughterhouse.'

'Massart?' Camille almost shouted. 'Why Massart, for heaven's sake?'

Johnstone rubbed his cheek, not knowing what to say.

'Come on, out with it.'

'Because Massart is smooth-skinned.'

Camille held out her cup like a machine and Johnstone spooned in another serving of grapes in cognac.

'What, you mean no body hair?'

'Have you seen him?'

'Once.'

'He's got no hair.'

'I don't get it,' Camille said, obstinately. 'He's got hair on his head like you and me. "He's got a black fringe right down to his eyes."'

'I said body hair, Camille. He's got no hair on his body.'

'You mean on his arms and legs and chest?'

'That's right. He's as smooth-skinned as a choirboy. Haven't seen it close up, but apparently he doesn't even need to shave.'

Camille screwed up her eyes the better to picture Massart standing beside his van the other day. She recalled the pallor of his forearms and face, which struck such a contrast with the swarthy skins of everyone else. Well, maybe yes, he might also have no body hair.

'And so what?' she said. 'What's that bloody well got to do with it?'

'You're not really into werewolves, are you?'

'Hardly.'

'You wouldn't know one if you saw one walking down the street.'

'No, I wouldn't And what *would* tell me that some poor old sod was a werewolf?'

'That's how. A werewolf is an unhairy man. You know why? Because his wolf-coat is on the inside of his skin.'

'Is that some kind of a joke?'

'Go read the old books written in your own old country. You'll see. It's all there in black and white. And there are loads of country-folk who know all the lore. The old bag included.'

'You mean Suzanne.'

'Suzanne.'

'And do they all know about the inside-outside nonsense?'

'It's not nonsense. It's the mark of the werewolf. The only mark. He's got his hair on the inside because he's an inside-out person. At night he turns himself round and his hairy coat reappears.'

'Which makes Massart nothing more than a fur coat worn with the silk lining on the outside?'

'If you like.'

'What about the teeth? Are they reversible too? Where does he store them during the day?'

Johnstone put his glass down on the table and turned to face Camille.

'Look, Camille, there's no point getting excited. And I'm not bloody well responsible for any of this. It's the old bag who's saying it.'

'You mean Suzanne.'

'Suzanne.'

'Of course,' Camille said. 'I'm sorry.'

She stood up, took the grape jar and poured the last dregs into her cup. One grape after another soon soothed stiff muscles. They'd been preserved by Suzanne. In her backroom at Les Écarts she had a still where she made spirits – her 'fire-water', she called it – in quantities way above the maximum allowance for vine growers. 'I don't give a toss for any bloody maximum allowances,' she said. Nor did she give so much as a tinker's fart for all other allowances, exemptions, taxes, quotas, insurance policies, safety guidelines, sell-by dates, communal burdens or parish meetings. Buteil, her farm manager, made sure the business did not wander too far from the bounds of legality and Watchee dealt with veterinary health. How could a woman like that, Camille wondered, a woman who could stamp on social norms as easily as she would barge through a barn door, how could she believe in something that came so close to being collectively acceptable? She screwed the cap back on the jar and paced up and down, clutching her cup. Unless Suzanne, by dint of standing up to the rules of the collectivity, had ended up creating her own order of the world. Her own order, her own laws, her own explanations of how the world worked. While everyone else went chasing after a monster animal, marching to the same drummer, in thrall to the same idea, she, Suzanne Rosselin, stood her ground as the undying opponent of whatever is unanimously agreed. She defied consensus and used a different logic – no matter whether it was good logic or bad, just so long as it wasn't the same as everybody else's.

'She's crazy,' said Johnstone to sum up, as if he had been following Camille's train of thought. 'She's living in her own world.'

'So are you. You live in the snow with your bears.'

'Except that I'm not crazy. Maybe I should be, but actually I'm not. That's the difference between me and the old bag. She doesn't give a damn. She doesn't even give a damn about stinking of lanolin.'

'Leave off about the smell, Lawrence.'

'I'll not leave off about anything. She's dangerous. Think of Massart.'

Camille passed her hand across her face. He was right. If Suzanne was off the wall with her were-wolves, that was her affair. You can be crazy whatever way you want. But pointing the finger at someone else was quite another kettle of fish.

'Why Massart?'

'Because he's smooth-skinned,' Johnstone repeated patiently.

'No, that won't do,' Camille said. 'Apart from the hair. Forget the bloody hair. Why do you think she's getting at him? He's quite like her – a loner, out on his own, and unloved. She ought to be on his side.'

'Quite. He's a bit too much like her. They plough the same furrow. She has to get rid of him.'

'Stop thinking grizzly bears.'

'But that's how things work. They're a pair of fierce competitors.'

Camille nodded.

'What did she tell you about Massart? Body hair aside.'

'Nothing. Soliman came in and she shut up. Didn't learn anything more.'

'You picked up a fair bit all the same.'

'More than enough.'

'What's to be done?'

Johnstone came closer to Camille and put his hands on her shoulders.

'I'll tell you what my father always said.'

'OK,' Camille said.

'*Steer clear and keep your trap shut.*'

'Sure. And then?'

'We stay shtumm. But if by any mischance people outside of Les Écarts got wind of the old bag's claim, then it'd be a bad lookout for Massart. You know what people did to suspected were-wolves, not more than a couple of hundred years ago, in your country?'

'Tell me. Might as well know it all.'

'They sliced them open from neck to crotch to see if the hair really was on the inside. By then, it was a bit too late to say sorry about the mistake.'

Johnstone gripped Camille's shoulders.

'It mustn't go one centimetre beyond the fence of her sodding farm,' he impressed on her.

'I don't think other people here are as brainless as you imagine. They wouldn't jump on Massart. They know perfectly well that the killer is a wolf.'

'You're right. In normal times you would be completely right. But you're forgetting one thing: this is no ordinary wolf. I saw its bite marks. And you can believe me when I tell you that this is one hell of a beast, Camille. I've never seen anything like it in my life.'

'I believe you,' Camille whispered.

'And I won't be the only person who knows that for much longer. The lads aren't blind, they're even quite knowledgeable, despite what the old bag says. They'll catch on soon enough. They'll know they're dealing with something out of the ordinary, something they've not seen before. Do you see, Camille? Do you see the risk? Something not normal. So they'll be afraid. And that'll be their downfall. Fear will make them believe in idols and burn loners at the stake. And if the old bag's gossip gets around, they'll hunt down Massart and slice him open from throat to crotch.'

Camille gave a taut nod. Johnstone had never said so much in one go before. He wouldn't let go, it was as if he was trying to protect her. Camille felt his hands warm on her back.

'That's why we absolutely must find the animal, dead or alive. If they find it, it'll be dead, and if I find it, it'll still be alive. But until then, mum's the word.'

'What about Suzanne?'

'We'll go and see her tomorrow and tell her to keep her trap shut.'

'She doesn't like being told what to do.'

'But she likes me.'

'She might have told someone else already.'

'I don't think so. I really don't.'

'Why not?'

'Because she thinks the inhabitants of Saint-Victor are fuckwits one and all. I'm different because I'm a foreigner. And also she told me because I know about wolves.'

'Why didn't you say anything on Wednesday evening when you got back from Les Écarts?'

'I thought the trackers would raise the beast and that all this would be forgotten. I didn't want to demolish your view of Suzanne for nothing.'

Camille nodded.

'She's a nutcase,' Johnstone said gently.

'I'm fond of her all the same.'

'I know.'

CHAPTER 10

Next morning at seven-thirty Johnstone kick-started his motorbike. Camille was hardly awake, but she got on the pillion, and slowly they covered the two kilometres to Les Écarts. Camille held Johnstone by the waist with one hand, and in the other she held the empty grape jar. Suzanne did not supply grapes in alcohol unless you brought the old jar back. That was the rule.

Johnstone turned left up the stony path leading to the shack.

'Police!' Camille yelled, shaking Johnstone by the shoulder.

Johnstone signalled that he had seen, stopped the engine and dismounted. He and Camille took off their helmets and looked at the blue van parked at the farm, just as it had been the other day, with the same two *gendarme*s, the tall one and the medium one, going from the vehicle to the building and back again.

'Shit,' Johnstone said.

'Bloody hell,' said Camille. 'Another savaging.'

'God almighty. This isn't going to settle the old bag's nerves.'

'You mean Suzanne.'

'I mean Suzanne.'

'If only it had happened somewhere else.'

'The wolf does the choosing,' said Johnstone. 'Not chance.'

'He chooses?'

'Sure he does. He starts off sniffing around until he finds the right place. Somewhere easy to break into, somewhere far from other houses, and where the dogs are kept on the chain. So he comes back for more. And he'll carry on coming back. If he makes a habit of it, it'll be easier to corner him.'

Johnstone laid his helmet and gloves on the motorbike seat.

'Come on,' he said. 'Let's go check the gashes. See if they're the same.'

Johnstone shook his long fair hair like a waking animal, which he often did when he was in difficulty. Camille thrust her clenched fists deep into her trouser pockets. The path smelled of thyme and basil and, to Camille's mind, of blood. Johnstone reckoned that it smelled most of all and as always of lanolin and rancid piss.

They shook hands with the medium policeman, who looked worn and overwhelmed.

'Can I see the wounds?' Johnstone asked him.

The *gendarme* shrugged. 'Nothing may be touched,' he said as if by rote. 'Nothing may be touched.'

But at the same time he waved them on in with a weary flap of his arm.

'Careful', the policeman said, 'it's not pretty. Really not.'

'Sure it's not pretty,' Johnstone said.

'Did you come for the grapes?' he asked, seeing the empty jar in Camille's hand.

'Sort of,' Camille said.

'Well, it's not the right time for that. Not the right time at all.'

Camille wondered why the *gendarme* said everything twice. It must take a lot of time to say everything in duplicate; you could waste half the day as easy as pie. Whereas Johnstone who scarcely articulated one third of his sentences saved a great deal of time. But it could also be argued that he was wasting his time too. Camille's mother used to say that time wasted is time gained.

She looked up towards the sheep-pen, but this morning neither Watchee nor Soliman was standing guard. Johnstone was already inside when she entered the low building. He turned, looking as pale as a sheet in the gloom, and held out both hands to stop her coming in any further.

'Stay where you are, Camille,' he breathed. 'It's not a sheep, for heaven's sake.'

But Camille had already seen. Suzanne was lying on her back in the messed straw with her arms asplay and her dress up over her knees. Blood had gushed from a ghastly wound on her neck. Camille closed her eyes and ran out. She ran straight into the medium *gendarme*, who held her back.

'Whatever happened?' she bawled.

'The wolf,' the policeman said. 'The wolf.'

He took her by the arm, helped her to the van, made her sit down in the front seat.

'I'm all cut up about it, too,' the *gendarme* said. 'But I mustn't show it. It's against standing orders.'

'Did Suzanne take a blind bit of notice of your standing orders, I wonder?'

'No, of course not, dearie.'

He took a flask from the glove-compartment and offered it to her, clumsily.

'I don't want any hooch,' she wept. 'I want grapes. I came for grapes.'

'Come on, don't be a baby. Don't be a baby.'

'Suzanne,' Camille moaned. 'My big fat Suzanne.'

'She must have heard the animal,' the *gendarme* said. 'She must have come up to see what the mayhem in the sheep-pen was about. She must have had the beast cornered, and then it jumped her. Jumped her. She was too brave by half, she was.'

'And Watchee?' Camille growled. 'What the fuck was Watchee doing?'

'Don't be a baby,' the *gendarme* said once more. 'Watchee was out. There was one lamb missing, new-born this spring. He spent part of the night looking for it, then when he was too far away to come back in the dark he slept in a meadow. Got back here at seven this morning and called us straight away. So watch it, dearie.'

'Watch what?' Camille said, looking up.

'You mustn't take it out on Watchee when he's grieving. You mustn't say "And what about Watchee? What about Watchee? What the fuck was he doing?" or any other rubbish like that. You're not from hereabouts, so you don't say anything, anything at all, without thinking it through very carefully first. For Watchee Suzanne was like a saint. So watch what you say. Watch it.'

Camille was impressed by the medium *gendarme*. She nodded her assent and wiped her eyes with the back of her sleeve. The policeman proffered a paper handkerchief.

'Where is he?'

'At the back of the pen. Keeping watch.'

'And Soliman?'

The *gendarme* shook his head in resignation.

'He's locked himself in the toilet. In the toilet. He says he'll die there. They're sending us someone from psychology. Can be useful, in special cases.'

'Has he got a gun with him?'

'No, no weapon on him.'

'I mended the leak, last Wednesday,' Camille said glumly.

'Yes. The leak. Do you know how Suzanne came to adopt Soliman Melchior when he was a baby?'

'Yes. I've been told all about it.'

The *gendarme* nodded knowingly.

'The baby wouldn't have anyone but Suzanne. He laid his wee head right there and stopped bawling. That's what they say. I wasn't there. I'm not from these parts. *Gendarme*s don't have the right to be from the whereabouts, so as not to get too involved.'

'I know,' Camille said.

'But you do get involved, all the same. Take Suzanne, for instance. Nobody –'

The *gendarme* stopped in mid-sentence as he saw Johnstone coming, in sombre mood, his head sunk in his shoulders.

'Sure you didn't touch anything?' he asked.

'Your colleague never took his eyes off me.'

'Well?'

'Could be the same animal. Can't be certain.'

'The big wolf?' the *gendarme* queried defensively, screwing up his eyes.

Johnstone pursed his lips. He raised his hand and spread out his thumb and ring finger.

'Big, yes. At least that much between his carnassial and his canine. Can't see easily in there. One gash in the shoulder, one in the throat. Couldn't have had time to pull the trigger.'

Two vehicles were bumping their way up the drive.

'Here come the technicians,' said the *gendarme*. 'With the medic behind them.'

'Come on,' Johnstone said, putting a hand on Camille's shoulder and shaking her gently. 'Let's not stay around.'

'I'd like to talk to Soliman,' Camille said. 'He's shut himself up in the toilet.'

'When people have shut themselves in the john there's no way you'll get anything out of them.'

'I'm going to have a try even so. He's all on his own now.'

'I'll wait for you by the bike.'

Camille went into the silent and ill-lit house, climbed the stairs and stood in front of the closed door.

'Sol,' she said, knocking on the panel.

'You fuckwits can all go to hell!' the young man screamed at her.

Camille nodded. Soliman would keep the tradition alive.

'Sol, I'm not trying to get you out.'

'Fuck off!'

'I'm upset, too, you know.'

'You don't know what upset means! You know nothing, got that? You've not even got the right to be here. You weren't her daughter, OK? So get out! Bloody hell, just fuck off, will you!'

'Of course I don't know what upset means. I was just a friend of Suzanne's, that's all.'

'So there! You see?' Soliman roared.

'I used to mend her plumbing and in return she supplied me with veg and liquor. And anyway I'm not bothered whether you stay in there or not. We'll slide slices of ham under the door to keep you going.'

'Oh, terrific!' the young man shouted.

'So this is the position, Sol. You're going to stay in the toilet. Watchee won't leave the pen, and Buteil is stuck in his shack. Nobody's moving, not anywhere. The sheep will all die.'

'I couldn't care less about those bloody woolsacks! They're totally stupid!'

'But Watchee's an old man. He won't come out, and he won't move either, and he's stopped saying anything. He's gone as stiff as his crook. Don't let him drop, Sol, or else I'll have to have him looked after in an old people's home.'

'What do I care?'

'Watchee's gone like that because he was in the hills when the wolf attacked and he wasn't able to come to Suzanne's aid.'

'And I was in bed! Asleep!'

Camille could hear Soliman burst into tears.

'Suzanne always insisted you slept lots. You were doing what she wanted you to do. It's not your fault.'

'Why didn't she wake me?'

'Because she didn't want you to get in harm's way. You were her little prince.'

Camille leaned her hand on the door.

'That's what she said, you know.'

Camille went out and walked back up towards the pen. The medium *gendarme* stopped her half way.

'What's he up to?' he asked.

'He's crying,' she replied wearily. 'It's difficult having a conversation with someone locked in the toilet.'

'I know,' the *gendarme* agreed, as if he had frequently tried to converse with people locked in their toilets. 'Psychology's late,' he said with a glance at his watch. 'Don't know what they're playing at.'

'What's the doctor saying?'

'Same thing as your trapper. Throat cut. Cut. Between three and four this morning. Toothmarks still can't be seen properly. Have to clean her up first. But he says it won't be very clear in any case. It's not like the teeth had been stuck into modelling clay, right?'

Camille nodded. 'Is Watchee still inside?'

'Yes. We're afraid he'll turn into a statue.'

'You could ask psychology to take a look at him.'

The *gendarme* shook his head, adamant.

'No, it's not worth it,' he declared. 'Watchee is as tough as old bootleather. Psychology would have about as much effect on him as peeing on a tree-trunk.'

'Is that right?' Camille said. 'Would you mind telling me your name?'

'Lemirail. Justin Lemirail.'

'Thank you.'

Camille went on her way, swinging her arms.

She joined Johnstone beside the motorbike and put on her helmet without a word.

'Can't remember where I put the bloody jar,' she muttered.

'I don't think that's a big issue,' Johnstone said.

Camille nodded in agreement, hopped onto the pillion and clasped the big man around his middle.

81

CHAPTER 11

Johnstone drew up in front of the house and kept the bike still while Camille dismounted.

'Aren't you coming in?' she asked. 'I'll make coffee, all right?'

Johnstone shook his head without relaxing his grip on the handlebars.

'Are you going straight back into the hills? Do you really want to go on looking for that foul wolf?'

Johnstone hesitated, then took off his helmet and shook his mane.

'Off to see Massart,' he said.

'Massart? At this time of day?'

'It's already nine,' he said, glancing at his watch.

'I don't get it,' Camille said. 'What have you got against the guy?'

Johnstone made a face. 'Last night's attack doesn't make good sense to me, for a wolf.'

'But it must have, to the wolf.'

'Wolves are frightened of humans,' Johnstone persisted. 'They do not stand up to people.'

'If you say so. But last night's wolf stood up to Suzanne.'

'Look, the old bag was the size of a battleship and made one hell of a noise. She was determined and she was armed. She would have to have got the wolf in a corner with no way out.'

'If you say so. That's what she did do, Lawrence. She trapped the wolf in a corner. Everyone knows that wolves go on the attack when they're cornered.'

'That's just what worries me. The old bag wasn't born yesterday, she knew damn well not to back a wild animal into a corner with no way out. She'd have stayed outside the pen, she'd have gone round the back, and then taken aim through one of the window openings. That's how the old bag would have shot the wolf and killed it stone dead. But for the life of me I cannot imagine her going inside the sheep-pen and backing the creature into a corner.'

Camille frowned.

'So tell me just what it is you're thinking.'

'Not yet. Not sure I'm right.'

'Say it all the same.'

'Bloody hell. Suzanne accused Massart and now Suzanne is dead. She could easily have been to see Massart and thrown all that werewolf nonsense at him. She wasn't scared of anything.'

'So what, Lawrence? Given that Massart is *not* a werewolf. What would he have done about it? He'd have had a good laugh, don't you think?'

'Not necessarily.'

'He's already got a bad reputation and kids keep away from him. What more could Suzanne's accusations do to him? He's supposed to be hairless, impotent, queer, crazy and God knows what else besides. So what, if people say he's a werewolf as well? He can take that on the chin, I reckon. He's been through worse already.'

'Good grief, you really don't get it.'

'Well, tell me straight out what's on your mind. This is no time for swallowing your words.'

'Massart doesn't give a damn for gossip, I agree. Fine. But what if the old bag was right? What if Massart really had been savaging sheep?'

'You're losing it, Johnstone. You told me you didn't believe in werewolves.'

'Not in werewolves, no.'

'You're forgetting the gashes, for heaven's sake. You're not telling me those were made by Massart's front teeth?'

'No, I'm not.'

'There you are, then.'

'But Massart has a dog. A very large dog.'

Camille shivered. She'd seen that dog on the village square. It was a remarkable, long-legged, brindled dog with a massive head that stood as high as a man's waist.

'A mastiff,' said Johnstone. 'The largest breed there is. The only dog that can grow as big or even bigger than a male wolf.'

Camille rested her foot on the kick-stand and sighed.

'Johnstone, why can't it just be a wolf?' she asked. 'A plain old wolf? Why can't it be Crassus the Bald? You couldn't find him yesterday.'

'Because the old bag would have shot him from behind. Through the window. I'm off to see Massart.'

'Why not Lemirail?'

'Who's Lemirail?'

'The medium *gendarme*.'

'Good God. Too soon for that. I'm just going to have a chat with Massart.'

Johnstone revved his engine and soon was vanished over the hill.

He did not come back until lunchtime. Camille was feeling knocked out, she wasn't hungry, she'd just put out bread and tomatoes and was nibbling as she leafed without paying much attention through yesterday's newspaper. Even the *A to Z* would not have aroused her interest today. Johnstone came in without a word, put his gloves and helmet on a chair, glanced at the table, added some ham, cheese and apples to the spread, and sat down. Camille did not attempt to spring the conversation to life as she usually did. As a result Johnstone ate in silence, shaking his locks now and again, casting eyes wide with amazement at Camille from time to time. Camille wondered what would become of them if she did not take a verbal initiative. Maybe they would stay at the same table for forty years eating tomatoes in silence until one of them dropped dead. Maybe. The prospect did not seem burdensome to Johnstone. Camille cracked after twenty minutes.

'So, did you see him?'

'Vanished.'

'Why do you say "vanished"? He's entitled to go out for a while.'

'Sure.'

'Was the dog around?'

'No.'

'There you are, then. He was out. And anyway, it's Sunday.'

Johnstone raised his head.

'Apparently he goes to seven o'clock mass every Sunday', Camille said, 'in some other village.'

'He would have been back already. I combed the whole area around his place for two hours. Didn't come across him.'

'There's lots of room in the mountains, you know.'

'Stopped at Les Écarts on the way back. Soliman's come out of the john.'

'The psychologist?'

Johnstone nodded. 'He's not well. The doctor gave him tranquillisers. He's now asleep.'

'Watchee?'

'Apparently he's moved.'

'Good.'

'All of three feet.'

Camille sighed, tore off a crust of bread, and chewed it absent-mindedly.

'What do you make of Watchee, then?' she asked.

'A pain in the backside.'

'Really. I'm rather impressed.'

'Impressive types are always a pain.'

'That's possible,' Camille conceded.

'I'll go back to find Massart this evening, at his dinner time. Mustn't miss him.'

But that evening Johnstone did not find Massart at home. He waited for more than an hour and half, watching the sun go down over the mountains. Johnstone was a champion waiter. He had once held out for twenty hours on the trot waiting for a bear to come by. When darkness had fallen completely he made tracks back to Saint-Victor.

'I'm worried,' he told Camille.

'You're getting too worried about that one. Nobody knows what he does with his time. It's hot. Maybe he spends his days away up on the mountainside.'

Johnstone pursed his lips. 'He's due at the slaughterhouse tomorrow. Should have been back.'

'Calm down about Massart.'

'Three possibilities,' Johnstone said, holding out a hand with three fingers extended. 'One, Massart is as innocent as a new-born lamb. He's gone for a walk in the mountains and got lost, and is fast asleep with his back propped against a tree-trunk. Or he's got his foot caught in a trap. Or he's fallen into a gully. Even wolves sometimes slip and fall into gullies. Or two . . .'

Johnstone paused for a long while. Camille shook his knee, as if she was jiggling an ill-wired lamp to make it come back on again. It worked.

'Or two: Massart is innocent again, but Suzanne came to talk to him, and this morning he learns she's dead. He takes fright. What if the whole village came to get him? What if the old bag had shared her accusations with other people? He's afraid he's going to be sliced open from his neck to his crotch. So he goes into hiding, with his dog.'

'I don't buy that,' Camille said.

'Or three: Massart is a killer. He killed the sheep, he and his dog. Then he murdered Suzanne. But Suzanne might have talked – to me, for instance. So he scarpers. He's on the run. He's mad, he's bloodthirsty, and he carries out his killings with the jaws of his mastiff.'

'I don't buy that one either. And all this because the poor guy has no body hair. Just because he's ugly and on his own. Even without all this nonsense he can't have much fun up there on his own without any hair.'

'No, that's not it,' Johnstone cut in. 'It's all because the old bag was far from stupid and because the old bag would not have trapped a wolf in a corner. And it's also all because Massart has vanished. I'm going back at dawn. Before he sets off down to Digne.'

'Do me a favour, Lawrence. Leave the poor man alone.'

Johnstone took Camille's hand in his own. 'You always take the other guy's side,' he smiled.

'Yes.'

'That's not the way the world works.'

'Yes it does. No it doesn't. I don't care. Leave Massart alone. He's not done anything.'

'You don't know that, Camille.'

'Don't you think you would do better to go and look for Crassus?'

'Absolutely. Maybe Massart has got Crassus.'

'What do you mean? That he's killed him?'

'No. Tamed him.'

'Why do you say that?'

'Nobody's seen Crassus for nearly two years. He must be somewhere. He was only a cub when he went missing. Could have been tamed. Could have been tamed by a man who's not afraid of a giant mastiff.'

'So where would he have hidden it?'

'In the wooden shack where he keeps the dog. Nobody goes near Massart, let alone his mastiff's kennel. No danger that anyone would ever see the wolf.'

'So how would he have fed it? Wolves need a bundle of feeding. And that would have been noticed.'

'He has to get loads of meat for the mastiff anyway. And remember, Massart does his shopping at Digne. Where he's virtually unknown. He might go hunting, as well. And he works in a slaughter-house. He could easily have raised Crassus without being found out.'

'But why should he have raised a wolf?'

'Same reasons as for keeping a mastiff. Power and vengeance. And to be special. Once knew a nutter who'd brought up a female grizzly. You know what? He thought he was lord of the universe. Having your own grizzly must be a great pick-me-up. Would make your head swim.'

'Same as a wolf, is that what you think?'

'Just the same. Especially if it looks like Crassus. Maybe he uses Crassus to do the killing.'

Camille pondered Johnstone's three possibilities. The thought of Massart ordering Crassus to attack in the dark of night sent shivers down her spine.

'No,' she said. 'Massart is caught in a trap. There are folk about laying traps for him all over the mountain.'

'Maybe you're right,' Johnstone blurted out, with a shake of his hair. 'Maybe the old bag turned my head the other night. Have to accept that for once she was out of her mind and backed the wolf into a corner. So the wolf jumped at her. And Massart is out walking. That leaves one question: where the hell is Crassus the Bald?'

CHAPTER 12

On Sunday, 21 June it was raining cats and dogs on Paris. it had not stopped since dawn. At his bedroom window on the fifth floor of an unmodernised block in the Marais whose façade had a dangerous slant towards the street, Jean-Baptiste Adamsberg stood watching the swirling rainwater pushing rubbish along the gutters and down the drains. Some bits of waste put up stubborn resistance, while others yielded without demur. So life's unfairness was reflected even in the unrecognised world of urban litter. Some people could stand up to pressure, others couldn't.

He had been withstanding it for five weeks now. Not water pressure, but three girls who wanted to get him in the neck. One of the three in particular. A tall, scrawny redhead, usually but not always on dope, about twenty-five, with her escort – two pitiful, wasted, determined, twenty-year-old wraiths under her spell, for ever at her side, ever ready to do her bidding. The redhead was the only one who was really dangerous. She had shot at him ten days ago, in the street, in broad daylight; the bullet had missed his shoulder by barely an inch. One day or another she would finally manage to get a nice heavy bullet through his hide. That was all that girl had on her mind. She had let him know many times, on the phone, in a voice full of muffled rage. A nice heavy bullet, just like the one he had put in the big guy's guts. The guy the girls called Dickie the D., but whose real name was plain Jérôme Lantin.

Under the swaggering pseudonym of Dickie the D., the man had turned a handful of boys and girls who could hardly stand up any more into a pathetic and servile gang that was supposed to provide protection. But Dickie was a dealer to be reckoned with. With his radical methods, he could twist other guys round his little finger. A plump, short brute with enough insight to do business, but not enough to realise that other people existed. He wore spiked bracelets and leather trousers. The initial 'D' perhaps stood for Dictator, or Divine, or Demon. By some miserable twist of fate, the redhead had given herself body and soul to Dickie the D. He was her supplier, her man, her protector, her god and her undoing. This was the man that *Commissaire* Adamsberg had brought down in a cellar at two o'clock one morning.

A bloody battle was already raging between Dickie's gang and the Oberkampf hoodlums when the *flics* burst through the door with their weapons raised. The guys weren't play-acting – they were all armed to the teeth. Dickie was taking aim at

92

a policeman, Adamsberg was about to shoot him below the waist. And at that point some idiot threw a cast-iron café table at the *commissaire*. It knocked Adamsberg three yards back and threw his shot off target, into the guts of Dickie the D.

The final score was one dead and four injured, two of them policemen.

Since which time *Commissaire* Adamsberg had been living with a man's death on his conscience and a girl on his tail. It was the first time he had ever killed a man, in twenty-five years in the force. Certainly he had damaged some arms, legs and feet with the object of keeping his own, but he had never previously done a guy in for good. Certainly it was an accident. Of course it was the cast-iron table the idiot had thrown. Of course Dickie the Dunce, Dickie the Deranged, Dickie the Dread would have mown them all down if he had had the chance. Of course he was a real bad apple, and of course it was an accident. But it was a fatal one.

And now the girl was out to get him. After Dickie's death the gang had evaporated, save for the angel of revenge and attendant cherubs. The avenging female possessed significant amounts of hardware that she had appropriated when the gang broke up, but her lair had not yet been found. Every time she had been arrested lying in wait on one of Adamsberg's probable paths, she had managed to get rid of her weapon before she could be charged with unlawful possession. She always lay in wait next to a dustbin with her hands behind her back. By the time the *flics* had their hands on her, the gun was already somewhere else. It was a stupid set-up, but there was still no way of getting her charged with anything. Anyway, Adamsberg discouraged his colleagues from trying too hard. One day or another she would come out from behind the dustbin and shoot. So for heaven's sake let's leave her out there and wait for her to shoot. You'll find out soon enough whether she'll have the last word, or whether Adamsberg will. Basically, the avenging angel seeking to kill him expunged his own guilt. Not that he had resigned himself to being shot. But this long-drawn-out hunt, day in day out, kept him alert and on his toes.

Adamsberg could see her now, standing on the other side of the street. She was soaking wet, and was leaning against the door of the building opposite. Sometimes she hid, and sometimes she altered her appearance with make-up or even dressed up in disguise, like in a fairy tale. But when she came out in the open, like today, Adamsberg did not know whether she had a weapon on her or not. She often kept visible watch on him like that – to try his nerves, he reckoned. Adamsberg's easygoing nature kept him at a steady rhythm, which was always slow, almost detached. It was not easy, therefore, to know whether he was taking a genuine interest in something or whether he didn't give a damn. More out of indolence than courage,

Commissaire Adamsberg did not know what it was to be scared.

His imperturbable low key had an almost magical calming effect on other people, and brought about genuine miracles in the interrogation of suspects. But it could also seem irritating, unfair, even offensive. People like Inspector Danglard, who felt all of life's big and little bumps in his bones, like a cyclist for ever riding a new leather saddle, despaired of getting Adamsberg to react to anything. Just to react! That wasn't asking for the moon, was it, now?

The redhead, whose name was Sabrina Monge, was quite unaware of the *commissaire*'s unusual rubber soul. Nor did she know that almost as soon as she had begun her tail the police had opened up an escape route for Adamsberg which led from the building's basement through underground passageways into the open two streets away. Nor did she know that he had a plan to deal with her and was working at it quite hard.

Adamsberg cast a last glance at her before going out. He sometimes felt sorry for Sabrina, but all the same she was potentially lethal and not to be taken lightly – but for only a short while yet, he reckoned.

He sauntered towards a bar he had discovered two years ago barely six hundred metres from his flat and which constituted, to his mind, a kind of perfection. The Waters of Liffey was a brick-built Irish pub where there was always a tremendous din. *Commissaire* Adamsberg liked solitude, he liked to let his mind wander far out to sea, but he also liked people and the movement of people, and he fed on their presence around him like a flea. The only burdensome aspect of other people was that they would talk non-stop, and their conversations constantly interrupted Adamsberg's musings. So he found himself obliged to retreat, but retreating from the crowd meant that he had to resume the loneliness he had wanted to suspend for a few hours.

The Waters of Liffey provided a first-rate solution to his dilemma. The only people in the bar were noisy, boozy Irishmen speaking what was for Adamsberg a completely hermetic tongue. He thought he must be one of the last people left on the planet to know not a single word of English. Such old-fashioned ignorance allowed him to fit happily into the Liffey, where he could enjoy the stream of life without being in any way inconvenienced by it. In this precious hidey-hole Adamsberg spent many an hour dreaming away, peacefully waiting for ideas to rise to the surface of his mind.

For that is how Adamsberg found his ideas – simply by waiting for them to turn up. When one rose before his eyes like a dead fish on the crest of a wave, he picked it up, turned it over, asked himself whether he needed this item at the moment, whether it was of any interest. Adamsberg never thought actively, he found it quite sufficient to day-dream and then to sort his catch, like a fisherman scrabbling about clumsily in the bottom of a net and finally picking the prawn out of the mess of sand, seaweed, pebbles and shells. Adamsberg's thoughts contained plenty of seaweed and sand, and he didn't always know how to avoid getting caught in the mess. He needed to jettison a lot of it, evacuate great heaps. He was aware that his own mind produced a mixed bag of mental items of uneven size and value, and that things did not necessarily happen the same way for other people. He had noticed that the difference between his thinking and the mental products of Danglard, his number two, was identical to the difference between a netful from the river-bed and a fish-monger's neatly laid-out slab. He couldn't help it. Anyway, he always ended up fishing something useful out of his glory-hole, as long as people gave him enough time. That is how Adamsberg used his brain, like an ocean that you trust entirely to feed you well, but which you've long ago given up trying to tame.

As he pushed open the door of the Waters of Liffey he reckoned it must be close to eight o'clock. Adamsberg never wore a watch and relied on his inner chronometer, accurate to within ten minutes, sometimes better but never worse than that. The tang of Guinness – or of Guinness-induced vomit – hung heavy in the bar-room air which the large ceiling fan had never managed entirely to refresh. Your elbows stuck to the lacquered tables permanently tacky from spilled beer too rapidly wiped away. Adamsberg put his spiral notepad onto one such table to bag his place, and stuck his jacket unceremoniously over the chair-back. It was the best table in the room, standing under a huge wall-sign bearing three crudely painted silver turrets being consumed by heraldic flames. The arms, so he had been told, of Baile Áthe Cliath, the Gaelic Dublin.

He gave his order to Enid, a strapping, fair-haired waitress endowed with uncommon resistance to Guinness, and asked her to do him a favour by allowing him to watch the evening television news. People knew he was a *flic* and granted him the privilege, when he needed it, of using the little set that was kept tucked inside the bar. Adamsberg knelt down and switched on.

'Trouble brewing?' Enid asked in her thick Irish accent.

'There's a wolf eating lambs, but a long way away.'

'Why's that anything to do with you?'

'Dunno.'

'Dunno' was among the most frequent of Adamsberg's utterances. He fell back on it neither from laziness nor from lack of wits, but because he really did not know the right answer and was ready to admit it. The *commissaire*'s passive ignorance bemused and maddened his deputy, who could not conceive of the possibility of taking any appropriate steps in full ignorance of the facts. Wavering was

Adamsberg's most natural element, however, and his most productive by far.

Enid went off, arms laden with dishes to serve customers seated at tables, and Adamsberg concentrated on the broadcast that had just begun. He put the volume right up as that was the only way of making out the commentary over the Waters's hubbub. He had been following the national news since Thursday, but there'd been nothing more about the wolves of the Mercantour Wildlife Reserve. Story over. He was surprised by the apparently abrupt ending, and convinced that it was more a truce than a final victory. The story was going to pick up again, and go on in a not necessarily very nice manner towards some ineluctable fatality. Why it should do so he did not know. And why it should hold his interest he knew even less. Which is what he had said to Enid.

Adamsberg was therefore only half-surprised to see a view of the now-familiar village square of Saint-Victor-du-Mont on the screen. He bent low and put his ear to the set so as to hear the voice-over. He stood up five minutes later somewhat groggy. Was that what he had been looking for? A woman slaughtered in her own sheep-pen? Had he not been expecting it all week long, at some deeper level of intuition? Only at moments like this one, when the lower depths of his mind were validated by reality, did Adamsberg lose his inner poise and become almost scared of himself.

He had never been entirely at ease with his lower depths. He thought them approximately as wholesome as ingrained dirt on the bottom of a witch's cauldron.

He walked slowly back to his table. Enid had already served his regular plate, a good old baked potato with cheese filling, and Adamsberg sat down to consume it mechanically. He wondered why the death of that woman had not surprised him. Good grief, wolves do not attack humans, they scarper, like the clever good beasts they are. Maybe they might, at a pinch, go for a small child, but they would never take on an adult. The woman would really have had to have given the wolf no alternative at all. And who is dumb enough to corner a wolf? But still, that's what must have happened. The pedantic vet from the previous broadcasts had come on screen again. Science lesson time. He'd given another demo of the carnassials, here, there, you see? The first tear, the second tear. The man was a bore. But he seemed to know his job, and he virtually certified that the woman had been done in by the teeth and jaws of a wolf, of *the* wolf, the big bad wolf of the Mercantour. Yes indeed, that ought to have surprised him, Adamsberg thought.

Adamsberg frowned, pushed away his empty plate, put sugar in his coffee. Maybe it had all seemed odd from the start. Too wonderful or too poetical to be true. When poetry bursts into real life you may be amazed and delighted, but it is never very long before you see that you have been had by a con or a scam. Maybe he had thought it unreal for a wolf out of hell to turn up and lay siege to a whole village. But for heaven's sake, those really were the marks of a wolf's bite. Maybe it was a mad dog? No, the vet had been clear it could not be that. Of course, it was not easy to make a positive identification on the basis of mere bite-marks, but no, it was not a dog. Domestication, mongrelisation, lesser height, shortening of muzzle, overlapping of pre-molars – Adamsberg had not got all of the explanation in detail, but the gist of it was clear: the sheer distance between the two halves of the bite made it impossible to pin the crime on a dog. Save for the special case of the giant mastiff, or bloodhound. But was there a mastiff running wild in the mountains? No, there was not. It was therefore a wolf, and a big one.

On this occasion spoor had been found – a left front paw imprinted in sheep dung, just to the right of the corpse. A print about ten centimetres wide, the size of a wolf's tread. When men put their left foot in shit, it's supposed to bring luck. Adamsberg wondered if it also worked for wolves.

You would really have to be rather dim to corner an animal of that kind. That's what happens if you take it too fast. People always want to go faster, to get things over with. Never does any good. Sin of impatience. Or else this was not an ordinary wolf. Not just a big one, but psychotic too. Adamsberg opened his sketch-pad, pulled a chewed pencil from his pocket, and looked at it with moderate interest. Must be one of Danglard's. He could chew away a warehouseful of pencils. Adamsberg rotated it in his fingers and dreamily studied the deep incisions in the wood made by the teeth of man.

CHAPTER 13

Camille heard the motorbike starting up at dawn. She had not even heard Johnstone getting up. He was a very quiet Canadian and mindful of Camille's sleep. For himself, he did not mind much whether he slept or not, but Camille considered sleep as one of life's key values. She could now hear the engine fading into the distance. She glanced at the alarm clock, and wondered what all the hurry was about.

But of course, it was about Massart. Johnstone was trying to catch him before he left for the slaughterhouse at Digne. She turned over and went straight back to sleep.

At nine o'clock Johnstone returned and shook her shoulder.

'Massart didn't sleep at his place last night. His car is still there. Didn't go to work.'

Camille sat up and rubbed her hair.

'Gonna tell the police.'

'Tell them what?'

'That Massart has gone AWOL. Have to search the mountains.'

'You won't say anything about Suzanne?'

Johnstone shook his head.

'Gonna go through his place first,' he said.

'Search his house? Are you crazy?'

'Have to find him.'

'What good would searching his place do?'

'Could tell us where he's gone.'

'What do you think you'll find? His werewolf suit on a hanger in the closet?'

Johnstone shrugged. 'Camille, put a sock in it, for God's sake. Come on.'

Forty-five minutes later they walked into Massart's little shack, built half of cinder-block and half of planks. The door wasn't even locked.

'I prefer it that way,' Camille said.

There were only two rooms: a barely furnished, gloomy main room, a bedroom and a bathroom. In one corner of the main room a large freezer provided the only visible trace of the modern world.

'Filthy,' Johnstone muttered as he looked around. 'The French are filthy. Have to look in the freezer.'

'Do it yourself,' Camille said, defensively.

Johnstone collected what was on top of the freezer and put the whole lot – a cap, a pocket lamp, a newspaper, a road map and some onions – on Massart's dining table. Then he opened the lid.

'And so?' asked Camille, who had retreated to the opposite side of the room.

'Meat, meat and more meat,' Johnstone reported.

He rummaged among the contents with one hand, right down to the bottom.

'Hare, rabbit, beef, and a quarter-carcass of a deer. Massart's been poaching. For himself, or for his dog, or for both.'

'Any pieces of lamb?'

'No.'

Johnstone dropped the lid back down. Camille was relieved, and sat down at the table to unfold the map.

'Maybe he marks his tracks through the mountains,' she said.

Johnstone moved silently to the bedroom, lifted the mattress, then the base of the bed, opened the drawers in the bedside table and the chest of drawers, looked into the little wardrobe. All filthy.

He came back into the main room wiping his hands on his trousers.

'It's not a local map,' Camille said. 'It's a map of France.'

'Anything written on it?'

'Dunno. Can't see anything in this light.'

Johnstone shrugged, opened the table drawer and emptied its contents onto the oilcloth.

'Stuffs his drawers with piles of shit,' he said. 'Utter crap.'

Camille went to the open front door and looked at the map in the light of day.

'He's marked a route in red pencil,' she said. 'All the way from Saint-Victor to . . .'

Johnstone surveyed the scattered objects briefly, then stuffed the lot back into the drawer and blew away the dust that had settled on the table. Camille was unfolding the other half of the map.

'. . . to Calais,' she concluded. 'Then it crosses the Channel and ends in England.'

'A trip,' Johnstone decided. 'Irrelevant.'

'Along secondary roads. It would take days and days.'

'So he likes the byways.'

'But not people. What's he going to England for?'

'Forget it,' said Johnstone. 'No connection. Anyway it could have been ages ago.'

Camille folded the map in half again and took another look at the area of the Mercantour.

'Look at this,' she said.

Johnstone looked up at her.

'Come and see,' Camille repeated. 'Three pencilled Xs.'

Johnstone bent over the map.

'Can't see them.'

'There,' Camille said, pointing with her finger. 'They're hardly visible.'

Johnstone took the map outside and creased his brow as he studied the red marks in full daylight.

'The three sheep farms,' he said between his teeth. 'Saint-Victor, Ventebrune, Pierrefort.'

'Can't be sure. The scale's too big.'

'Yes, we can,' Johnstone said with a shake of his long hair. 'Sheep farms.'

'But so what? All it proves is that Massart is interested in the savagings, same as you, same as everyone. He wants to work out how the wolf is moving around. You've done exactly the same thing, you've plotted the sites on the map of the Mercantour.'

'In that case he'd have put crosses on the other savagings, the ones that happened last year and the year before.'

'But if he's only interested in the big wolf?'

Johnstone folded the map in a trice, put it in his jacket and closed the door behind him.

'We're off,' he said.

'What about the map? Aren't you going to put it back?'

'Taking it. To have a closer look.'

'And what about the *flics*? What if they discover what you've done?'

'Do you think the *flics* are bloody well going to care about a map?'

'You're talking like Suzanne.'

'I told you. She turned my head.'

'Turned it a bit too far. Put the map back.'

'Camille, you're the one who's trying to protect Massart. It's better for him if we slip his map out from under.'

When they reached home Camille opened the shutters wide while Johnstone spread the map of France on the wooden table.

'This map stinks,' he said.

'No, it doesn't,' Camille said.

'It stinks of grease. Dunno what you French

have up your noses so as smells never bother you.'

'We've been deep-fried in two thousand years of historical fat, that's what. You uncooked Canadians can't understand.'

'Has to be something like that,' said Johnstone. 'Has to be why old countries always stink. All right,' he added, handing her a magnifying glass, 'you give that a good look. I'm going down to see the *flics*.'

Camille bent over the map and studied the roads, moving the glass slowly over the whole Mercantour area.

Johnstone took a whole hour to get back.

'They kept you a while,' Camille said.

'Yeah. Wondered why I was fussing over Massart. How did I know he'd run off. Nobody round here gives a damn for that man. Couldn't tell them about the werewolf.'

'So what did you say?'

'I told them Massart had made a rendezvous with me on Sunday to show me a big paw-print he'd spotted near Mont Vence.'

'Not bad.'

'And there was nobody there in the morning, or in the evening. So I got worried, and went back to see this morning.'

'Sounds logical.'

'In the end, they got worried too. Rang the slaughterhouse at Digne. Nobody's seen him there either. So they've just called in the men from

Puygiron and given them instructions to comb the area around the shack. If they haven't found Massart by two o'clock, they'll call in the *gendarmes* from Entrevaux as well. I want to eat, Camille. I'm starving. Fold the map away. Did you find anything else?'

'Four more *X*s, very faint. All of them between RN202 and the Mercantour.'

Johnstone raised his head interrogatively.

'They correspond roughly to Andelle and Anélias, east of Saint-Victor, to Guillos, ten kilometres north, and to La Castille, at the very edge of the National Park.'

'Doesn't fit,' said Johnstone. 'Never been a savaging in those farms. You sure of those locations?'

'Pretty much.'

'Doesn't fit. Must mean something else.' Johnstone pondered. 'Maybe that's where he sets his traps,' he suggested.

'Why mark them on a map?'

'To log catches. To record good poaching grounds.'

Camille nodded in agreement and folded the map away.

'We'll have lunch at the village café,' she said. 'There's nothing in the larder.'

Johnstone scowled as he looked in the fridge for confirmation.

'You believe me now?' Camille said.

Johnstone was a loner who did not like mixing in public places; he especially disliked eating in cafés in front of other people, amid the clatter of cutlery and the sounds of mastication. Camille liked the noise and whenever she could she dragged Johnstone to the village café, where she went almost daily whenever he disappeared up into the Mercantour hills.

She went up to him and kissed him on the lips.

'Come on,' she said.

Johnstone gave her a hug. Camille would run away if he tried to cut her off from the rest of the world. But that meant making a big sacrifice.

As they were finishing their lunch, Larquet, the roadman's brother, burst into the café, out of breath and apoplectic. Everyone fell silent. Larquet never set foot in the café as he always took his tiffin in a dixie and ate on the hoof.

'What's up, old fellow?' said the barkeeper. 'You look like you've seen the Virgin Mary.'

'I ain't seen no virgin, you idiot. I saw the vet's wife coming back up from Saint-André.'

'Not quite the same thing, I grant you,' said the bar-keeper.

The vet's wife was a medical auxiliary and had stuck needles into just about every backside in Saint-Victor and the surrounding area. She was much sought after because she had such a gentle touch that you hardly felt the injection. Others claimed her popularity stemmed from her sleeping with all the not entirely repulsive males whose rumps she perforated. More charitable souls said it was not her fault if she had to give injections in men's behinds, it could not be much fun to do that for a living and just put yourself in her shoes for a moment.

'And so what?' asked the barkeeper. 'Did she tip you in the ditch and have it off with you?'

'You're a brainless oaf, you are,' Larquet snorted with contempt. 'You want to know something, Albert?'

'Tell me, do.'

'She refuses to treat you, and that's what you can't stand. So you sling mud at her because that's the only thing you know how to do.'

'You finished your sermon?' the barkeeper retorted with a flash of anger in his eyes.

Albert had very small blue eyes set in a broad, baked-clay face. He was not particularly appealing.

'Yes, I've finished, but only because I don't want to offend your lady wife.'

'That's enough of that,' said Lucie, putting her hand on Albert's arm. 'What's going on, Larquet?'

'The vet's wife was on her way back from Guillos, she was. Where three more sheep have been done for.'

'Guillos? Are you sure? That's a long way off!'

'Of course I'm sure, I ain't making this up. It was Guillos. That means that the beast can strike anywhere. If it wants, it can be at Terres-Rouges tomorrow and Voudailles the day after. Whenever it likes, wherever it likes.'

'Whose sheep were they?'

'Gremont's. He's all churned up about it.'

'But it's only sheep!' someone bellowed. 'Are you going to cry your eyes out just for sheep?'

Everyone turned to see who it was. It was Buteil, the farm manager at Les Écarts, looking distraught. Bloody hell: Suzanne.

'None of you's shed a tear for Suzanne, and she ain't even in her grave! But you're sniffling over bloody baa-baas! You're all swine!'

'No, Buteil, we're not sniffling,' said Larquet, holding his hand out. 'We may all be swine, specially Albert, but nobody's forgotten Suzanne. But it's the same foul beast that done her in, and bloody hell, we've got to find it!'

'Right,' someone said.

'Right. And if the lads from Guillos find it first, we'll look pathetic.'

'We'll get it first. The Guillos lot have gone soft since they switched to lavender.'

'Don't kid yourselves, my friends,' said the postman, who was something of a nervous wreck. 'We're past it too, same as the blokes from Guillos or wherever. We've lost the knack, we've forgotten how to do it. We aren't going to catch the beast until it drops in here for a drink at the bar. Even then we'll have to wait until it's good and sozzled, and we'll need to be ten strong to keep it down. Meanwhile it'll have eaten up the whole county.'

'Heigh-ho, what a jolly fellow you are.'

'That story about a wolf coming in for a drink at the bar is farcical.'

'We should call in a 'copter,' said someone else.

'A 'copter? To look down on the mountains? Are you completely out of your mind?'

'Looks like we've lost Massart as well,' someone butted in. 'The *gendarmes* are looking for him on Mont Vence.'

'Not what I'd called a great loss,' Albert said.

'Fuckwit!' Larquet said.

'Enough of that!' Lucie said.

'How do you know Massart hasn't also fallen prey to the beast? What with his habit of going out at night.'

'Yeah, right enough, when we find Massart, we'll find him in little pieces. You mark my words.'

Johnstone grasped Camille's wrist. 'Let's get out of here,' he said. 'They're driving me crazy.'

When they got into the open air Johnstone took a deep breath, as if he had just emerged from a cloud of poison gas.

'A binful of loonies,' he growled.

'They're not loonies,' Camille said. 'They're just fearful, and sorrowful, and some of them are tipsy anyway. But I agree that Albert is a nasty piece of work.'

They walked home under the burning sun.

'What do you think about it?' asked Camille.

'About what? About their being sozzled?'

'No. About the place where the wolf attacked, Guillos. It was marked with an *X* on the map.'

Johnstone stopped and looked Camille in the eyes.

'How could Massart have known?' she said under her breath. 'How could he have known *in advance*?'

Barking dogs could be heard in the distance. Johnstone stiffened.

'*Gendarme*s looking for him,' he said with a grin. 'Fat lot of good it'll do. They won't find him. Last night at Guillos, tomorrow he'll be at La Castille. He's the killer, Camille. He's doing the killing, with Crassus.'

Camille made as if to say something, but stopped short. She could not find anything to say in Massart's defence.

'With Crassus,' Johnstone continued. 'On the run. They'll slaughter sheep, women, children.'

'But for heaven's sake, why?' she whispered.

'Because he has no hair.'

Camille looked at him in disbelief.

'And it's made him crazy,' Johnstone concluded. 'We're going to the police.'

'Wait,' said Camille, holding him back by the sleeve.

'What? You want him to murder more Suzannes?'

'Let's wait until tomorrow. To see if they find him. Please.'

Johnstone nodded and walked on up the street in silence.

'Augustus has had nothing to eat since Friday,' he said. 'I'm going up again. Back tomorrow noon.'

Next day at noon Massart was still missing. The lunchtime news reported three sheep savaged at La Castille. The wolf was on his way north.

★　★　★

114

In Paris, Jean-Baptiste Adamsberg made a note of the news. He had got hold of a Landranger map of the Mercantour, and he pulled it out of the bottom drawer where he kept files on murky muddles and dicey stratagems. He put a red line underneath the name of La Castille on the map. Yesterday he had underlined Guillos. He gazed at the map for a good while with his elbow on the table and his cheek in his hand. Pondering.

Danglard watched him at it, slightly aghast. He could not understand why Adamsberg had become so interested in the wolf business when he was up to his neck in a complicated manslaughter case in the Latin Quarter (a claim of self-defence which was just a bit too neat to be true) and when a raving madwoman had sworn she would put a bullet in his guts. But that's the way things were. Danglard had never grasped the peculiar logic that lay behind Adamsberg's decisions. In his view, of course, it was no logic at all, just an unending kaleidoscope of hunches and surmises which inexplicably gave rise to undeniably first-rate results. That said, Danglard's nerves could not stand the strain of keeping in step with Adamsberg's thought processes. For not only were the *commissaire*'s thoughts of indeterminate substance, hovering between the solid, liquid and gaseous states, but they were forever agglutinating with other thoughts without the slightest rational link. So while Danglard with his well-honed mind sorted sheep from goats, put things in little boxes, found the missing links, and thereby solved problems with method, Adamsberg put one thing with another, or turned them upside down, or scattered what had been brought together and threw it up in the air to see where it would fall. And despite his amazingly slow pace, he would, in the end, extract truth from that chaos. Danglard therefore supposed that *Commissaire* Adamsberg, like a genius or a mental patient, was endowed with what people call 'his own kind of logic'. For years he had been trying to get used to it, but he remained torn between finding Adamsberg's mind admirable, and finding it exasperating.

Danglard was indeed a divided man. Adamsberg, on the other hand, had been cast (rather hurriedly, at a guess) from a single mould and from a single, separate and slippery substance, which meant that the real world could never get a grip on him for very long. Strange to say, he was easy to get on with. Except for people who tried to get a grip on him, of course. And there were plenty of those. There always are people who want to get a grip on you.

Commissaire Adamsberg measured the distance between Guillos and La Castille with index finger and thumb, then pivoted on the latter to see where this nomadic bloodthirsty wolf might strike next in its search for new territory. Danglard watched him working at it for a few minutes. Despite the swirling mists and mirages of his mental landscape, Adamsberg could sometimes be disturbingly precise on technical matters.

116

'Something wrong with the wolves, then?' Danglard kicked off.

'With the *wolf*, Danglard. He's all alone, but he's as dangerous as a pack of ten. An uncatchable man-eater.'

'Is that any of our business? In any way you care to state?'

'No, Danglard, it's none of our business. How could it be?'

Danglard got up and looked at the map over Adamsberg's shoulder.

'All the same', the *commissaire* muttered, 'it's going to have to be somebody's business, sooner or later –'

'That girl, Sabrina Monge,' Danglard interrupted. 'She's found the underground exit. We're busted.'

'I know.'

'Must head her off before she tops you.'

'She can't be stopped. She has to shoot, she has to miss, and then we can pick her up. And get to work properly. Any news of the kid?'

'We've got a lead in Poland. But that could take a long time. She's got us trapped.'

'No, she hasn't. I'm going to disappear, Danglard. That'll give us time to find the kid before she tries to put a bullet in me.'

'Disappear where?'

'You'll soon find out. Tell me where the mastermind of the Gay-Lussac murder hangs out, if that's what he really is.'

'Avignon.'

'Then that's where I'll go. I'm off to Avignon. Nobody needs to know save you, Danglard. I've got the green light from the authorities. I need Sabrina off my tail so as to work in peace and quiet.'

'Makes sense,' said Danglard.

'Watch out, Danglard. When she realises I've gone off screen, she'll lay traps. And she's a very clever girl. So not a word to anyone, not even if my own mother were to whine at you on the phone. Mind you, my mother never whines, nor do any of my five sisters. Danglard, you'll be the only person to have my number.'

'While you're gone, sir, should I carry on with the map?' asked Danglard as he pointed to his boss's desk.

'No, my friend. Bugger the wolf.'

CHAPTER 14

When Johnstone got to the *Gendarmerie* at Puygiron he insisted on speaking to the most senior officer present. The conscript on desk duty did not give in straight away.

'What's your superior officer?' Johnstone asked.

'He's the sort of bloke who'll have you out on your ear in no time at all if you give him grief.'

'No, I meant, what rank has he got? What form of address to use, you know, what should I call him?'

'You should call him "Head Deputy".'

'Well then, that's the man I want to see. I want to see the Head Deputy.'

'And on what account do you wish to see the Head Deputy?'

'On account of a horror story I have to tell him. Such horror as to make you send me in to see your superior officer as soon as you've heard it, and to make your super send me up to his boss as soon as he's heard it. But I'm a busy man. I'm not going to waste my time telling the story four times over, I'm going straight to see the Head Deputy.'

The conscript frowned, unsure of his ground.

'What's makes this story such a horror, then?'

'Listen, young man,' said Johnstone. 'You know what a werewolf is?'

The *gendarme* looked at him. 'Of course,' he smirked.

'Well, you can wipe that grin off your face, because the tale I have to tell is about a werewolf.'

The conscript hesitated before throwing in the towel.

'I don't think I'm qualified to deal with that.'

'I'm afraid not,' said Johnstone.

'I'm not even sure that the Head Deputy is qualified to deal with it.'

'Now look here, young man,' Johnstone replied with false patience. 'We'll find out soon enough what the Head Deputy is and is not qualified to do. The best way to find out is to go see him. Is that clear?'

The conscript went off and came back five minutes later.

'The Head Deputy is ready to see you,' he said, pointing the way to a door.

'You can go in on your own,' Camille said abruptly to Johnstone. 'I don't like grassing on people. I'll wait for you in reception.'

'Bloody hell, you're deserting me so I play the part of the bastard solo, right? You really don't want to share the part, do you?'

Camille shrugged.

'Shit, Camille, this isn't about giving a man away. This is about stopping a lunatic.'

'I know.'

'So come in with me.'

'I can't. Don't ask.'

'You know you're ratting on Suzanne.'

'Emotional blackmail won't work, Lawrence. Go on in on your own. I'll be waiting.'

'Do you disapprove of my doing this?'

'No.'

'Then you're a coward.'

'I am a coward.'

'Have you always known?'

'For heaven's sake! Of course I've always known.'

Johnstone smiled and followed the conscript. Just before Johnstone went in to see the Head Deputy, the conscript tugged at his sleeve and said in a whisper:

'Seriously, though, is it a real werewolf? A bloke who when you open him up he's got . . .'

'Too soon to say,' said Johnstone. 'That's the kind of thing you can only prove at the very end, if you get my meaning.'

'Receiving you loud and clear, sir.'

'Glad to know that.'

The Head Deputy was a well-groomed man with a thin yet flabby face, leaning back in his plastic chair with his hands folded on his stomach and a sardonic curl to his lips. Johnstone recognised the man sitting at a side table with a typewriter – it was Justin Lemirail, the medium *gendarme*. Johnstone greeted him with a gesture.

'So we've come across a . . . how should I say . . . a lycanthrope, have we?' asked the Head Deputy with a sly grin.

'Don't see what's funny about that,' Johnstone answered gruffly.

'Now, now,' said the Head Deputy in the sugary tone that people use to mollify half-wits. 'Where did you come across your lycanthrope, then?'

'At Saint-Victor-du-Mont. Five sheep were savaged there last week, on Suzanne Rosselin's farm. Your assistant was there.'

The Head Deputy gestured towards the Canadian with an arm movement more likely to be seen at a *thé dansant* than in the paramilitary police.

'Family name, given name, ID,' he requested without ceasing to beam.

'Lawrence Donald Johnstone. Canadian citizen.'

Johnstone hauled a wodge of papers from his jacket pocket and put them on the table. Passport, visa, residence permit.

'Are you the scientist who's working on the Mercantour?'

Johnstone nodded.

'I see there are . . . how should I say? . . . extension requests. Run into trouble, have we?'

'No problems. I'm hanging around, that's all. Rooting in.'

'Can you say why?'

'Wolves, insects, woman.'

'As good a set of reasons as any.'

'Guess so,' said Johnstone.

The Head Deputy signalled to Lemirail to start typing.

'You know who Suzanne Rosselin is?' asked Johnstone.

'But of course, M. Johnstone. It's that poor woman who was killed . . . how should I say? . . . on Sunday.'

'And you know who Auguste Massart is?'

'We've been looking for M. Massart since yesterday.'

'Last Wednesday, Suzanne Rosselin accused Massart of being a werewolf.'

'Any witnesses?'

'I was.'

'You and who else?'

'No-one else.'

'What a pity. Can you give me a reason why the good lady should have confided in you alone?'

'Two good reasons. Suzanne believed that anyone from Saint-Victor was by definition an ignorant blockhead.'

'I can confirm that,' Lemirail interrupted.

'So in the first place I'm an outsider, and in the second place I know about wolves,' Johnstone concluded.

'And on what did Mme Rosselin base her . . . how should I say? . . . accusation?'

'On the fact that Massart has no body hair.'

The Head Deputy furrowed his brow.

'Suzanne was murdered', Johnstone continued,

'during the night of Saturday to Sunday. Massart went AWOL on Sunday.'

The deputy smiled. 'Or got lost in the hills,' he said.

'If Massart had got lost or trapped or whatever', Johnstone objected, 'his mastiff would not have gone missing as well.'

'The mastiff is surely at his side, guarding his master.'

'But he'd have been heard. He'd be howling.'

'Are you insinuating that a lycanthrope named Massart murdered a woman called Rosselin and thereafter . . . how shall I say? . . . ran away?'

'I'm insinuating that he killed Suzanne, yes.'

'And are you proposing we should take hold of this individual and then slice him open from the neck to the . . .'

'Bugger that,' said Johnstone. 'That's bullshit. This is a serious matter.'

'That's better. Now lay out your case and support it with convincing arguments.'

'I think Suzanne was not killed by a wolf, because Suzanne would never have pushed a wolf into a corner. I think Massart is not lost in the hills but on the run. I think Massart is not a werewolf but a hairless lunatic who kills sheep with his mastiff or with Crassus the Bald.'

'And who might that be?'

'Crassus is a very large wolf who's not been spotted for two years. I think Massart caught him when he was still a cub and tamed him. I think

Massart lost control of his bloodlust when the wolves came over into the Mercantour. I think he domesticated the cub and trained it to attack. I think that now he's murdered a woman, the flood-gates are wide open. I think he could kill again, especially women. I think that Crassus is an exceptionally large wolf and very dangerous. I think you must stop combing Mont Vence and hunt for Massart further north, above La Castille, which is where he was last night.'

Johnstone stopped and took a deep breath. That was a whole lot of speaking. Lemirail was typing away at high speed.

'To my mind,' said the Head Deputy, 'things are not quite so involved. We have enough on our hands dealing with the wolves, M. Johnstone, and we can do without imaginary wolf-tamers into the bargain. Wolves, M. Johnstone, are not liked in these parts. And in these parts, people do not kill sheep.'

'But Massart kills sheep, at the slaughterhouse.'

'That is to confuse killing and slaughtering. You don't believe Suzanne Rosselin died accidentally, but I do. That Rosselin woman was the sort of person who might well provoke a wild animal without thinking of – how shall I say? – the consequences. She was also likely to swallow almost any story doing the rounds. You don't believe Massart has got lost in the hills, but you don't know the area, believe you me. In the last fifteen years three experienced hikers have died around here from accidental falls. One of them has never been found. Massart's shack has been properly searched. We found his walking boots missing, as well as his stick, his backpack, his rifle, his ammo pouch and his how shall I say hunting jacket. But he did not take a change of clothes or a toilet bag with him. What that means, M. Johnstone, is that the man Massart has not gone AWOL, as you allege, he went for his how shall I say Sunday stroll in the hills. It's possible he was out hunting.'

'A man on the run doesn't always remember to take his toothbrush,' Johnstone said gruffly. 'He's not on an excursion. Did he leave any money in the house?'

'No.'

'Why would he have taken all his money with him if he'd gone out hunting?'

'How do you know there was cash in the house anyway? We have no reason to suppose he took any with him.'

'And the mastiff?'

'The mastiff stayed with his master and fell with him into a ravine. Or else the dog fell and the master tried to save him.'

'Damn it, let's suppose you're right,' Johnstone said. 'But what about Crassus? How could a wolf like that just disappear at such a young age from the whole Mercantour National Park? He's never been seen again, anywhere.'

'Crassus no doubt met his maker and his bones lie gleaming somewhere in the Park forest.'

126

'Damn it,' Johnstone said. 'Let's suppose you're right.'

'You let your imagination run away with you, M. Johnstone. I don't know what things are like where you come from, but in this how shall I say country, I have to tell you, there are precisely four causes of criminal violence capable of giving rise to the death of the victim: being betrayed by a spouse, being disappointed by a will, excessive consumption of alcohol, and trouble with the people next door. Wolf-taming and lady-killing are not among them, as you see, M. Johnstone. What exactly do you do for a living, in your own country?'

'Grizzly bears,' Johnstone said, gritting his teeth. 'I study grizzly bears.'

'You mean you live among these how shall I say bears?'

'Yeah, right.'

'A team job, I imagine?'

'No. Most of the time I'm on my own.'

The Head Deputy put a look on his face that said 'Poor fellow, now I can see why you went off the rails like that'. In fury, Johnstone got Massart's road map out of his pocket and laid it on the desk.

'Look at this, Head Deputy,' he said slowly and deliberately. 'Here is a map that I found in Massart's shack yesterday morning.'

'Did you of your own free will enter the Massart residence in the absence of the owner?'

127

'The door wasn't locked. I was worried. Could have been dead in bed. Duty to help. There's a witness.'

'And you knowingly purloined this map?'

'No. I looked at it and put it back in my pocket without realising. Later on, at home, I noticed these markings.'

The Head Deputy pulled the map over to his side of the desk and inspected it with care. After a few minutes he pushed it back to Johnstone's side, with no comment.

'These five Xs mark the hamlets where the latest sheep savagings have taken place,' Johnstone explained as he pointed them out. 'The Xs for Guillos and La Castille were marked *before* the attacks took place yesterday and last night.'

'And then there's a whole itinerary to England,' the Head Deputy observed.

'Could be his way of leaving the country. The marked route stays off all main roads. He'd thought it all through.'

'Hadn't he just!' the *gendarme* laughed, leaning right back in his chair.

'Meaning?'

'Meaning, M. Johnstone, that M. Massart has a kind of brother in how shall I say England, where he runs the main slaughterhouse in Manchester. The trade runs in the family. Massart had long been planning to join his brother over there.'

'How do you know that?'

'Because I'm a Head Deputy in the *gendarmerie*,

128

M. Johnstone. Anyway, it's common knowledge in these parts.'

'In that case, why did he work out a route on minor roads?'

The deputy beamed even more broadly.

'It's quite unbelievable how much I have to teach you, M. Johnstone! Where you come from people do five hundred kilometres of motorway just to have a beer. But over here people do not necessarily go from A to B in a straight line. Massart spent twenty years as an itinerant bottomer, working the markets, with one day here and one day there. He knows hundreds of villages and thousands of people. The minor roads of France are his home patch.'

'Why did he give up rushing chairs?'

'He wanted to come back to his roots. He found a job at the slaughterhouse and came back here six years ago. But you can't say people put out the flags for him. Hatred of the Massart clan has deep roots around here. It must go back to an old and ugly story that has to do with his how shall I say father, or grandfather, I don't recall.'

Johnstone shook his head in a way that showed his impatience.

'And the *X*s?' he asked.

The Head Deputy smiled as he tapped the map with his fingertip.

'This whole rectangle here – between the mountain range and the main road, and the gorges of the rivers Daluis and La Tinée – is Massart's pick-up area for the abattoir at Digne. Saint-Victor, Pierrefort, Guillos, Ventebrune and La Castille are where you'll find his main suppliers of lambs for the slaughter. That's what your Xs are.'

Johnstone folded up his map without saying a word.

'Ignorance, M. Johnstone, is the mother of the maddest ideas.'

Johnstone put the map back in his pocket and gathered up his documents.

'So there's not the faintest chance of an investigation?'

The Head Deputy shook his head.

'Not the faintest,' he agreed. 'We'll proceed in the normal way with a search that we'll keep up until there's no chance of finding him alive. But I fear that the how shall I say mountain has already had the better of him.'

He held out his hand to Johnstone without standing up. The trapper shook it in silence and began to leave the room.

'One moment, please,' said the Head Deputy.

'Yes?'

'What exactly does "bullshit" mean?'

'It means cow-crap, bison-dung, and bloody nonsense.'

'Thank you for this information.'

'You're welcome.'

Johnstone opened the door and went out.

'He's not very civilised,' the Head Deputy remarked.

'They're all like that over there,' Lemirail explained to his superior. 'All of them. They're not bad folk, but they're rough. Not refined. Not at all.'

'Plain ignorant,' said the Head Deputy.

CHAPTER 15

Camille did not switch on the light. Johnstone was grabbing a bite in the greyness before setting off again to the Mercantour. Mercier was expecting him, so were Augustus and Electre, so was the whole crowd. He wanted to trap rabbits for the old paterfamilias and to see the others at sunrise. He would come back down later for the fat lady's funeral, or so he had said. He was grim-faced and sick at heart as he chewed his sandwich.

'That stupid Head Deputy is too big for his bloody boots,' he muttered to himself. 'He can't bear anyone knowing more than he does. Can't stomach an ignorant Canadian having anything at all to teach him about a local. Because he thinks all Canadians are ignorant and smear themselves with bear-fat. But *he* stinks of sweat.'

'Maybe things will ease off,' Camille said.

'Things aren't going to ease off at all. Only after Massart has had his wolf savage a dozen women – if he doesn't manage to murder them with his own bare hands – will they get off their backsides and do something.'

'I think he'll stick to sheep,' Camille said. 'He

killed Suzanne in self-defence. Maybe he'll make a beeline for Manchester and stop. It was village life that made him go crazy.'

Johnstone looked at her and stroked her hair.

'You're really weird,' he said. 'You see no evil anywhere. I'm afraid you're blind.'

'Could be,' Camille shrugged, sounding ruffled.

'Haven't you understood what's going on? Have you really not understood?'

'I've understood as much as you have.'

'No, you haven't, Camille. You haven't understood a thing. You haven't twigged that Massart murdered only female sheep. He never touched a wether or a lamb, and certainly never any tetchy rams. Camille, he only ever goes for *ewes*. But that passed you by completely.'

'It could have,' said Camille, who was in fact beginning to grasp what had quite passed her by.

'And the reason you missed it is because you're not a ram. You don't see the female in a ewe. So you aren't aware of the sexual violence in the savagings. You think Massart's going to stop. My poor darling. Massart *can't* stop. Don't you see that the stupid slaughterer is basically a rapist?'

Camille nodded. She was beginning to see.

'Now that he's upgraded from ewes to women, do you really think he's going to calm down when he gets to Manchester? For heaven's sake, he's not going to slack off one bit! He's not got the slightest chance of a spot of peace. He'll go on seeking whom he may devour. Massart may have no body hair and he may not be carrying a cutting tool, but he's got his wolf with him, and the wolf is a hundred times hairier than any man, and has jaws ten times sharper than any knife. He'll let his own beast loose on the women he chooses and watch it gnaw their flesh in his stead.'

Johnstone stood up and shook his hair with a jerk, as if to dispel all that violence. He smiled as he put his arms around Camille.

'That's how it is,' he whispered. 'Animal life.'

Johnstone disappeared from sight down the road, but Camille went on sitting where she was for another fifteen minutes, deep in silent thought, besieged by unpleasant images.

Music time. She switched on the synthesiser and put on the headphones. She still had two themes to come up with before she could finish episode eight of the romantic soap.

The only way she could compose music of this kind to order was to bury herself in the emotional lives of the characters in the soap, but given the silliness of the scrapes they got into, that was no easy task. The plot was based entirely on the dramatic friction between two dilemmas. On the one hand you had a middle-aged aristocrat recently retired from the military who had sworn never to remarry because of some unexplained tragedy in his past; and on the other, a much younger female classics teacher who'd sworn never to love another man because of a similarly unidentified upset in her past.

The aristocrat spends his time giving an education to his two children within the confines of his estate with its castle in the valley of the Loire (it wasn't clear why these kids couldn't go to school). Which is how he comes across the classics teacher. Fine. From which there arises an unspoken, unexpected, and irresistible physical attraction between the squire and the schoolmarm, putting the protagonists' oaths of celibacy to a pretty demanding test.

That was where Camille was up to and much of the time she felt stuck. She was as sick of the squire pacing back and forth before the flaming logs in the baronial fireplace as she was of the teacher standing at the blackboard, both of them visibly holding themselves back with clenched fists from their natural inclinations. Camille detested the pair of them. The best mental trick she had found for allowing herself to compose a halfway decent sound-track was to replace the laird and the lady teacher with Mother Water-Rat and Father Water-Rat from the storybooks she loved as a child, when she still believed in love. She could close her eyes and summon up an image of Father Rat dressed in workman's overalls standing proudly on his firm hind legs and gazing amorously at Mother Rat in her red blouse, while the two Baby Rats gambolled at their feet gobbling up Greek verbs. She could work better with that in her mind. She could create suspense and tension over an unexplained absence of M.

or Mme Rat just as she could warm up the emotions when they got back together again. The producers had so far expressed satisfaction with the tapes she was sending in. Very good fit with the subject, they said.

The death of Suzanne had made it damn hard to bother about Mummy Water-Rat, Daddy Water-Rat and their two juniors getting all tangled up over nothing at all.

Camille paused quite often with her fingers at rest on the keyboard. To her mind, what had really upset Johnstone as far as Massart was concerned was not just the horrible savagings, but the fact that he was making use of a wolf. He was bringing the beasts into disrepute, he was demeaning them, he was cheapening them. Massart had done more harm to the cause of the wolves in a week than sheep farmers had done in six years' lobbying. Johnstone would never forgive the man for that.

But there was nothing that could be done about it now. Massart was on the road, the *gendarme*s were looking for his remains on Mont Vence, Johnstone was back up in the Mercantour, and Camille was once more confronted with a quartet of weepy mammals.

It was only one in the morning, but she took off her headphones, closed her manuscript book, lay down on the double bed and opened *The A to Z of Tools for Trade and Craft* at the page describing an *Emery grinder Ø125mm 850W with left and right handles & worn brush safety cut-out.*

Now that would have sorted out a lot of the classics teacher's little problems, if only she had taken the trouble to find out about it.

There was a gentle knock at the door, twice over. Camille sat up with a start. She kept dead still and waited. Then two more knocks as well as rustling from the other side of the wooden panel. No sound of voice, nobody calling. Another short interval, then two more knocks. Camille saw the door latch going down then coming back up again. She slipped out of bed with her heart pounding. She had the door locked from the inside, but anyone who really wanted to get in could easily shove a shoulder through the windowpane. Massart? Massart could have seen them when they went into his shack. Or even when they went to talk to the police. Who's to say that Massart hadn't waited for Johnstone to leave before coming to deal with her, in the dark, man to woman? With the wolf?

She made herself take deep breaths and tiptoed over to her tool-bag. Dear lovely old bag, with your hammers, your heavy-duty universal pliers, your metal oil-squirter and its reservoir of engine oil. She took the oilcan in her left hand and a mallet in her right, and moved carefully towards the telephone. She imagined the hairless man was there on the other side of that door, quietly seeking a means of entering the room.

'Camille?' Soliman called out suddenly. 'Are you there?'

137

Camille dropped her arms and opened the door. In the shadows she could make out the young man's silhouette and the bewilderment on his face.

'Were you mending something?' he asked. 'At this time of night?'

'Why didn't you say it was you?'

'I didn't know if you were awake or not. Why didn't you answer the knock?' Sol stared at the oilcan and the mallet. 'I gave you a scare, right?'

'Maybe,' Camille said. 'Now come on in.'

'I'm not on my own.' Sol hesitated. 'Watchee's with me.'

Camille raised her eyes and made out the silhouette of the ancient, straight-backed shepherd standing four paces behind the young man. Watchee's being down in the village and not up on the sheep farm meant that something quite exceptional was under way.

'What on earth has happened?' she whispered.

'Nothing's happened. We want to see you.'

Camille drew back to let Sol and Watchee come in. The old man greeted her stiffly, with a nod of the head. Camille put down the oilcan and the mallet, though her hands were still shaking, and waved them to a seat. The old man's stare made her feel awkward. She got out three glasses and filled them to the brim with a brandy that had no grapes in it. There had not been any grapes since Suzanne died.

'What were you scared of?' Soliman asked.

Camille shrugged.

'Nothing. I just got the shivers, that's all.'

'But you're not a scaredy-cat, usually.'

'Sometimes I am.'

'What were you scared of?' Soliman insisted.

'Wolves. I was frightened of the wolves. Satisfied?'

'Do you know any wolves who knock twice at the front door?'

'All right, Sol. What's it matter to you, anyway?'

'You were scared of Massart.'

'Massart? The one who is lost on Mont Vence?'

'That's right.'

'Why should I be scared of him? Apparently he's come a cropper on the mountainside and the *gendarme*s are out searching for him.'

'You were scared of Massart, that's all there is to it.'

Soliman swallowed a slug of brandy and Camille squinted at him.

'How come you know so much?'

'On the village square they're talking about nothing else,' Sol answered tensely. 'Seems you and the trapper went to Puygiron to tell the *flics* that Massart was a werewolf, that he'd savaged the sheep, murdered my ma, and was on the run.'

Camille said nothing. She and Johnstone had overtaken the locals and made an accusation against one of their number. There had obviously been a leak. And they were going to pay for that. She gulped down a mouthful of spirits and looked up at Soliman.

'It was supposed to be confidential.'

'Well, the confidence was broken. It's the sort of leak a plumber can't fix.'

'Well, that's just tough, Soliman,' she said, standing up. 'It's true. Massart is a murderer. It was he who drew Suzanne into the trap. I don't give a damn whether it suits you or not, it's the truth.'

'Yeah, sure,' Watchee said, all of a sudden. 'The truth it is.'

His voice was muffled and guttural.

'It is the truth,' Soliman repeated, leaning forward towards Camille, who sat down again in some doubt. 'He saw through it all, he did,' the young man went on, gabbling. 'The trapper knows about animals and he knows about men. The wolf would not have attacked my ma, my ma would never have cornered a wolf, and Massart's mastiff is supposed to have come back down from the mountain. Massart has run away with his dog because Massart killed my ma, because she knew *who* he was.'

'A werewolf!' said Watchee, slapping the table with the flat of his hand.

Soliman was getting steadily more excited.

'And they're saying the *flics* won't even investigate, they didn't believe a word the trapper said. Is that true, Camille?'

Camille nodded.

'No two ways? They really won't lift a finger?'

'Not a pinkie,' Camille confirmed. 'They're looking for him dead or alive on Mont Vence, and when they

140

don't find him in a few days' time they'll call off the search and close the case.'

'Do you know what he's going to do next, Camille?'

'I suppose he'll follow the road until he gets to England, killing a few ewes as he goes.'

'But I reckon he's going to kill a lot more than a few ewes.'

'Aha. You think so too?'

'Who else thinks that, then?'

'Lawrence.'

'M. Johnstone is right.'

'Because Massart is a werewolf!' Watchee proclaimed, bringing the flat of his hand down on the table again.

Soliman finished his glass.

'Camille', he said, 'am I the sort of guy who would let his mother's murderer get away to England?'

Camille looked at Soliman with his dark, shining eyes and his quivering lips.

'No, you don't really look the part,' she conceded.

'Do you know what happens to the poor souls who've been killed without being avenged?'

'No, Sol. How am I supposed to know that?'

'They rot in the stinking crocodile swamp, and never can their spirit pull itself out of the mud.'

Watchee put his hand on the young man's shoulder. 'Can't be sure it's quite like that,' he pointed out, in a whisper.

'All right,' Soliman said. 'I'm not even sure they're in a swamp.'

'Don't make up any of your African stories, Sol,' said Watchee, still whispering. 'It'll confuse things for the young lady.'

Soliman turned his eyes back to Camille.

'So, do you know what we're going to do, Watchee and me?'

Camille raised her eyebrows and waited for the rest of it. Soliman was overexcited, and that worried her. He was usually a quiet young man. Last Sunday he had locked himself in the toilet; this evening he was out and about but almost beside himself. Suzanne's death had unhinged the youngster and shaken the old man.

'We're going to sit on his shadow,' Soliman declared. 'Since the *flics* won't track him down, we will.'

'We won't let him get away,' Watchee chimed in.

'And we'll catch him by the tail.'

'And then what?' asked Camille warily. 'Are you going to hand him over to the police?'

'My arse we will!' said Soliman, proving himself a true heir to Suzanne's vigorous turn of phrase. 'If we hand him over to the police, the police will let him go, and we're back to square one. Watchee and me aren't going to spend our whole lives tracking this vampire. All we want is to avenge my ma. So we're going to nab him, and when we've nabbed him we'll deal with him.'

'Deal with him?' Camille repeated.

'Do him in, that's what we'll do.'

'And when's he dead right and proper,' Watchee

filled in, 'we'll open him up from his neck to his balls to see if his hair's on the inside. He's dead lucky we ain't gonna do it while he's alive.'

'Be grateful for small mercies, I suppose,' muttered Camille.

She looked into Watchee's beautiful amber eyes.

'Do you buy this body hair business? Do you really buy it?'

'The body hair business?' Watchee repeated in his muffled voice.

He screwed up his face and said no more.

'Massart is a werewolf,' he mumbled a moment later. 'Your trapper said so too.'

'Lawrence said nothing of the sort. Lawrence said that anyone who believes in werewolves must be a mentally challenged turd-brain. He said that anyone who so much as mentions slitting a guy open from his throat to his balls would have to walk through a bullet from his hunting rifle first. And Lawrence also said that Massart used a mastiff or else a large wolf that went missing two years ago, Crassus the Bald, to do his murdering for him. The bites come from the wolf, not from Massart's teeth, for heaven's sake!'

Watchee pursed his lips and straightened his back even straighter.

'Anyway,' Soliman butted in. 'He killed my ma. So me and Watchee are going to sit on his shadow and catch him by the tail.'

'He won't get away from us.'

'And when we nab him, we'll do him in.'

'No, you won't,' Camille said.

'Why shouldn't we?' Soliman asked, rising to his feet.

'Because if you do you won't be any better than he is. But nobody will give a damn about you because you'll be in the slammer for the rest of your twatty lives. Maybe Suzanne will have got away from her stinking crocodile swamp, I don't rule that out. But whether you slit him open or not, whether he's got hair inside or not, Massart will get his due and you two will be convicted of his murder and have nothing to do for the rest of your days except to count sheep all night long in your prison cell.'

'We won't get caught,' said Soliman, with a defiant thrust of his chin.

'Yes, you will. You'll get caught all right. But that's no business of mine,' Camille said abruptly as she stared at one and then the other of the pair. 'I don't know why you came to tell me all that, but I don't want to know. I don't talk to avengers, assassins or body-slitters.'

She went to the door and opened it for them.

'Goodbye,' she said.

'You don't understand,' Soliman said, swithering. 'We didn't make ourselves clear.'

'I don't care.'

'We're upset.'

'I know.'

'He could kill other people.'

'That's for the police to resolve.'

'The *flics* are sitting on their hands.'

'I know. We've been over that already.'

'So, me and Watchee . . .'

'Are going to sit on his shadow. I got that, too, Sol. I see the whole picture.'

'Not all of it, Camille.'

'So what's missing?'

'You're missing, Camille. We forgot to say that you're part of this picture. You're coming with us.'

'Well . . . that's if you'd care to,' added Watchee, courteously.

'Is this some kind of a joke?' Camille said.

'You tell her,' Watchee said to Sol.

'Camille', said Soliman, 'could you please let go of the bloody door and come and sit down? Sit down with us, like a friend.'

'We're not friends. You're murderers and I'm a plumber. Miles apart.'

'But don't you want to sit down? As a plumber among murderers?'

'In that case, all right,' Camille said.

She slammed the door, sat on a stool, put her elbows on the kitchen table, and stared at the two men at the other end.

'Look,' said Soliman. 'Watchee and me, we're going to sit on his shadow and catch his tail.'

'Fine,' Camille said.

'But to trail him we need transport. We're not going to go after him on foot, right?'

'You can go after him however you like. On foot, on skis, or riding a ram. I don't give a sou.'

'Massart must be driving a car,' Soliman went on.

145

'He's not driving his own, it seems,' Camille said. 'His van is still at the shack.'

'The vampire isn't stupid. He's taken some other car.'

'Fine. He's taken another car.'

'So we have to have one to follow him with. Make sense?'

'Makes sense. You're going to sit on his shadow.'

'But we don't have a car.'

'That's right, we don't have a car,' said Watchee.

'Well, get hold of one, then. You could borrow Massart's.'

'We haven't got a driver's licence.'

'That's right,' said Watchee. 'We haven't got a licence.'

'What are you getting at, Sol? I haven't got a car either. And Johnstone has only got a motorbike.'

'But we do have a lorry,' said Sol.

'You mean the cattle wagon?'

'Yes, we do. You might not believe it, but it is a lorry.'

'Well, that's all right then, Sol,' Camille said. 'Take the cattle wagon and catch the man by his tail. May the wind be in your back.'

'But as I said, Camille, we haven't got a licence.'

'Indeed we haven't,' Watchee said.

'Whereas you do have a licence, don't you? And you've already driven HGVs.'

Camille looked at them in stark disbelief.

'It took a while for the penny to drop,' said Soliman.

'I don't want that penny to drop.'

'Then I'll explain it in more detail.'

'Leave the detail be. I don't want to hear another word about it.'

'Hear me out, please, there's just one more thing. You'll drive the lorry. But you won't do anything else at all. You'll just be the driver and nothing more. Watchee and me will take care of everything else. All we're asking of you, Camille, is to do the driving. Just drive, and you can be blind and deaf to all the rest.'

'Blind, deaf and out of my mind.'

'If you say so.'

'If I have understood you correctly', Camille summed up, 'the main drift of it is that I drive the cattle wagon with you and Watchee sitting up front to egg me on, catch up with Massart, and then run him over accidentally on purpose. Watchee then slits his guts from top to crotch, to clear his mind, whereupon we deliver the man's remnants to a police station and drive all the way home for a nice hot bowl of onion soup with croutons and grated cheese?'

Soliman started to jump up and down.

'No, Camille, we don't mean it exactly like that . . .'

'But you could say that it will be something like that,' Watchee concluded.

'Find someone else to drive the crate,' Camille said. 'Who usually drives it?'

'Buteil. But Buteil is staying at Les Écarts to

look after the flock. And Buteil's got a wife and two kids.'

'Whereas I've not got anything.'

'If you want to put it that way.'

'Find someone else for your stupid road movie.'

'Your what?' asked Watchee.

'Our road movie,' Soliman said. 'It comes from the cinema. It means like when someone drives across the Mojave looking for someone else.'

'Thanks,' said Watchee, still puzzled. 'I do like to understand.'

'Camille, nobody in the village will want to give us a hand. They don't give a damn about Suzanne. But you were really fond of her. Lemirail the *gendarme* was too, but we can't ask Lemirail to help us out, can we?'

'No, we cannot,' said Watchee.

'Don't play on my feelings, Sol,' Camille said.

'So what am I supposed to play on, then? I've only got one hand, Camille. I'm banking on your feelings and I'm relying on your HGV licence. If you don't help us, Suzanne's soul will stay stuck in that bloody stinking crocodile swamp.'

'Don't do my head in with that swamp, Sol. Give me another glass of brandy and let me think.'

Camille stood up and went to stand facing the now-cold hearth, turning her back on the two men. Suzanne's soul in a swamp, Massart on the road all hairless and deranged, the *flics* sitting on their backsides. Get Massart and remove his fangs. Well, why not? But to drive a lorry with forty cubic

148

metres of loading area around hairpin bends . . . well, perhaps.

'What sort of lorry is it?' she asked, turning to face Soliman.

'A 508D,' said Sol. 'Less than 3.5 metric tons. You don't need an HGV licence for it, in point of fact.'

Camille turned back to the fireplace and silence reigned. So, driving the lorry. To release Soliman and Watchee from torment, to reassure Johnstone and do his wolves a good turn. Getting the lorry so close you can breathe down the murderer's neck . . . It was a crazy idea. Not a chance of working. Really stupid. But what's the alternative? Stay at home, wait for news, eat, drink, worry about the incomprehensible crises of M. and Mme Water Rat, and wait for Johnstone. Hang around. Hang on. Get bored. And scared. Lock the door at night in case Massart comes prowling by. Then wait some more.

Camille went back to the table, took her glass and wetted her lips.

'I'm interested in the lorry,' she said. 'I'm interested in Suzanne. I'm interested in Massart – but not in his mortal remains. I'll bring him back alive, or not at all. Up to you. If I drive the lorry, then Massart comes back in one piece, in the unlikely event we actually catch up with him. If I'm not driving, then you can bring him back as werewolf soup for all I care, but I won't have any part of it.'

'You mean we have to hand him over to the

flics without so much as a squeal?' said Soliman, miserably.

'That would be the legal thing to do. Splitting a guy in two goes beyond the legal limit of violence between neighbours.'

'Fuck legal limits!' said the younger of the two men.

'I'm aware of your feelings on that point. But the law's not the issue. Massart's life is the issue.'

'Comes to the same difference.'

'Up to a point.'

'Fuck Massart's life!'

'Well no, I don't.'

'You're asking for too much.'

'Think of it as a question of taste. Me plus Massart in one piece, or Massart soup minus me. I'm really not keen on people soup.'

'We got that,' said Soliman.

'Of course you did,' Camille said. 'I'll leave you to think it over.'

Camille sat at her synthesiser and put on her headphones. She drummed her fingers on the keyboard for show, because her overexcited imagination was a thousand miles away from well-groomed Water Rats. Going after Massart? Like three sheep lost in the woods? What were they, if not three lost sheep?

Soliman signalled to Camille, who took off her headset and came back to the table. Watchee spoke first.

'Young lady', he asked, 'have you ever squelched a spider?'

Camille clenched her fist and laid it on the table between Soliman and Watchee.

'I've squashed bucket-loads of spiders in my time,' she said. 'I've destroyed hundreds of wasp nests too, and I've terminated entire anthills by throwing them in the river with ten pounds of quick-setting cement around their base. I will not discuss capital punishment with tossers like you two. The answer is no, and always will be no, from now to eternity.'

'Are you calling us two tossers?' said Soliman.

'That's what she said,' said Watchee. 'Don't make her repeat it.'

'Repeat that, Camille.'

'Tossers. A pair of dickheads.'

Sol was about to stand up, but Watchee restrained him by the forearm.

'Have some respect, Sol. The young lady's not wrong. You should reckon she's not wrong, really.' He turned back towards Camille, stretched out his hand, and said, 'It's a deal.'

'Not so much as a scratch on Massart?' Camille remained uncertain, and did not shake the offered hand.

'Not a scratch,' Watchee replied in his gruff voice, and once again offered his hand.

'Not a scratch,' Soliman repeated, ungraciously.

Camille nodded her head.

'When do we set off?' she asked.

'My ma's funeral is tomorrow. We'll leave after lunch. Buteil will have the lorry ready. Come over in the morning.'

Soliman bounded to his feet, Watchee rose stiffly.

'Just one more thing,' Camille said. 'There's a clause to add to the contract. There's no reason to suppose we will actually find our man. If we get nowhere in ten days, or thirty days, what do we do then? We're not going to sit on his shadow for the rest of our lives – or are we?'

'Yes we are, young lady,' said Watchee.

'I see,' said Camille.

CHAPTER 16

All night long a nagging awareness that something was amiss kept Camille on edge even as she slept. As soon as she woke up she realised what it was that was wrong. Last night she had agreed to take part in a murder hunt at the wheel of a livestock transporter. This morning she had begun to see all of the project's chief flaws: that it was a childish idea, that it would be dangerous, and that it was not going to be pleasant living at close quarters with two men she barely knew and who were neither of them exactly on an even keel.

Yet, strangely, the idea of just backing out of last night's undertaking never crossed her mind. On the contrary, she paid serious and thoughtful attention to gearing up, like someone on the brink of taking on a really difficult job. The ploddingly simple task in question had only one plus, but it tipped the scales – it would get her on the move. Chasing after Massart in this simple-minded manner was far better than sitting around intelligently and waiting for him to turn up. The sheer attractiveness of movement – of rational movement, since Camille

153

was incapable of travelling without a purpose – had won her over last night. She had been parked at Saint-Victor for a while now and it had begun to tie her up in knots, besides bearing fruit that was rather bland. Then there was that story about the crocodile swamp with Suzanne's soul trapped inside it. Camille did not take it any more seriously than Soliman did, but Suzanne's murder and Massart's disappearance were somehow like two open doors giving rise to a nasty draught that blew right through her. And it struck her that taking the lorry to follow the trail of that man and his wolf might well be a way of shutting off the draught.

Camille finished packing her rucksack, stuffed her score in the right flap pocket and the *A to Z* in the left-hand one, and hoisted it onto her shoulders. She picked up her toolbag, checked the house over one last time, and closed the door behind her.

At Les Écarts things seemed to be happening in slow motion, the way they do in the run-up to a funeral. Buteil and Soliman seemed like rag dolls as they set about kitting out the lorry. Camille went up to them and dumped her rucksack. Seen close up, the lorry looked more like a livestock pen than anything else. Buteil was training the hose on the floor and panels of the loading platform, making a thick black gunge of straw and animal shit squirt out of the side panels and onto the ground. Soliman was unfolding the lengths of

154

tarpaulin that were intended to make a roof over the loading area. Because the lorry – and Camille only now grasped what this meant – was going to serve as their sleeping quarters too.

'Don't worry,' Buteil shouted over the hiss of the water jet. 'This lorry's like Beauty and The Beast, it can metamorphose. I'll have it turned into a three-star hotel in a couple of hours.'

'Buteil has often taken his family for outings in the lorry,' Soliman explained. 'Trust him, you'll have your own bedroom in no time at all, and all mod cons.'

'If you say so,' Camille said doubtfully.

'But I can't hide the fact that it does smell a bit. We can't get rid of the odour completely. It's ingrained in the wood.'

'I see.'

'And in the metal too.'

'Indeed.'

Suddenly the pressure in the hose died. Soliman looked at his watch. Ten thirty.

'Must get changed,' he said in a quavering voice. 'It's going to be time.'

Sol and Buteil encountered Johnstone driving his motorbike dead slow the other way up the unmade road. He was wearing a dark suit. He put the bike on its kick-stand and took Camille in his arms.

'You weren't at home,' he said. 'Is there an emergency at Les Écarts?'

'I'm going with Soliman and Watchee after the

funeral. They want to track down Massart, but they haven't got a licence.'

'I don't see the connection.' Johnstone stepped back to look at Camille.

'I can drive.'

Johnstone shook his head. 'You must have done that on purpose,' he said with stifled emotion. 'You got your HGV licence on purpose. Couldn't resist it, could you?'

Camille shrugged. 'It just happened. When the band was on tour in Germany, the road manager didn't want to drive all day and all night. So he taught me, to help out, as we went along.'

'A trucker, my god, a girl trucker,' Johnstone said as Camille and Camille alone obliged him to remove great chunks from his ideal of womanhood.

'Lorry driving is not beneath one's dignity,' she said.

'It's not frightfully refined, either.'

'Can't deny that.'

'Anyway, what's all this about chauffeuring Soliman and Watchee? Where are you going to set them down?'

'That is the question, Lawrence. I'm not taking them anywhere in particular. I'm driving them wherever and for as long as it takes for them to lay their hands on Massart.'

'You mean to say those two guys really have decided to look for Massart?' said Johnstone with growing disquiet.

'That's right.'

'And you're taking them in a truck? You're going away?'

'Yes. Not for too long,' she added uncertainly.

Johnstone put his two hands on her shoulders.

'Are you leaving?' he asked again.

Camille raised her eyes. An expression of pain flitted across the trapper's face. He shook his hair.

'But not straight away,' he said as he gripped Camille's shoulder tightly. 'Stay by me. Stay for tonight.'

'Sol wants to set off straight after the funeral.'

'One night.'

'I'll be back. I'll call.'

'It's senseless,' Johnstone muttered.

'The police aren't doing anything and the man will kill again. You said so yourself.'

'God! I'm telling you to stay.'

'Neither of them can drive.'

'I want you to stick around,' Johnstone almost commanded.

Camille shook her head slowly. 'They're counting on me,' she said in a whisper.

'Jesus fucking Christ,' Johnstone swore as he moved off. 'An old man, a boy-child and a girl stalking a man like Massart! Who the hell do you three imagine you are?'

'I don't imagine anything. I'll just do the driving.'

'You imagine you're going to catch Massart!'

'Could happen.'

'Don't make me laugh. Catching a murderer isn't like playing tag. You need leads.'

'If he savages any more sheep, we'll follow his trail.'

'Trailing behind isn't catching up.'

'We can find things out, find out what car he's driving. When we've got that, we'll have a chance of spotting him. It could take a few days, perhaps.'

'Is that all they want to do with him?' Johnstone asked suspiciously.

'Soliman was supposed to kill him and Watchee was going to open him up from his neck to his balls, but only when he was dead, as a humanitarian gesture. I told them I wouldn't drive their bloody lorry unless we brought Massart back in one piece.'

'It's dangerous,' Johnstone said, his temper rising from frustration. 'It's a grotesque and dangerous idea.'

'I know.'

'So why do it?'

Camille paused. 'Things just clicked,' was all she said by way of explanation. For the moment she couldn't think of any better reason.

'That's bullshit,' Johnstone growled as he approached her again. 'You'd better get things to unclick.'

Camille shrugged. 'Sometimes things just click for all sorts of lousy reasons, but loads of good reasons just can't unclick them ever again.'

Johnstone felt quite defeated. 'All right,' he said gloomily. 'Which truck are you driving?'

'That one,' said Camille, with a nod towards the livestock transporter.

'That object', Johnstone said professorially, 'is a livestock transporter. It is a cattle wagon. It reeks of shit and sheep grease. It is not a truck.'

'Yes it is, apparently. Buteil says that after a good wash and dry behind the ears, with the back kitted out and the ragtop on, it'll be like a three-star hotel on wheels.'

'It'll be a stinking hovel and nothing else. Camille, have you really thought this through?'

'Yes.'

'And you're going to sleep with those two guys in the same small space? Have you thought that through too?'

'Yes. Things went click, that's all.'

'Have you thought about being spotted by Massart?'

'Not yet.'

'Well, you *should* think about it. That flimsy canvas isn't going to give you much protection against him in the dark of night, is it?'

'We'll hear him coming.'

'So what, Camille? What will an old man, a boy-child and a girl do when they hear him coming?'

'I don't know. Put our heads together, I suppose.'

Johnstone threw his arms wide in a gesture of utter impotence.

CHAPTER 17

After the funeral a wake for Suzanne Rosselin was held at Les Écarts. There was a lot to say. The burial had been a disturbingly plain affair, in accordance with the instructions Suzanne had left with her lawyer four years beforehand, stipulating that she would have no truck 'with flowers and gold-plated handles', that she'd rather 'the kid kept her savings so as to go and visit the land of his forefathers', and lastly that her old ewe Mauricette be laid to rest beside her when her time came – 'because though you couldn't say she was a bright spark Mauricette had been a loving and faithful companion and could the priest please say a word about her in his sermon.' The lawyer pointed out that this last pagan wish stood not the slightest chance of being fulfilled and Suzanne said she did not give a damn for dogma and she'd go and see the damnfool priest herself to sort out the matter of Mauricette.

The priest apparently remembered the earful he had had from Suzanne and did make a clumsy reference to the deceased's great attachment to her flock.

By four the last car had driven away from Les Écarts. Camille's head was buzzing as she went back to the lorry where Buteil was still at work. The more she thought about how the transporter was being got ready the more it worried her.

Buteil was sitting on the running board at the back of the lorry, smoking a nostalgic cigarette.

'She's ready,' he said as he saw Camille approaching.

Camille looked the vehicle over. The tarpaulin was stretched over the roof bars and halfway down the sides. The grey bodywork had been cleaned, up to a point.

Buteil slapped the side panel with the flat of his hand and made the whole rust-bucket resound like a drum, as if he were about to introduce a circus artiste.

'Just twenty years old and in her prime,' he declaimed. 'A 508 is a sturdy lass, but she does have a few drawbacks. She has drum brakes, so you do have to stand on them on long downhills; there's no power steering, so you do have to lean on it hard to get round bends. Apart from which the steering is really soggy. And the pedals have lost their spring. That's the only thing about the lorry that shows her real age.'

Buteil turned to Camille and looked her up and down with an expert eye. It was an elongated body with thin arms and delicate wrists.

He made a clucking noise with his tongue, and said, 'It's all very well for a woman to have arms

161

like that, but it's not so fine for a lorry-driver. I don't know if you'll be able to control her.'

'I've driven things like that before,' Camille said.

'Round here the bends are damn sharp. You have to really spin that wheel.'

'So I'll spin it.'

'Get in, I'll show you around. I always set it up like this when I take the kids for a drive.'

Buteil pulled down the tailgate with a clang and clambered up. Inside the transporter the heat was stifling and Camille was overcome by the odour of natural lanolin.

'Smells less when she's moving,' Buteil explained. 'She's been cooking in the sun all afternoon.'

Camille nodded and Buteil took that as an encouragement to play the major-domo and give a guided tour of the facilities. The loading platform was more than eighteen feet long, so Buteil had set up four camp beds lengthways, two up front and two at the rear, with a canvas curtain separating the two pairs.

'Like that you've got two bedrooms, each with natural light, too,' he complimented himself. 'If you want to see outside – or if you want to see anything inside, comes to the same thing really – all you have to do is raise the canvas, like a Venetian blind. And when you want to be private, you drop it down again.'

Buteil raised the tarpaulins to demonstrate, and light flooded in through the slats that made up the side-wall, illuminating the whole of the back of the transporter. 'And here', he said as he moved towards the rear and pulled aside a thick canvas curtain, 'you have the bathroom.'

Camille inspected the home-made shower assembly with its thirty-gallon water tank made from a recycled boiler.

'Where's the pump?' she asked.

'Over here,' said Buteil. 'You'll need to fill her up every other day. And there's the toilet. Same system as on the railways of old, you release as you go. Now at the other end we have the bottle-gas cooker – you've got a full bottle, by the way. In the larger box here you'll find cooking utensils, bed linen, pocket lamps, the whole caboodle. Over there are the folding stools. Under the beds there's a drawer for your personal belongings. It's all there. All been thought out. It all works.'

'I believe you,' Camille said.

She sat down on one of the two beds at the rear, the one on the off-side. She let her eyes wander over the 120 square feet of baking hot interior space that the livestock transporter provided. The white sheets and pillowcases that Buteil had put on the bunks stood out in sharp contrast to the black floor, the peeling paintwork and the shabby canvas. She was slowly becoming accustomed to the smell. She was beginning to make the soggy mattress she was sitting on a thing of her own. She was coming to think of the lorry as hers. Buteil looked at her with pride and concern.

'It all works,' he repeated.

163

'It's perfect, Buteil,' she said.

'And don't worry about the smell. It goes off when you get the old girl moving.'

'And when she's not moving? When we're asleep?'

'Well, when you're asleep you can't smell a thing. Seeing as you're asleep.'

'I'm not worried.'

'Do you want to try her out?'

Camille signalled agreement and followed Buteil round to the driver's door. She climbed the two footholds and settled into the driving seat, adjusted the position, and stretched out her arms to grasp the large, hand-scorching steering wheel. Buteil handed over the key and withdrew. Camille switched on, engaged first gear and steered the hulk slowly down the sheep farm's unmetalled drive. First gear, full lock, stop; clutch, reverse, reverse lock, go, stop; clutch, first, and back up the drive. Switch off.

'I'll manage just fine,' she said, climbing down from the cab.

Buteil gave Camille the vehicle papers as if she had just earned them by executing a three-point turn. And at that moment Soliman turned up, dragging his heels, with a drawn expression on his face and bloodshot eyes.

'We'll be off as soon as you're ready,' he said to Camille.

'Aren't we eating before we go?'

'We'll eat in the lorry. The more time we lose, the further away the vampire gets.'

'I am ready,' Camille said. 'Get your things and bring Watchee with you.'

Ten minutes later Camille was smoking a cigarette, sitting beside Buteil at the back of the van, when she saw Soliman return with a rucksack on his back and a dictionary under his arm.

'Your bed is front off-side,' Buteil determined.

'Fine,' said Soliman.

'Sol's a finicky lad,' said Buteil. 'He'll take an age to sort his drawer.'

'Buteil', Soliman shouted from inside the truck, 'your transporter hasn't stopped smelling of livestock, you know.'

'So what am I supposed to do about that?' said the major-domo somewhat aggressively. 'We don't grow courgettes, do we now? We raise sheep!'

'Calm down, I was only saying there's a pong.'

'Apparently it disappears when we're on the road,' Camille put in.

'Exactly.'

Johnstone was coming towards them with Watchee in tow.

'*Love*,' Soliman declared as he leaned against the lorry with his hands on his hips. 'A. That state of feeling with regard to a person which manifests itself in concern for the person's welfare, pleasure in his or her presence, and often also desire for his or her approval. B. Sexual passion combined with liking and concern for the other. C. Strong attachment to a person of the opposite sex.'

165

Camille was taken aback and turned to look at the young man.

'It's the dictionary,' Buteil explained. 'He's stored it all up here,' he added, pointing to his head.

'I'm going to say my goodbyes,' Camille said, standing up.

Watchee took his turn to inspect the converted transporter. Buteil showed him his drawer – the first on the right as you come in – and the old man put his things away in it in no time at all. Then he hopped down and stood waiting next to Soliman, by the cab steps, filling in time by hand-rolling a cigarette from shag. Straight after the funeral Watchee had got back into his baggy cords and his shapeless jacket and put on his hiking boots and his time-worn hat with its traditional black ribbon, all impregnated with dust. He had trimmed his hair and shaved and then put a clean white shirt over his undervest. It felt a bit stiff. He was standing as straight as a ramrod with his cigarette hanging on his lower lip and his left hand at rest on his crook. His dog lay at his feet. Watchee got out his pocket-knife and started to strop the blade on his trouser-leg.

'So when are we going to start up this here road movement?' he asked gruffly.

'This what?' Soliman queried.

'This road movement. Road *movie*.'

'Oh, I see. Soon as Camille has stopped saying goodbye to the trapper.'

'In my day young women did not kiss men in front of me on unmade roads.'

'It was your idea to get her to come too.'

'In my day', Watchee went on, as he folded away the blade of his pocket-knife, 'young women did not drive lorries.'

'If you'd learned to drive, we wouldn't be in this pickle.'

'I didn't say I was against it, Sol. I'm actually for it.'

'For what?'

'Having a young lady's hands on the wheel. I'm for it.'

'She's pretty,' Soliman said.

'She's more than just pretty.'

Johnstone was watching them from the distance, holding Camille in his arms.

'The old man's putting his best foot forward for you,' he said. 'He's got a spotless shirt tucked into his filthy trousers.'

'He's not filthy,' she said.

'Well, all you can now do is pray to heaven he doesn't bring his dog along for the ride. That dog must reek.'

'Possibly.'

'For God's sake, are you sure you want to go?'

Camille looked at the two anxious and worried men waiting for her by the running board. Buteil was putting the finishing touches to the equipment – securing a moped to the bodywork on the near side, and a pedal cycle to the off-side.

'I'm sure,' she answered.

She kissed Johnstone; he hugged her close, then let her free with a nod of his head. From the driver's cab she watched him going back to his motorbike, start up and ride away down the track.

'So, what's next?' she asked the two men.

'We sit on his shadow,' said Watchee with a commanding stare and his jaw set stiffly at the angle of determination.

'Which way? He was at La Castille on Monday night. That means he has almost forty-eight hours' head start.'

'Let's roll,' said Soliman. 'I'll tell you what the idea is as we go.'

Soliman was a featherweight youngster, and, with his dainty hands, his long arms and his slouch, he seemed all the time to be holding his sharp, handsome profile up to the stars. His complexion was smooth, and his face, like a child's, seemed almost transparent. But there was always a glint of irony or perhaps of impish fun in those eyes, as if the young man was straining not to let some huge joke – or some great message – out of the bag, or as if he was constantly talking to himself and saying 'Now wait till you've heard this one . . .' Camille imagined that the combined effects of the dictionary and of African folklore were responsible for Soliman's strangely knowing smile, which gave his face an ambiguous light and made it look in turns obedient, then kindly, then dark, then dictatorial. She wondered what kind of smile he might have acquired from concentrating instead on the *The A to Z of Tools for Trade and Craft*. Probably not a very nice one.

Camille tossed her own rucksack into the lorry, unpacked it neatly into the drawer under her bed – the rear left-hand bed, Buteil had said – closed the tailgate and clambered into the cab where the two men were already settled, Sol next to the driver's seat and Watchee by the near-side door.

'You'd better lay your crook on the floor,' she advised the old man, leaning towards him. 'If I have to brake hard, it could smash your jaw.'

Watchee hesitated, pondered, then lay his shepherd's crook flat on the cab floor.

'Belt, please,' Camille added amiably as she wondered whether Watchee had in fact ever been in a motor vehicle before. 'You have to click it in here. In case I brake sharply.'

'It'll trap me,' said Watchee. 'I don't like being trapped.'

'It's the rule, I'm afraid. Compulsory.'

'Fuck compulsory, that's what we say,' said Soliman.

'All right,' Camille said as she switched on the ignition. 'What direction of travel?'

'Due north, towards the Mercantour.'

'Via?'

'The Tinée valley.'

'Good, that's the way I'm heading, too.'

'Eh?' said Sol.

'Yes. I'll tell you what the idea is as we go.'

The transporter clanked and snorted down the dirt and gravel track and onto the metalled road. Buteil, leaning back against the old wooden gate, gave them an unenthusiastic wave. He had the worried look of a man watching his own home wandering over the fields and far away.

CHAPTER 18

Camille turned very slowly onto the main road.

'Did you have to bring the dog?' she asked.

'Don't worry about him,' said Watchee. 'He's a real sheepdog. He goes for wolves and foxes and all kinds of shit including werewolves, but he never lays a paw on women. Woof respects women.'

'I wasn't worrying,' Camille said. 'It's just that he smells.'

'He smells of dog.'

'As I said.'

'You can't expect a dog not to smell of dog. Woof will look after us. You can rely on him to catch the scent of that lousy werewolf five miles off. Nobody needs to know his teeth have been filed.'

'Filed?'

'He's a sheepdog. Has to be prevented from harming the flock. Mustn't get used to the taste of blood, either, because he'd have to be put down. But Woof has a fine nose. He's taken the scent from Massart's shack, and he'll find the man.'

171

Camille nodded, keeping her eyes on the road. She had changed up to third and for the time being she had the lorry under control. It made an enormous racket on the road. The metal bars holding together the side-slats rattled with every bump. You had to shout in the cab to be heard. The windows were down and the tarpaulins rolled up to get some air through the vehicle.

'Woof? Is that his name?' she asked.

'I picked it from the dictionary, arbitrarily, when he was born,' Soliman explained. '*Woof. n.* A. The threads that cross from side to side of the loom. B. A woven fabric. C. The texture of a fabric.'

'I see,' Camille said. 'What time is it?'

'Past six.'

'Tell us your idea, Sol.'

'It's Watchee's, too.'

The lorry was now rolling along a minor road that ran beside the north-flowing river. Camille wasn't pushing the vehicle, she was taking her own good time to get accustomed to the controls. Bends were not easy.

'Massart left his pick-up at Mont Vence,' Soliman began. 'He had to, if he wanted people to believe he'd gone missing in the mountains. So for the meantime the vampire had to go on foot.'

'Or by bike,' Watchee added.

'Tell him to shout louder, Soliman, I can't hear a word he says with all the racket the lorry's making.'

'Say it louder!' Soliman told the shepherd.

'Or by bike,' Watchee boomed.

'Has he got a bike?'

'Certainly has,' said Watchee. 'At any rate he had one, a few years back. He used to keep it in the kennel. I went over to look last night and the bike's not there.'

'You mean Massart is riding round on a bike with a mastiff and a wolf padding along beside him?'

'He's not riding around, dear girl. He's proceeding. And proceeding to murder.'

'It's too visible,' Camille objected. 'He'd be spotted a mile off if he tried to get near a sheep farm.'

'That's why he only moves at night,' said Soliman. 'He hides during the day and moves at night, with his creatures.'

'Even so,' Camille said. 'He won't get far with a crew like that.'

'He's not going far, dear girl. He's going to Loubas, just past Jausiers.'

'I can't hear you!' shouted Camille.

'To Loubas,' bellowed Watchee. 'It's eighty kilometres the other side of the Mercantour. That's where he's heading.'

'Is there anything special at Loubas?'

'There certainly is.'

Watchee leaned out of the window and spat noisily. Johnstone's warning flashed across Camille's mind.

'There's his cousin,' he continued. 'Sol, you explain.'

'He needs a car,' Soliman said. 'He can't hang around out in the open with his animals in tow. He only abandoned his pick-up because it's part of a plan. Massart's cousin is a crook who lives at Loubas, runs a shady garage and sells used cars. A cousin who can be relied upon to keep his mouth shut.'

'Fine,' Camille said, who was concentrating on the tight bends in the narrow road. 'Let's say Massart has gone to Loubas to get a car. Fine. But why didn't he just rent one?'

'So as not to get caught.'

'For heaven's sake, no-one is looking for him! Nobody's going to stop him going wherever he pleases.'

'He's not a wanted man yet, but he could be. But the main thing is that Massart wants to be thought dead.'

'To carry on doing the werewolf business in peace and quiet,' Watchee said.

'Exactly,' Sol said.

'If that's so', Camille pointed out, 'he'll need an alternative ID.'

'His cousin's bent,' Watchee said. 'The garage is a front.'

'That's what people say,' Soliman confirmed.

'The cousin can forge official documents?'

'He can get hold of false identity papers.'

'How?'

'You can buy anything if you know where to shop.'

Camille slowed down and brought the lorry to a halt in a lay-by.

'Are we stopping already?' Watchee said.

'My arms need a break,' said Camille, getting down from the cab. 'The steering is heavy and the road is nothing but bends.'

'I can see,' said Sol. 'I realise.'

'I'm going to show you a map,' she said. 'We found it at Massart's place. It's got a whole route marked out on it. You're going to show me where Loubas is on that map.'

'Just past Jausiers.'

'Well, show me where Jausiers is.'

'You don't know Jausiers?' said Soliman, evidently astonished.

'No, I don't.' Camille was leaning on the driver's door. 'I do not know where Jausiers is. I'd never even been to this baking-hot region until earlier this year. And this is the first time I've driven a three-ton wreck round a bloody switchback. And I've no idea what the Mercantour looks like. All I know is that the Mediterranean is down at the bottom and that it has a tide that goes neither up nor down.'

'Wow,' said Soliman. He was really impressed. 'Where have you been living so as to not learn all that?'

Camille went to her drawer to look for the map, closed up the tailgate, climbed back into the cab and sat down beside Soliman.

'Listen, Sol,' Camille said, 'did you know that

there are places – thousands of places – in the world where cicadas never go?'

'I had heard tell,' Sol said, pursing his lips sceptically.

'Well, that's where I was living.'

Soliman shook his head, half in admiration, half in pity.

'All right then,' Camille said as she unfolded Massart's map. 'Show me where this Loubas is.'

Soliman put a finger on the map. 'What's this red line?' he said.

'I told you, it's Massart's route. All the Xs match sheep farms where he's savaged the animals, except Andelle and Anélias where nothing has happened. I reckon he hit the road before he had time to attack there. They're too far east. At the moment he's making his way along his red route to the north. By the banks of the Tinée, through the Mercantour, and by way of Loubas.'

'And then?' asked Soliman, with an inquiring frown.

'Look. The itinerary wiggles along minor roads as far as Calais, and then over the Channel to England.'

'Whatever for?'

'He's got a step-brother working in a slaughter-house in Manchester.'

Soliman shook his head. 'No,' he said. 'Massart is not trying to start a new life like your average fugitive. Massart is beyond the living already. He's out of the light, he's living in the night. He's dead to the police, he's dead to the village, he's dead to everyone and maybe even to himself. He's not after a new existence, he's after an altered state.'

'My, what a lot you know!' Camille said.

'He wants a new skin,' Soliman added.

'A hairy one,' said Watchee.

'That's right,' said Soliman. 'Now the man is dead, the wolfman can kill as he pleases. I just don't see him going to look for a decent job in Manchester.'

'In that case, why cross the Channel? Why work out an itinerary if it's not to follow it somewhere?'

Soliman rested his head on his hands and thought, letting one eye wander over the map. 'It's like a vanishing point. He's on the move because he can't stay where he is. He will cross to England, maybe he'll look for a helping hand over there. But he'll keep on moving wherever he is, all round the world. You know what "werewolf" means?'

'Lawrence told me that lycanthropy wasn't my strong point.'

'It means a wolf that wanders far and wide. Massart won't hide under a stone, he'll keep going, moving on each night. He knows the little roads like the back of his hand. He knows where he can go to ground.'

'But Massart is *not* a werewolf,' Camille said.

There was a brief silence in the cab. Camille could feel Watchee making an effort not to respond.

'Well, at least he thinks he's a wolf,' Soliman said. 'That's sufficient.'

'Probably.'

'Did the trapper show this map to the *flics*?'

'Obviously he did. They take it to refer to an ordinary trip to Manchester.'

'And the *X*s?'

'Just simple job-related marks, they say. It holds water, if you're convinced that Suzanne was savaged by a wolf, and only a wolf. And the police *are* convinced of that.'

'Idiots,' said Watchee authoritatively. 'Wolves do not attack humans.'

Another pause. The memory of Suzanne lying in her own blood flashed through Camille's mind.

'No,' Camille mumbled.

'We hunt him down,' said Watchee.

Camille switched on the ignition and manoeuvred the lorry out of the lay-by. She drove on for a good while with her arms taut on the wheel before anything more was said.

'I've worked it out,' Soliman said at length. 'Massart can do between fifteen and twenty kilometres a night without overstretching the animals. He must be on the northern edge of the Mercantour now, let's say around the level of the Col de la Bonette. So tonight he'll have an easy downhill walk towards Jausiers, about twenty-five kilometres. That's where we'll expect him tomorrow morning, if we haven't crossed his path already, higher up.'

'Do you want us to spend all night driving round the Mercantour?'

'I'm simply suggesting we pitch camp at the Col.

We'll take turns to keep watch on the road, but I don't expect any result. He knows the goat-tracks and the passes. At five thirty in the morning we'll drive down to Loubas and that's where we'll pounce on him.'

'What exactly do you mean by "pounce"?' asked Camille. 'Have you ever tried to pounce on someone who has a mastiff and a trained wolf for bodyguards?'

'We're going to set ourselves up properly first. We'll identify his car. Then we tail him until he savages another flock. We'll catch him at it, red-handed. That's when we pounce.'

'We means you and who, Sol?'

'We'll sort that later. It's a nuisance you don't know Jausiers.'

'Why?'

'Because that means you don't know the road either. It climbs to almost three thousand metres, with a hairpin every few hundred metres. It's barely wider than the lorry. There's a sheer drop over the side and the barrier wall's got a gap in it every few feet. What we've done so far is a picnic compared to what's up ahead.'

'I see,' Camille said. 'I didn't think the Mercantour was quite like that.'

'What did you think it was like, then?'

'I imagined a hot and slightly hilly sort of area, with olive trees. That sort of thing.'

'Well, no. It's cold and hilly to the utmost extreme. There are larches, but when it gets too high for them to survive, there's nothing at all, just us three, and a lorry.'

'How jolly,' Camille said.

'Didn't you know that olive trees can't grow above six hundred metres?'

'Six hundred metres above what?'

'Above sea level, for heaven's sake. Olive trees stop at the six hundred metre line, everyone knows that.'

'Where I come from there aren't any olive trees.'

'You must be joking. So what do people live on?'

'Beet. Beets are brave, you know. They never give up, and they go right round the world.'

'If you were to plant beets up on the Mercantour, they would die.'

'Fine. That's not what I was aiming to do. How far is it to the top of the bloody Col?'

'About fifty kilometres. The last twelve are the worst. Do you think you can manage it?'

'I've no idea.'

'Can you give a real heave with those arms?'

'Yes, I can heave with these arms.'

'Do you think you can make it?'

'Leave her alone, Sol,' Watchee growled. 'Leave her in peace.'

CHAPTER 19

It was seven in the evening and the day's heat was slowly waning. Camille kept her hands on the wheel and her eyes straight ahead. The road was still wide enough for two cars to pass, but the unending switchbacks were wearing her arms out. The trouble was that she had virtually no margin for error.

The road went ever up. Camille wasn't saying a word, and Soliman and Watchee had fallen silent too, their eyes glued to the landscape. The familiar foliage of hazelnut and oak was long behind them. Now serried ranks of dark *sylvestris* pines marched over the hillsides. Camille found them as sinister and as disturbing as columns of black-clad soldiers. Further up you could make out the start of the larch forest which was a little lighter in colour but just as regimented and military, then the green-grey grass of the high plateau and then, higher up still, bare rock reaching to the summit. The higher you go the harsher it gets. She relaxed for a few moments on the descent into Saint-Étienne, the last village at the head of the valley before the big climb to the Col. The last inhabited outpost. Much more sensible to stop here, call it off, settle down. Taking this cattle truck up two thousand metres over the next twenty-five kilometres was not going to be a piece of cake.

Camille pulled up just after Saint-Étienne, took the water bottle, drank slowly, and let her arms hang loose. She wasn't sure she could control the lorry in these conditions. She did not like sheer drops and felt that she was at the limit of her physical abilities.

Soliman and Watchee said nothing. They were peering intently at the mountainside, and Camille was not sure whether they were trying to make out the bent shadow of the werewolf, or whether they were fretting about what the lorry might fall into. But since they looked pretty confident Camille reckoned they must be on the lookout for Massart.

She glanced at Soliman, who smiled back.

'Obstinacy,' he said. 'The quality or condition of being obstinate; stubbornness; persistency.'

Camille started the engine and the livestock transporter moved on, away from the village. A sign told them this was the start of Europe's highest road. Another sign advised caution. Camille took a deep breath. It stank of sweat, dog and sheep, but in the circumstances that homely if stomach-turning blend was almost comforting.

A little more than two kilometres further on they crossed into the Mercantour National Park. Much as Camille had feared, the corkscrew road narrowed until it seemed no wider than a shoelace, no more significant than a scratch on the mountainside. The engine roared and the bodywork rattled as the sheep wagon nosed its way up, with less thunderous moments only on the flatter curves of left-hand hairpin bends. The near-side wing was inches from the sheer rising cliff, and from her window Camille could see straight down to the bottom of the ravine. She tried to keep her eyes off that spectacle and watched out instead for the kilometre posts by the roadside. Above 2,000 metres' altitude the trees grew sparser, and the engine began to pink in the thinner air. Gritting her teeth to keep on going, Camille kept a wary eye on the water temperature gauge. It wasn't a foregone conclusion that the lorry would make it to the top. A brawny lass, Buteil had called her, but he had had lots of practice nursing her from pasture to mountain pasture. Camille would not right now have said no to a helping hand from him, just to get to the top of this Col.

At 2,200 metres the last puny larches gave way to verdant carpets of grazing set against the grey slopes. A harsh kind of beauty, to be sure: a vast, noiseless, lunar landscape in which people, not to mention their sheep, were mere specks. Lonely, old, tin-roofed sheepfolds were dotted around the fields. Camille glanced at Watchee. With his face overshadowed by his faded hat, he sat so still and steadfast, like a ship's captain standing at the bridge, that he almost seemed to be drowsing. She thought him admirable. She was awed by his having spent more than half a century living in these immense uninhabited spaces, no bigger than a flea on a mammoth's back, without making the slightest fuss about it. People always seemed to be hinting at something dark when they said that Massart had never had a wife; Watchee had not been married either, but nobody commented on that. Always on his own up in his mountains. Two thousand six hundred and twenty metres. Camille cautiously overtook two cyclists weaving out of exhaustion, only yourself to blame, and then double-declutched into first for the last round of tight bends before the top. Her whole chest was aflame with aching muscles.

'Summit,' Soliman shouted above the engine noise. '"The top, the highest point; utmost elevation, as of rank, prosperity, etc." Pull in over there, Camille, there's a parking area at the peak.'

Camille nodded.

She brought the lorry to a halt in the lengthening shade, switched off the engine, let her arms fall to her side and closed her eyes.

'Break,' Soliman said to Watchee. '"Respite from labour, pause in activity, downtime, rest." Let's get down and make dinner while she's getting her strength back.'

It wasn't so easy to get out of the cab and Soliman had to lend the old shepherd a helping hand and almost lift him down the two steps.

'Don't treat me as if I was ready for the scrap-heap,' Watchee said sharply.

'You're not ready for the scrap-heap. You're just

184

very old, very stiff, and quite knocked about, and if I don't give you a hand you'll most likely break your neck. Then we'd have to look after you for the rest of the trip.'

'Bugger off, Sol. Let go of me now.'

One hour later, Camille joined the two men for dinner in the open, sitting on the folding stools set around the tea chest. It was getting dark. Camille looked over the peaks and pine trees that filled the landscape as far as the eye could see. Not a hamlet, not a shack, not a single human being could be seen moving in what was the wolves' natural habitat. At this moment the two cyclists panted over the top of the Col and disappeared down the other side.

'There we are now,' she said. 'All on our own.'

'There are three of us on our own together,' said Soliman as he passed her a plate.

'Plus Warp,' Camille added.

'Woof,' Soliman insisted. 'Threads that cross from side to side of the loom.'

'Yes,' Camille said. 'Sorry.'

'There are four of us,' Watchee said by way of correction.

Sitting up straight on his stool he gestured towards the high pastures.

'We three, and him,' he said. 'He's about. He's gone to ground, but he's lurking. In an hour's time, when it's completely dark, he'll move off with his animals. He'll be looking for meat to feed them, and himself.'

185

'Do you think he too eats the flesh of the sheep he kills?' Soliman said.

'He has to drink their blood, at least,' Watchee asserted. 'We forgot to get the wine out,' he added without a pause. 'Go and get it, Sol. I put a whole case behind the canvas curtain, by the toilet.'

Sol came back with an unlabelled bottle of white wine. Watchee held it out for Camille's approval.

'*Vin du pays*,' he said as he took the corkscrew from his pocket. 'Our own, from the vineyards of Saint-Victor. Doesn't travel at all. It's a miracle, like a gift of life. It's got a fair nose, good legs, and a broad bottom. It's all the wine we need.'

Watchee raised his elbow and took a swig.

'You're not all on your own up here,' said Sol, pulling down the shepherd's arm. 'You've got company. Don't drink like a pig. From now on we'll use wine glasses.'

'I was going to share it,' said Watchee.

'That's not the point,' said Soliman. 'The point is glasses.'

He gave a tumbler to Camille who held it out for Watchee to fill.

'Careful,' the old man said as he poured. 'It's got a tail.'

It certainly was an unusual wine – sweet and slightly sparkling; and it had been warmed right through in the back of the lorry. Camille could not decide whether it would keep them alive for the rest of the trip or kill them off in three days. She held out her glass for more.

'Be careful about that sting in the tail,' Watchee warned again with raised index finger.

'We'll take turns at sentry duty over there,' said Soliman, pointing to the bare knoll on their right. 'From there you can keep an eye on the whole mountainside. Camille, you take first watch until half past midnight, I'll do second watch. I'll call reveille at five thirty.'

'The young lady should get some sleep,' Watchee said. 'She's got to get us all down the mountain in the morning.'

'That's true,' said Soliman.

'I'll be fine,' Camille said.

'We haven't got a gun,' said Watchee with a resentful glance at Camille. 'What do we do if we see him?'

'He won't come over the Col by the road,' said Soliman. 'He'll use a sidetrack. All we can hope for is to catch sight or sound of him. If we do, we'll know to within the hour when we can expect to nab him at Loubas.'

Watchee rose with the help of his crook, folded his canvas stool and put it under his arm.

'I'll let the dog stay with you, young lady,' he said to Camille. 'Woof defends women.'

He shook her hand very formally, the way tennis players do at the end of a match, and got into the lorry. Soliman watched him with mistrustful eye, and then went on in after him.

'Hey!' he said when he was inside. 'Don't sleep starkers. Did that occur to you? You can't sleep in the altogether.'

'I'll do as I please in my own bed, Sol. Bugger off.'

'You won't be *in* your bed, you'll be *on* your bed in this stifling tin can.'

'So what?'

'She has to come past to get to her bed. I don't see why she should have to set her eyes on you in your birthday suit.'

'How about you?' Watchee said.

'I'm in the same boat,' said Soliman haughtily. 'I'll keep a whatsit on.'

Watchee sighed and sat on his bunk. 'If it makes you happy, OK,' he said. 'You're a complicated fellow, Sol. Makes me wonder how you got to be like that.'

'Civilisation,' said Sol. 'Meaning . . .'

Watchee shut him up with a wave of his hand. 'Stop that dictionary nonsense for now.'

Soliman jumped down from the back. A few yards away Camille stood gazing into the dusky distance. She was side-on to Soliman, with her hands stuffed in her trouser back pockets. She had a clean profile, a strong chin, a long neck and dark hair cut short at the back. He had always thought of Camille as delicate, pure and almost perfect. The idea of sleeping so near to her made him uneasy. He had not thought of it ahead of time. Camille was supposed to be the driver, and

Soliman had never thought about what sleeping with a trucker might mean. Because once the lorry was parked Camille ceased to be a trucker and suddenly became simply a woman dropping off to sleep on a sheet a mere two metres away from you just behind a canvas screen, and a piece of canvas is not a big deal at all. Whereas a woman like Camille sleeping two metres away from you is a very big deal indeed.

Camille turned towards him. 'Do you know if there's any water or suchlike around here? 'she asked.

'An unending supply,' said Soliman. 'Fifty metres down the road there's a spring and a pond. We went and washed there while you were asleep. Take your turn before the night turns really cold.'

His stomach tightened at the thought that Camille might be going to take off her jacket and jeans and boots. He imagined her freshening up in the mountain stream no more than fifty metres away, a pale, vulnerable, naked form in the gloom. Without her boots or her jacket or her T-shirt or her truck. It was as if a protective boulder had suddenly rolled back and put Camille almost within reach. Disarmed and therefore unprotected. Fifty metres is no big deal.

Almost within reach. Everything always hangs on that 'almost'. If you could only jog a carefree fifty metres to riverbanks where naked women bathe, and if naked women were always happy to see you, then quite a lot of the world's miseries might evaporate. But things are not like that. They never have been like that. The last fifty metres are unimaginably complicated, from the start through the middle to the finish. Nothing doing.

Camille walked past with a towel round her shoulders. Soliman was sitting cross-legged on the ground, and he hugged his knees a little harder.

Almost within reach. The hardest last straight in the world.

CHAPTER 20

Jean-Baptiste Adamsberg had reached Avignon the previous evening and already found the perfect spot on the opposite bank of the River Rhône where he could go to let his mind drift on its own tide. Wherever he was, he could sniff out by instinct, almost immediately, like a pointer, the kind of haunt he needed to keep himself going. So when he had to travel he never really worried about where he would land. He knew he would find a bolthole of his own. Adamsberg's private perches were always quite similar despite differences in climate, vegetation and the lie of the land, whether he happened to be in Avignon or at the other end of the universe. What he needed to find was a spot that was sufficiently uninhabited, untended and unseen to let his mind unbutton and unbelt itself, but also sufficiently unprepossessing for him not to have to look at it and declare it to be beautiful. Breathtaking landscapes aren't good for thinking in. You are obliged to take notice and you cannot put your muddy feet anywhere you have a mind to.

Adamsberg spent the entire day on the premises

of Avignon police HQ laying siege to the wily businessman whose brother-in-law was the lad murdered in the Latin Quarter. The *commissaire* had not yet played all his cards, the time was not ripe. But he had lured the man into a free-flowing, easygoing chat that had drifted rather further than the suspect would have wished, like little ripples on the water drawing a kayak away from the bank and into deep water. And when the canoeist looks around, all of a sudden it's too late, he's gone too far, he's now got no way of getting back to the shore. Adamsberg frequently encircled his targets in difficult cases, but he had no idea how to explain what he was doing or even to give the technique a name, even when someone as precious to him as his colleague Danglard asked him to teach him the basic steps.

He did not know how to explain it. He just did it, because there was nothing else you could do with some people. Which people? Well, the sort of person he had got right now at Avignon.

For the time being the man was vaguely aware that the *commissaire* was leading him down paths he ought to avoid like the plague, into deep waters where he might drown. He was fighting back and ducking for cover in fits and starts. Adamsberg reckoned it would take him another ten hours or so to catch the man off balance and pin him down. When he did finally confess to the murder Adamsberg would feel that brief pang of satisfaction that always came when his intuition was vindicated by reason.

He smiled. He was frequently unsure of himself, but not in this case. The man would go down. It was just a matter of time.

Adamsberg was sitting on the riverbank a few yards from a side road that followed the Rhône, in a little clearing blocked off by a willow hedge, and he was struggling to make a long branch that he had picked up and dipped in the water resist the river's flow. The current eddied around the obstacle and then resumed its course downstream, brushing leaves over and under the branch. This was obviously not going to keep him occupied for the rest of his life.

He had called Paris. Sabrina Monge had not yet made a move to find out where he had gone to ground. Since she had not seen Adamsberg go home last night she had put one of her young slaves on sentry duty at the main entrance and taken up her own position near the basement exit. The second slave was ferrying supplies to the pair of them. However, said Danglard, as Adamsberg had not appeared this morning at either door, it seemed that Sabrina was getting concerned.

'Actually, she's worried sick about you,' Danglard had said on the phone. 'I can't really make out any more if what she wants is to top you, or to marry you.'

Adamsberg knew which was the right answer. She wanted to kill him.

He pulled the branch back out of the water and

consulted his mental clock. Between twenty and half past eight. He had forgotten to listen to the eight o'clock news on the radio.

So he had not got an update on the big wolf.

He laid the branch down in the long grass, which almost hid it. Perhaps he would be happy to find it there again tomorrow, who knows, who can tell? It was a long, solid bough, an excellent tool for discussing things calmly with rivers. He stood up and brushed some of the grass off his crumpled trousers. He would go and find somewhere to eat in town, back in the noise, with people, and with a bit of luck he would find himself next to a party of English speakers.

He shook his head. He was a little distraught at having missed the big bad wolf.

CHAPTER 21

Sitting cross-legged on a flat stone, with the dog nestled against her feet, Camille watched night fall on the Mercantour. Wherever she cast her eyes the mountains loomed in their dense, dark, opulent and hopeless solidity.

Sooner or later he would have to come down from the mountains. Sooner or later Massart would have to abandon their sanctuary. In all likelihood. The Loubas garage theory was interesting. But maybe they were all making a mistake about that. Maybe Massart would avoid roads and vehicles altogether. Maybe he would stay holed up in the Mercantour for ever. This no longer seemed impossible, now that Camille could see this huge and primevally empty space for herself. Nothing but stone and almost virgin forest for seventy kilometres from end to end – but with all its slopes and inclines, all its cliffs and rock faces, the surface area must actually be immensely larger. A hundred times, maybe a thousand times bigger. What Massart had here was a vast and vacant territory where he just had to hold out a pitcher for water, and put out his fangs for as much meat and as many victims as he cared for.

But then there was the temperature. Camille huddled inside her jacket for warmth. Now that night had fallen it was 10°C at most, and Watchee had said that by dawn it would go down to 6°. And this was high summer, late June. She put out her hand for the bottle of white Saint-Victor wine and poured herself a thumbnail. Could Massart hold out against the cold? Months and months under snow? With no shelter beside a wolf's coat? He could light a fire, but then he would be spotted.

So he would be cold. So he would leave the Mercantour sooner or later. But not necessarily tomorrow, via Loubas, as Soliman and Watchee seemed convinced he would. Their certainty surprised Camille. They seemed to reckon they had the right plan and were bound to succeed. Whereas to Camille it sometimes seemed on the one hand a defensible and reasonable project, but on the other hand half-baked and brainless.

Massart might not come down from the Mercantour until the first frosts, in October. Were they going to camp out in the lorry outside Loubas for four months? Nobody spoke about that, nobody even mentioned that their pursuit of Massart had no foregone conclusion. Even had they been tracking a wolf with a transponder they still would not be any surer of finding it. Camille shook her head in the dark, turned her jacket collar up, and

196

took another swig of the wine with the tail. She was not at all confident. She could not see the story proceeding the way the young man and the shepherd thought it would. She saw something darker, more disorderly, something basically more fearful than the clockwork search they were clinging to with the map laid out in front of them.

Fearful and dangerous, too. Camille looked through the binoculars. She could not see a thing on the pitch-black mountainside. She would not even notice if Massart slipped past a few feet away with his wolf. Having the dog was a comfort. He would smell them coming long before they could get at her. Camille ran her fingers through his coat. He smelled of dog sure enough, but she was thankful to have him curled around her boots. Now what was his name? Wart? Hoof? And why did he always wrap himself around people's feet?

She switched on the torch, glanced at her watch, and switched it off again. In fifteen minutes she'd wake Soliman.

With her left hand hugging the dog and her right hand round her wine glass, she stared straight at the mountain. The mountain did not bother to stare back. It remained sublimely indifferent to her existence.

CHAPTER 22

Getting down the mountain in the half-light was no easier than going up had been, and it took almost as long. It was just before six when Camille brought the lorry to a halt thirty metres from Massart's cousin's garage at Loubas. She had sore arms and an aching back. The only thing to do now was to wait for Massart to appear.

Nobody had seen him from the Col and the dog had not even growled once all night long. Massart must have given them a very wide berth, Watchee reckoned.

Camille got out of the cab to make coffee at the back. Her eyes were stinging. She thought that Watchee had snored a lot during the five hours they had both been asleep, but it had not really bothered her. All in all she had not slept too badly on the old sprung bedstead, in a lorry that had been lubricated inside and out with wool fat. The smell had not actually wafted away with the draught. The notion of the odour disappearing was just one of Buteil's fantasies, and about as reliable as a magic carpet. She had had a dream of danger, she could still feel the lorry being bumped. Someone banging on the outside. But actually nothing had shifted in the truck. Soliman had been on watch no more than twenty metres away, and he had not seen anything. Nor had Wafty, or whatever his silly name was. Maybe Watchee had had a patch of insomnia and got up for a bit. He said that sometimes he stayed up until dawn with his flock. Camille picked up the pot full of coffee, the sugar and three tin mugs.

'What exactly is lanolin?' she asked as she got back into the cab. 'Does it come from their skins? Or from the wool?'

'Lanolin,' Soliman piped up immediately. 'Fatty matter permeating sheep's wool. Also called wool-fat, wool-wax, wool-oil.'

'I see. Thanks,' Camille said.

Soliman shut his mouth as if it were a book, and the three of them, tin mugs in hand, returned to staring at the steel door of the garage. Soliman wanted six eyes instead of two trained on it. If a car were to shoot out all of a sudden, they'd need all their eyes to register the vital clues. Soliman had shared out the jobs: Camille was to catch the driver's face and nothing else, Watchee was to get the model and colour of the car, and he himself would log the number plate. They would fit the pieces together afterwards.

'At the beginning of the world,' said Soliman, 'people had three eyes.'

'Bugger that,' said Watchee. 'Lay off with your stories. Keep quiet.'

'They could see everything,' Soliman continued undeterred. 'They could see very far, they could see very bright, they could see in the dark, they could see colours below the wavelength of red and colours beyond purple. But men could not see into their womenfolk's minds, and that made them sad, and sometimes sent them crazy. So they went to ask the marsh god for help. He warned them, but the men pleaded so hard that he finally gave them their hearts' desire. From that day on people had only two eyes, and men could see into their womenfolk's minds. And what they saw there was so astounding that they quite lost the ability to see anything else properly. That's why people can't see straight nowadays.'

Camille was not a little upset and turned to face Soliman.

'He makes them up,' Watchee said with weary irritation. 'He makes up silly African stories to explain things. But they don't explain a thing.'

'You never know,' Camille said.

'Not a thing,' Watchee insisted. 'They make things more complicated instead.'

'Don't take your eyes off the steel door, Camille,' said Soliman. 'And my story doesn't make things more complicated,' he added for Watchee's benefit. 'It just explains why we need to be three to see one single thing. It's a clarification.'

'Pull the other one,' said Watchee.

★   ★   ★

By ten no car had appeared. Camille's back was aching and so she granted herself a short walk along the village road. At noon even Watchee began to lose heart.

'We've missed him,' Soliman said glumly.

'He's been and gone,' said Watchee. 'Or else he's still up there.'

'He could stay up there for weeks,' Camille said.

'No,' said Soliman. 'He'll move.'

'If he's got a car, he doesn't have to move at night any more. He can drive in the daytime. He could come out of that garage at five this afternoon, or he could come out in September.'

'No,' said Soliman. 'He'll travel at night and sleep by day. His animals might be heard, the wolf might howl. It's too risky for him. And anyway, he's a man of the night.'

'So what are we doing hanging round here in broad daylight, then?'

Soliman shrugged.

'Optimism,' he began.

'Switch on the radio,' Camille interrupted. 'He didn't do anything on Tuesday night, but maybe he did last night. Find a local station.'

Soliman twiddled the knob for a good while. Reception came and went through a crackle of static.

'Bloody mountains,' he said.

'Don't you blaspheme at the mountains,' said Watchee.

'All right,' Soliman replied.

He tuned in to a station, put his ear to the speaker, then turned up the volume.

'That's our boy,' he mumbled.

. . . pert who examined the earlier victims considers there is a good case for thinking that the same animal is involved, namely an un-usually large wolf. The beast has attacked several sheep farms over the past two weeks and also caused the death of an inhabitant of Saint-Victor-du-Mont who tried to kill it, Suzanne Rosselin. Now the wolf is believed to have reverted to its pattern of killing at a place called La Tête du Cavalier, in the canton of Fours, in the department of the Alpes-de-Haute-Provence, where last night five ewes from the local flock were savaged. The wardens of the Mercantour National Park believe it is a young male seeking new territory and think that within . . .

Camille grabbed the map. 'Show me where La Tête du Cavalier is,' she said to Soliman.

'On the other side of the Mercantour, right up north. He's over the pass.'

Soliman spread out his arms to unfold the map and laid it on Camille's lap.

'There,' he said. 'Among the high pastures. It's on the red route he'd pencilled in, two kilometres off that minor road.'

'He's just ahead of us,' Camille said. 'Bloody hell, he's only eight kilometres away.'

'Shit,' said Watchee.

'What are we going to do?' Soliman asked.

'Sit on his shadow,' said Watchee.

'Hang on a second,' Camille interrupted.

She frowned and turned up the volume on the softly sputtering radio. Soliman wanted to say something, but Camille motioned him to shut up.

'Just a second,' she said again.

> *. . . raised the alarm when the man failed to return. The victim, Jacques-Jean Sernot, is a retired teacher, aged sixty-six. His horribly mutilated body was found at daybreak on a country path near the village of Sautrey, in the department of Isère. His throat had been cut. Family and friends describe the victim as a quiet individual, and the tragedy remains a complete mystery. An investigation is being conducted by the coroner's office in Grenoble and it is believed that the facts . . .*

'Not our boy,' said Soliman as he jumped down from the cab. 'Sautrey's a god-forsaken hole at the other end of the universe, south of Grenoble.'

'How did you learn where everything is?' asked Camille.

'In the dictionary of proper names,' Soliman said, who was lifting and then lowered the moped from the hooks it was hanging on.

'Show me on the map.'

'There,' said Soliman, pointing it out with his

forefinger. 'Not our man, Camille. We can't take on every murder in the land. Sautrey is at least 120 kilometres from here.'

'That may be so. But it is also on Massart's itinerary, and the man had his throat cut.'

'So what? If you haven't got a gun the best way is either to strangle or to cut a throat. Forget about this Sernot, don't waste your energy, we're concentrating on ewes. La Tête du Cavalier is where he went. Maybe they spotted his car down there.'

Soliman pushed the moped for a few yards to get the motor to start.

'Pick me up on the other side of the village,' he said. 'I'll get some supplies: water, cooking oil and food. We'll eat in the cab.'

'Foresight,' he said as he rode away. 'The capacity to see ahead. Taking relevant action.'

At one thirty Camille drew up in a lay-by on the D900 outside Le Plaisse, the village nearest to the grazing land known as La Tête du Cavalier. All it contained was an old church with a tin roof, a café, and a score of dilapidated houses made of stones and planks patched up with cinderblock. The café kept going out of the locals' generosity, and the locals kept going out of the magnetic presence of a café. Camille hoped that a car stopping by the roadside at night around here stood a good chance of being noticed.

Watchee walked into the café with head held

high. Since crossing the Col de la Bonette he was outside his own patch and bonhomie was no longer appropriate. Strangers should be kept at a wary distance, initially, before making contact with any of them. He acknowledged the barman with a nod and looked around the small room where six or seven men were eating lunch. His eye came to rest on a man sitting hunched up in the corner. The hair beneath the man's cap was as white as Watchee's own. He was staring vacantly into space and had his hand gripped tightly around a glass of wine.

'Sol, go and get some white from the lorry,' the old man said with a sideways move of his head. 'I know that fellow. He's called Michelet, from Seignol. He often brings his flock up for summer grazing to La Tête du Cavalier.'

Watchee took off his hat respectfully, then took Camille by the hand – it was the first time he had touched her – and led her rather pompously to the shepherd's table.

'A shepherd who's had a sheep savaged', he said to Camille, not letting go of her hand, 'is a changed man. He can never be the same again. No two ways about it. It warps your mind.'

Watchee took a seat at the table and held out a hand to the hunchback shepherd.

'Five sheep, wasn't it?'

Michelet looked at him with empty blue eyes which spoke to Camille of real despair. He just held up his left hand with four fingers and his thumb outstretched to agree the figure, while he mouthed a silent sentence. Watchee put a hand on his shoulder.

'Ewes, were they?'

The shepherd nodded, tight-lipped.

'Nasty business,' said Watchee.

At this point Soliman returned with the bottle and put it down on the dining table. Without a word Watchee took Michelet's glass, emptied it out of the open window with a lordly sweep of his arm, and uncorked his own bottle of wine.

'You're going to down two glasses of this,' he said. 'We'll talk when you're done.'

'So you want to talk?'

'I do.'

'Not your usual style.'

'No indeed. Drink up.'

'Is it your local wine?'

'It is. Saint-Victor-du-Mont. Drink up.'

The shepherd drank two full glasses and Watchee poured a third.

'This one's to be drunk slowly,' he said. 'Sol, fetch some glasses for us.'

Michelet glared at Soliman with disapproval in his eyes. Like others he had not managed to come to terms with the idea of a Black being involved with Provence or its sheep. To his mind it would be a grisly state of affairs if the next generation were all to be like that. But he was not so daft as to open his mouth on that subject with Watchee present, because it was common knowledge that if you took it out on Soliman, you'd have Watchee's knife to reckon with.

Watchee finished pouring the round and stood the bottle on the table as straight up as he was.

'Did you see anything?' he asked.

'Not until this morning. When I went back up to the pasture I found them lying on the ground. That bastard didn't even eat them. He bit them in the throat, that's all. For fun, I reckon. The animal's cruel, Watchee, real cruel.'

'I know,' Watchee said. 'It got Suzanne. But was it the wolf? Would you swear to that?'

'Cross my heart and swear to die. Rips in the flesh as long as that,' he said, rolling up his sleeve to show his forearm.

'What time did you go back down yesterday?'

'Ten.'

'Did you see anyone in the village? Did you see a car?'

'A stranger, you mean?'

'Yes.'

'No, Watchee, I didn't.'

'Nothing on the way down?'

'No, nothing.'

'Do you know Massart?'

'The weirdo from Mont Vence?'

'That's the one.'

'I come across him here and there, at services. He won't attend Mass at the churches round your way. And he always comes for the St John's Day procession in midsummer.'

'He's a religious fanatic?'

Michelet looked away. 'You lot from Les Écarts have no respect, not even for Adam and Eve. Why are you asking after Massart?'

'He went missing five days ago.'

'Is there a connection?'

Watchee nodded.

'What are you saying?' asked Michelet. 'You mean the animal . . . ?'

'That's what's not clear. That's why we're asking.'

Michelet swallowed a mouthful of wine and whistled through his teeth.

'So you've not seen him around here, then?' Watchee said.

'Not since Mass a week ago last Sunday.'

'Tell us about the processions. Is he a fanatic?'

Michelet scowled.

'Could call it something worse. He's superstitious, know what I mean? Bowing and scraping and all that. You know what I mean.'

'Not sure I do. But I know what people say. That raw meat turned his head. What he has to do in the slaughterhouse really got to him and made him go all religious.'

'What I can tell you is that the fellow ought to have been a monk. They say he's never touched a woman.'

Watchee poured out another round.

'I've never known him miss a Sunday service,' Michelet went on. 'He spends fifteen francs on candles every week.'

'Does that make a lot of candles?'

'Five,' said Michelet, putting his hand up as he had done to number his lost sheep. 'He arranges them like the five points of an M,' he added, drawing the figure on the tablecloth with his finger. 'Maybe M stands for "Massart", or for "My God", or for "Mercy". I dunno, I never asked, and I don't give a damn anyway. Bowing and scraping, if you know what I mean. He does a complicated shuffle down the aisle as well – one foot forward, one foot back. God knows what he thinks he's up to. It don't look above-board or regular to me, that's for sure. Then he does a war-dance around the font. Bowing and scraping all the time. You know what I mean.'

'Would you say he's a raving lunatic?'

'Not lunatic, no, but he must be slightly barmy. A bit nutty. But he's OK. Never did anyone any harm.'

'Never did anyone any good either, did he?'

'No, he didn't,' Michelet agreed. 'In any case he doesn't talk to anyone. What's it to you that he's gone missing?'

'Don't give a damn about him being missing.'

'Well then, why are you asking after him?'

'It's him who slashed your sheep.'

Michelet opened his eyes wide and Watchee put a firm hand on the man's arm.

'Keep it to yourself. Shepherd to shepherd.'

'Is that what you mean? A werewolf?' whispered Michelet.

Watchee nodded. 'Certainly. Did you notice anything?'

'One thing.'

'What?'

'He ain't got no hair on his skin.'

An angel passed as Michelet let the news sink in. Camille sighed and emptied her glass of white wine.

'And you're after him?'

'We are.'

'With them two?'

'Sure.'

'Never met the lass,' Michelet said reproachfully.

'She's a stranger in these parts,' Watchee explained. 'She comes from the north.'

Michelet doffed his cap to Camille, perfunctorily.

'She's our driver,' Watchee added.

Michelet looked at Camille and Soliman steadily and thoughtfully. A pretty odd pair of escorts for old Watchee, he reckoned, but he wasn't going to criticise. In any case, nobody ever criticised Watchee. Soliman, Suzanne, women in general and whatever else, they were all off limits. Because of that knife.

Michelet watched the old man put his hat back on and stand up.

'Thanks,' said Watchee and a smile flashed across his lips. 'Warn the sheep farmers. Tell them that the wolf is moving eastwards, towards Gap and Veynes, and that he'll then head north towards Grenoble. Tell them to stay with their flocks by night. With a gun.'

'I know what you mean.'

'I hope you do.'

'How come you know so much about him?'

Watchee did not deign to answer and went over to the bar. Soliman went outside to get water from the fountain. It was two in the afternoon. Camille went back to the lorry, climbed into the driving seat, and switched on the radio.

Fifteen minutes later she could hear Soliman winding the hose back in at the rear of vehicle while Watchee was rummaging around among the bottles of wine. She got out of the cab, went round to the back, got in and sat down on Soliman's bunk.

'We're out of this dump,' said Watchee as he sat down opposite. 'Nobody's seen anything. No Massart, no car, no wolf.'

'Not a bloody thing,' Soliman confirmed, as he too sat down, next to Camille.

It was getting hotter in the back of the truck. The canvas sides had been half raised to let in a paltry breath of air. Soliman watched the fine hairs on Camille's neck waving up and down as if they were breathing.

'But there might be something,' said Soliman. 'What Michelet told us.'

'Michelet's an oaf,' Watchee said with hauteur. 'He was not courteous towards the young lady.'

He took out his tobacco and rolled three cigarettes. He licked the paper two or three times over, stuck it down, and handed one of the roll-ups to

Camille. She put the cigarette between her lips with a thought for Johnstone.

'What he said about Massart being a bigot', Soliman went on, 'and about his thing with candles. It's possible Massart can't manage without churches and candles, especially after a murder. It's possible he's been to light candles somewhere to beg forgiveness.'

'How could you tell which candles were his?'

'Michelet said he always puts five in the shape of the letter M.'

'Are you going to examine every church on the itinerary?'

'It would be one way of working out where he is. He can't be terribly far from here. Ten kilometres, fifteen at the outside.'

Camille pondered as she smoked, leaning her elbows on her knees, and said nothing. Then:

'I think he's a long way away. I think he killed the retired teacher in that village, Sautrey.'

'Good heavens,' Soliman exlaimed. 'So he's not the only crazy person around! Whatever makes you connect him to that old bird?'

'Same thing as connects him to Suzanne.'

'Suzanne had twigged, so he had to corner her. What makes you think a teacher in Isère saw through the werewolf?'

'He might have come across him unawares.'

'The vampire only kills females,' Watchee growled. 'Massart's not interested in old men. Not the tiniest bit interested, young lady.'

'Right. That's what Lawrence says too.'

'Well, that settles it,' Soliman said. 'We're going to scour the churches.'

'But I'm going to Sautrey,' said Camille as she stamped out her cigarette butt on the black floor.

'Hey!' said Soliman. 'Not on the floor!'

Camille picked up the butt and threw it out between the slats.

'We are not going to Sautrey,' Soliman said.

'Yes we are, because I am the driver. I listened to the two o'clock news. Sernot was killed in a quite particular way: his throat was torn open by means unspecified. A stray dog, they reckon. They've not yet connected it to the Mercantour wolf.'

'That makes a whole heap of difference,' Watchee said.

'What time did it happen?' Soliman asked as he stood up. 'It can't have been before three. The sheep here were killed around two in the morning, according to the vet.'

'The news didn't give a time.'

'And the man? What was he doing outdoors?'

'We'll go and ask,' Camille said.

CHAPTER 23

To get to Sautrey Camille had to nurse the lorry over yet another mountain pass. But it was an easier, wider road with fewer wiggles overall and more leeway on the hairpin bends. As they left the last slivers of Mediterranean landscape behind them and began the climb towards the Col de la Croix-Haute, about ten kilometres before the summit they drove into a bank of white, fluffy fog. Soliman and Watchee were entering an alien sector and they observed their new surroundings with hostility and fascination. Visibility was poor, Camille was driving slowly. Watchee cast disparaging eyes on the long, low houses that seemed to have been plastered onto these melancholy hillsides. They reached the summit at four and made it to Sautrey thirty minutes later.

'Woodpiles, woodpiles,' Watchee muttered. 'What the hell do they do with all those logs?'

'They have to keep fires burning nearly all year round,' Camille said.

Watchee shook his head with pity and disbelief.

★   ★   ★

214

The owner of the Sautrey café was about to shut up shop and set off home just before it turned eight. A short-haired dog gambolled at his feet. Dinner time.

'See here now, mutt,' said the café-keeper. 'It ain't right for a nice kind of girl to drive a truck, and no good'll come of it, you mark my words. Why can't those two beggars who are with her do the driving, eh? It's a right sorry sight. Ain't that what it is, mutt? I couldn't begin to tell you how clapped-out that truck is. And the girl sleeps inside it, with a Black and a crone beside her.'

The café-owner sighed as he draped his tea-towel over the sideboard.

'What do you think, mutt?' he continued. 'Which one do you think she sleeps with? You're not going to tell me she sleeps with nobody, 'cos I wouldn't believe you. Probably with the nigger-boy. It doesn't turn her off. The Black looks at her like she was a goddess. Anyway, what the hell are the three of them doing here getting up everybody's nose with all their bloody questions? What's old Sernot got to do with them, anyhow? You don't know, mutt? Well, nor do I.'

He switched off the last of the lights and buttoned up his coat as he left the premises. The temperature had fallen below ten degrees.

'Ain't that right, mutt? People who ask so many questions about a stiff can't be normal, can they.'

Because it was cold and windy Soliman set up their dinner-table inside the lorry, squeezing the

215

wooden box between the two bunks. Camille let Soliman look after the meals. He was in charge of the moped, food supplies and water. She held out her plate.

'Meat, tomatoes and onions,' Soliman announced.

Watchee uncorked a bottle of white.

'In times gone by', Soliman said, 'when the world was new, people didn't need to cook.'

'Oh, not that again,' Watchee groaned.

'And so it was for all the animals on earth.'

'Quite so,' Watchee butted in, pouring the wine. 'Then Adam and Eve got it together and ever since we've had to slave away and do the cooking all our life long.'

'No, no,' Soliman said. 'That's a different story.'

'You make up your stories from start to finish.'

'So what? Do you know any other way?'

Camille shivered, and went to fetch a pullover from her drawer. It wasn't raining, but the mist was so damp that it made you feel like a wet rag all over.

'There was food within arm's reach all around,' Soliman went on. 'But Man gobbled everything up, and the crocodiles began to complain about his selfishness and greed. To check up on what was really going on, the god of the stinking marsh turned himself into a crocodile and went to see for himself. The marsh god went hungry for three days, then he summoned Man and said: "From now on you're going to share and share alike." "Sod that," said Man. "We don't give a toss for the others." The god of the stinking marsh then

216

went into an awesome rage and took away Man's taste for blood, raw flesh and uncooked meat. Since when we've had to cook everything we put in our mouths. It took a long time to learn, and crocodiles have had the kingdom of raw meat all to themselves ever since.'

'And why shouldn't they?' Camille said.

'Man felt so humiliated being the only animal to have to cook his food that he dumped all the work on Woman. Except for me, Soliman Melchior, because I've stayed good and I've stayed black, and also I haven't got a woman.'

'You could put it that way,' Camille said.

Soliman fell silent and concentrated on his plate. 'People round here aren't very chatty,' he said.

He held out his glass for Watchee to fill.

'That's because they're in on it,' said Watchee as he poured.

'They didn't spill a single bean.'

'Because they've none to spill,' Camille said. 'They're as much in the dark as we are. They'd heard the radio, that's all. If they knew anything they'd have told us. Have you ever met a human being who knows something and doesn't end up blurting it out? Any one at all?'

'No.'

'So there you are. They've told us all they know. The guy had been a teacher at Grenoble, then he retired here.'

'Retired here,' Watchee repeated pensively.

'It's where his wife had her roots.'

'That's no excuse.'

'We've run into the sand,' Soliman said. 'We're going off as fast as windfallen figs. Aren't we?'

'Let's not get stuck in this woodpile,' said Watchee. 'On with the road movie. Sit on his shadow and catch him by the tail.'

'Stop talking rubbish, will you?' Soliman burst out. 'We've no idea where Massart's shadow is, for heaven's sake! We don't know if it's ahead of us, behind us, or down the bloody well!'

'Calm down, lad.'

'Can't you get it into your head that we've lost it? That we're in the dark? That we've no way of knowing if it was Massart or the man in the moon who killed Sernot? Could even be that the *flics* already know who did it – could have been the man's son, or his wife! What the bloody hell are we really doing in this sheep-wagon?'

'Eating and drinking,' Camille said.

Watchee filled her glass. 'Careful,' he said. 'It's got a tail.'

'We know nothing!' Soliman said excitedly. 'Patiently and persistently, we go on learning nothing. We've put hundreds of hours into learning nothing. And we'll sleep through the night and wake up in the morning knowing exactly the same amount of nothing.'

'Calm down,' said Watchee.

Soliman paused, then let his arms slump into his lap.

'Ignorance,' he said in a more collected tone.

218

'Lack of knowledge, general or particular. State of unknowing.'

'Exactly,' Camille said.

Watchee set himself to hand-rolling, licking and sticking down three cigarettes.

'Time to break camp,' he said. 'Might as well go and see the *flics* on the Sernot case. Where do we find them?'

'Villard-de-Lans.'

Soliman shrugged. 'Do you really think the *flics* will fall over themselves to help us with their case-notes? Do you think they'll be delighted to repeat everything the pathologist told them? To oblige a Black? To please a shepherd? Out of courtesy for a female trucker?'

'No,' Watchee scowled. 'I think they'll fall over themselves asking for our ID and then they'll kick us out.'

He gave one roll-up to Camille and one to Soliman.

'And we can't tell them we're after Massart, can we?' Soliman went on. 'What do you think the *flics* would do to three people like us if they knew they were tracking an innocent man so as to teach him a lesson?'

'They'd lock them up.'

'Quite.'

Soliman paused to inhale.

'Three people, three know-nothings,' he said after a while, with a shake of his head. 'The three know-nothings in the fable.'

'What fable?' asked Camille.

'The fable I'm about to make up, under the title "The Three Know-Nothings".'

'I see.'

Soliman got up and paced back and forth with his hands behind his back.

'What we really need', he resumed, 'is a special sort of policeman. A very special *flic*. A *flic* who'd pass on all the info without giving us any grief, and who'd let us carry on tracking the vampire down.'

'Stop daydreaming,' said Watchee.

'Daydream', said Soliman: 'Idea without substance. Wishful thinking.'

'Right.'

'But we're up the creek if we don't find the dream. Without the dream policeman we're wasting our time.'

The youngster went to open the tailgate and threw his cigarette stub out. Camille picked hers off the floor and dropped it through the slats.

'I once met a dream,' she said.

Camille had spoken almost in a whisper. Soliman turned to look at her. With her elbows propped up on her knees she was turning her wine glass in her two hands.

'No, Camille, I didn't mean a guy. I meant a *flic*.'

'So did I.'

'A special kind of *flic*. I meant getting to know a very special policeman.'

'I once met a very special policeman.'

'Are you serious?'

'Completely, utterly serious.'

Soliman cleared the dining table and opened the box that it actually was. He got down on his knees to rummage inside and pulled out a box of candles.

'Can't see a bloody thing in this cattle-truck,' he said.

He dripped some melting wax into a saucer and stood three candles up in it. Camille was still swirling white wine in the bottom of her glass.

Candlelight suited Camille. It made her silhouette stand out against the background of grey canvas at the top end of Soliman's bunk. What with night nearly upon them, and the prospect of more long hours lying only a few feet apart either side of the canvas curtain, Soliman was a little hesitant. He sat down opposite her, next to Watchee.

'Did you meet him a long time ago?'

Camille looked up at the young man.

'Maybe ten years ago.'

'Friend or foe?'

'Friend, I suppose. I don't know really. I haven't seen him for years.'

'What way is he special?'

Camille shrugged. 'He's different.'

'Really not like other *flics*?'

'It's worse than that. He's not like other people even.'

'Oh,' said Soliman, taken aback. 'So what is he like as a policeman? Unscrupulous?'

'He's very scrupulous, but quite unprincipled.'

'You mean he's bent?'

'No, he's not bent at all.'

'So what is he, then?'

'He's special, as I said.'

'Don't keep on at her,' said Watchee.

'And they let him stay in the force?'

'He's got gifts.'

'What's his name?'

'Jean-Baptiste Adamsberg.'

'Age?'

'What's that got to do with it?' Watchee interrupted.

Camille thought hard and added things up on her fingers.

'Around forty-five.'

'And where does your special *flic* hang out?'

'In Paris, at the police HQ in the fifth arrondissement.'

'He's an Inspector?'

'No, he's a *commissaire.*'

'Really?'

'Really.'

'Could this guy Adamsberg get us out of our hole? Does he have that much power?'

'He's got gifts, that's what he has.'

'Can you give him a call? Do you know his number?'

'I've no intention of ringing him.'

Soliman stared at Camille in surprise. 'And why don't you want to ring him?'

'Because I don't want to hear his voice.'

'Really? Why not? Is he a bastard?'

'No.'

'Is he an idiot?'

Camille shrugged again. She was passing her finger in and out of the candle's flame.

'Go on, then,' said Soliman. 'Why don't you want to hear his voice?'

'I told you. Because he is special.'

'Don't keep on at her,' Watchee said.

Soliman jumped up in sheer exasperation.

'It's her call,' Watchee reminded the young man, tapping Soliman's shoulder with the tip of his crook. 'If she doesn't want to see the fellow, she doesn't, and that's that.'

'Bugger that!' Soliman yelled. 'We don't give a toss for him being special!' He turned towards Camille and said: 'And what about Suzanne's soul, Camille? Have you thought about that? Stuck for all eternity in that bloody stinking pond with all those crocodiles? I'd call that a special position, and so should you!'

'The pond stuff's not altogether gospel, you know,' said Watchee.

'But don't you reckon Suzanne's relying on us?' Soliman went on. 'By now she must be wondering what the hell we're up to. Whether we've forgotten her. Whether we aren't just getting sozzled and don't give a damn any more.'

'No, Sol, I don't believe she is.'

'Really, Camille? So what the fuck are you doing here?'

'Have you forgotten? I'm here to do the driving.'

Soliman pulled himself up straight and wiped his brow. He was getting agitated. He was much too agitated about Camille. Perhaps because he fancied her and had no idea how to make it over the last fifty metres between him and her. Unless Camille made a move, but she had not given the slightest sign so far. Camille was pretty much all-powerful in the lorry and that was exhausting. She was mistress of seduction, she was mistress of the lorry, and she could be the mistress of the chase – if only she would call that special man of hers.

Soliman sat down again somewhat crestfallen.

'It isn't true you're only here as the driver.'

'No.'

'You're here because of Suzanne, you're here because of M. Johnstone, you're here because of Massart, to nab him before he tops anyone else.'

'Could be,' said Camille before emptying her glass.

'He might have killed again already,' said Soliman insistently. 'But we can't even find out if he has. We can't find out the first thing about a vampire that only we know. And that only we can head off.'

Camille got up.

'Unless you call that *flic,* of course.'

'I'm going to bed,' she said. 'Give me your mobile.'

'Are you going to ring him?' Soliman asked with a brighter face.

'No, I want to get hold of Johnstone.'

'Who cares about your trapper?'

'I do.'

'Think about it all the same, Camille. Pausing for thought is the privilege of the wise. Do you want to hear the story about the man who refused to pause for thought?'

'No,' said Watchee.

'No,' Camille concurred. 'I find wisdom boring.'

'All right then, don't think. Act. Boldness is the privilege of stout hearts.'

Camille smiled and gave Soliman a kiss. She paused, then shook Watchee's hand and vanished behind the canvas screen.

'Bugger,' said Soliman.

'She's hard to crack,' Watchee observed.

CHAPTER 24

Camille woke up by herself at around seven, which was a significant indication of inner tension and contradictions. Also a symptom of wine with a tail. Yes, it could be that too.

Last night she had been able to get in touch with Johnstone and she had enjoyed hearing the Canadian's voice, even if only in splinters. Johnstone had been more monosyllabic than ever on the telephone. Up in the Mercantour, Crassus the Bald remained untraceable. Almost all the other known wolves had been spotted in their ranges, but big Crassus was still missing. Augustus was gobbling down his ration of rabbits, Mercier was amazed that the old boy was holding up so well given the rotten state of his teeth. 'You see,' he told Johnstone, 'where's there's a will, there's a way.' And Johnstone had accepted that without a word. He had been concerned to hear of the death of Jacques-Jean Sernot. Sure, Massart had crossed his mind. But he did not like the ragged turn that Camille's pursuit of the man was taking. He did not like knowing that Camille was within spitting range of Massart, holed up but also vulnerable in that truck. In any case, he did not like Camille being stuck in that stinking vehicle with two men. With any man, actually, in any lorry. No, he wasn't against getting a *flic* involved. Quite the opposite, in fact. Hadn't they wanted to get the police involved from the start? Well, if she knew one, she should call him. Makes no difference if he's special or not, as long as he's a *flic*. He would be more effective than the three of them together, if he was prepared to get interested in the were-wolf. A big if. Johnstone was convinced that police involvement would put an end to the saga of the girl, the shepherd and the boy-child. That's what his heart most desired. He'd try to come to where the lorry was this evening, to have a talk with her, sleep with her. She must let him know if they decided to move.

Lying on her back Camille watched the slanted rays of the sun filter through the slats and light up the dust suspended in the air. That was no ordinary dust. There must be micro-particles of straw, sheep wax and sheep shit hanging there, shimmering in the morning light. A rare blend, for sure. A really beefy kind of dust. Camille pulled the blanket up to her chin. The night had been cool in this misty village, and they had needed the woollen blankets Buteil had provided. What would it cost her to call Adamsberg? Bugger all, as Soliman said. She did not give a toss for Adamsberg, he had fallen through the floor into the black hole of forgetting, where everything gets pulped and incinerated and turned into something else, like in those recycling plants where you make cane chairs out of old tractor parts. Basically, she had already recycled Adamsberg. Not into a cane chair, definitely not, she had no use for such things. She had turned him into wanderlust and musical scores, into 5cm sheet-metal screws, and into a Canadian, why not? Memory does whatever it wants with the rubbish you discard in it, that is memory's business, you have no right to go poking around down there. In any case, there was nothing left of the Jean-Baptiste Adamsberg she had once loved so much. Not a tremor, not an echo, not even a regret. There were a few images, of course, but they had no relief, no charge. At one point Camille had been deeply upset by memory's merciless pulping of people and sentiments. Seeing a man you had spent so much time worrying about transformed into a 5cm sheet-steel screw was enough to make you stop and think. And she had stopped for a while to think. Her memory had not done all that work in a day, of course. There was no denying it had been a lot of work. Long months of smashing and grinding. Then a period of thinking. Then nothing. Devoid of the slightest twitch or the batting of an eyelid. Just a few souvenirs from another world.

Well then, what was stopping her giving Adamsberg a call? Nothing. Just that she expected to be irritated by it. Just that she felt tired at the prospect of stirring the remnants of a past that was now a foreign land. The kind of weariness you feel when you realise you have to go all the way back to check on some piddling detail like a gas cut-off. Making a detour. Wasting time. Killing time. The sinking feeling that you're taking a sidetrack back down a burned-out memory lane.

But Soliman, with his suffering on his sleeve, his pressing glance, with his fables and stories and dictionary definitions – Soliman had begun to breach her defences, and Camille had spent all night exercising the privilege of the wise, taking pause for thought. And in addition, all through the night Massart with his fangs and Suzanne with her Black boy-child and her Watchee had mounted noisy attacks on her uncooperative and selfish mood.

Came the dawn, and she found herself sitting or rather wobbling on the fence, torn between two equally distasteful prospects – going back to Les Écarts in defeat, or calling Adamsberg.

On the other side of the screen Soliman and Watchee were up. She could hear the young man unhooking the moped, no doubt to go in search of fresh bread. Then Watchee putting on his shirt and trousers. Then the smell of coffee and the noise of the moped coming back. Camille slipped on her top, her jeans and her boots before putting a foot on the ground – walking around inside the back of the truck in bare feet was out of the question.

Soliman smiled when he saw Camille appear, and Watchee showed her her breakfast stool with the tip of his crook. The youngster filled Camille's mug, put in two sugar-lumps, and cut her slices of bread.

'I'm going to manage now,' Camille said.

'We thought you would, young lady,' said Watchee.

'We're going back,' Soliman declared. 'Retreat. "Act or action of retiring or withdrawing in face of difficulty." Retreat's not a defeat. The dictionary makes that quite clear. Doesn't mention being beaten.'

Camille frowned sceptically. 'Can't that wait?' she said. 'In a day or two there could be more sheep. Then we'd know where to go.'

'So what?' said Soliman. 'We'll always be one step behind. We're on his tail. And if we stay on his tail we'll never be able to head him off, right? To do that you have to be one step ahead. And to be ahead of him you have to have much more information than we have. We're useless. We're tracking him, we're closing in on him, but we can't actually touch him. We're going home, Camille.'

'When?'

'Today, if you're up to driving over those passes again. We could be at Les Écarts by nightfall.'

'At least the animals would be glad to see us back,' said Watchee. 'They don't feed properly when I'm away.'

Camille drank her coffee and ran her fingers through her hair.

'I'm not happy with that,' she said.

'But that's the way it is,' said Soliman. 'Stuff your pride down your boots. Do you know the

230

story about the three foolish men who tried to learn the secret of the tree with the 120 branches?'

'What if I rang?' Camille said. 'If I rang that policeman?'

'If you call that *flic*, then it'll be the story of the three idiots and the genius who tried to learn the secret of the man with no hair.'

Camille nodded and pondered for a few minutes. Soliman tried to chew silently, while Watchee sat bolt upright with his hands on his knees, looking at Camille.

'I'll call him now,' she said, getting up.

'You're the driver,' said Soliman.

CHAPTER 25

'I'm the one standing in for him,' Adrien Danglard said for the third time. 'Are you phoning to make a complaint? Or to report a theft? Threatening behaviour? GBH?'

'It's personal,' Camille said. 'Strictly personal.'

She had reservations about that word. She did not like saying 'personal' for fear it would be taking a liberty and create ties she did not wish to have. Some words are like that – like insurgents stealing fields not their own.

'I'm his stand-in,' Danglard said blankly. 'Please tell me what your call is about.'

'I cannot tell you what my call is about.' Camille remained imperturbable. 'I wish to speak to *Commissaire* Adamsberg.'

'Personal, is it?'

'I said so.'

'Are you in the fifth arrondissement? Where are you calling from?'

'From the side of the N75 in the department of Isère.'

'Then I'm afraid we can't help you,' said *Lieutenant*

Danglard. 'You'd do better to contact the nearest *gendarmerie.*'

He grabbed a sheet of paper, scribbled the name SABRINA MONGE in capitals, jerked his head, shoved the paper towards the man sitting on his right, and with a jab of his pencil turned on the speakerphone.

Camille thought of hanging up. By blocking her, the Inspector was providing an easy way out, making it seem like fate. She could say that they just would not put her through to Adamsberg and she wasn't going to fight to get put through. But once combat had been engaged, Camille, with her streak of not entirely commendable pride, was simply inept at giving up. A quirk that had often wasted a lot of her time and energy.

'I don't think you understand me,' she said patiently.

'Of course I do,' said Danglard. 'You wish to speak to *Commissaire* Adamsberg. But *Commissaire* Adamsberg cannot be spoken to.'

'Is he away?'

'He cannot be reached.'

'This is important,' Camille said. 'Tell me where I can get hold of him.'

Danglard gave another nod to his assistant. The Monge girl was giving herself away with astounding naivety. She really must think *flics* were complete idiots.

'He can't be reached,' Danglard said again. 'He's gone away. Flown the nest. There is no

Commissaire Adamsberg any more. I'm standing in for him.'

There was a pause at the other end of the line.

'Is he dead?' Camille inquired in a quavering tone.

Danglard's forehead puckered into a frown: Sabrina Monge's voice wouldn't go wobbly like that. He was quite astute. He had not heard the fury or the mistrust he would have expected in the voice of Sabrina. The girl he was listening to was simply incredulous and taken aback.

Camille waited tensely, more stunned than anxious, as if she had seen the tide come to a halt. It could not be. She would have seen it in the papers, she would have heard about it. Adamsberg was a name.

'No, just away,' Danglard informed her in a different tone of voice. 'Leave me your name and number. I'll get him to call you back.'

'That won't work,' Camille said as her nervous tension returned to normal. 'This mobile is nearly out of power and I'm in the middle of nowhere.'

'Your name, please,' Danglard insisted.

'Camille Forestier.'

Danglard sat up straight, waved his assistant out of the room and switched off the speaker-phone. So it was Camille, Mathilde's girl, Queen Matilda's only daughter. Adamsberg had patches of trying to find out where on earth the girl was, but it was like trying to pin down a cloud, so he let it drop. Danglard took a fresh sheet of paper with the excitement of a boy who's been fishing at sea for days and suddenly feels a tug on the line.

'I'm listening,' he said.

Cautious Danglard quizzed Camille for fifteen minutes before he was satisfied that it was she. He had never met her but he had known the mother well enough to be able to test Camille on a file's worth of details that Sabrina Monge could never have known even if she had done all her homework. And what a beautiful mother Mathilde had been!

When Camille hung up she felt dizzy with all Danglard's questioning. The way Adamsberg was being protected made it seem as if a team of killers was after him. She reckoned the memories of her mother had done a lot to bust the policeman's barrage. She smiled. Queen Matilda was a pass key all to herself, and always had been. Adamsberg was in Avignon: she had the name of his hotel and his number.

Camille paced up and down beside the main road for a while, deep in thought. She had a vague idea in her head of where Avignon was on the map of France, and that it was relatively near. Tackling Adamsberg viva voce suddenly seemed infinitely preferable to speaking to him on the telephone. She did not trust a device unsuited to even moderately delicate circumstances. Telephones were fine for heavyweight and middleweight conversations but quite useless for the featherweight stuff. Calling a man you've not seen for years – and who is probably under deep cover – to ask him to help you find a werewolf that nobody else believes exists suddenly seemed a risky, not to say clumsy, way to proceed. Bumping into him seemed much more hopeful.

Soliman and Watchee were waiting at the back of the lorry in what had become their customary positions – the younger man sitting on the metal foothold, the straight-backed shepherd standing beside him, and the dog curled round his feet.

'He's at Avignon,' Camille said. 'I couldn't get through. I guess we ought to be able to get there.'

'So you don't know where Avignon is either?' asked Soliman.

'I do, in flashes. Is it far?'

Soliman looked at his watch.

'You go down to Valence and join the motorway south,' he said. 'Then follow the Rhône gently downstream. Should get there by one. Aren't you going to call ahead?'

'No. Better see him first.'

'Why?'

'Special reason,' Camille said with a shrug.

Watchee put his hand out to request the mobile phone.

'It's almost dead,' Camille said. 'Needs recharging.'

'I won't take long,' mumbled Watchee as he wandered off.

'Who's he calling?' she asked Soliman.

'The flock. He's having a wee word with the flock.'

Camille raised her eyebrows.

'So who picks up?' she asked. 'A ewe? Mauricette?'

Soliman shook his head crossly.

'Don't be silly. Buteil picks up. But after . . . well . . . Buteil puts one or two sheep on the line. He did it yesterday. He rings every day.'

'You mean to say he talks to the sheep?'

'Of course he does. Who else is he going to talk to? He tells them not to let themselves get down in the dumps, he tells them to eat properly, he tells them to keep their spirits up. He mostly talks to the leading ewe. As you might expect.'

'Are you telling me that Buteil shoves the mobile into the ear of the leading ewe?'

'Bloody hell. Yes, he does,' said Soliman. 'How else is he going to talk to the sheep?'

'All right,' Camille said. 'I didn't mean to upset you. I just wanted to know, that's all.'

She stared at Watchee pacing up and down with the mobile to his ear. His face had a caring expression and he was making soothing gestures with his free arm. His baritone carried all the way over and Camille could make out louder expressions like 'Listen to what I'm telling you, old girl'. Soliman followed Camille's gaze.

'Do you reckon a *flic* could take on board all that sort of thing?' he asked, waving generally at the mountains, the sheep wagon and the three of them.

'I wonder,' Camille said. 'It's not obvious.'

'I know what you mean,' Soliman said.

CHAPTER 26

At around three in the afternoon Camille left the city walls of Avignon behind her and crossed the bridge to the right bank of the Rhône. She sauntered along the down-stream towpath in search of Adamsberg, under a broiling sun. Nobody knew exactly where he was to be found. The hotel people did not know, nor did anyone at police HQ, where he had spent half the night and which he had left at around two. All they knew was that the *commissaire* hung around on the far side of the water.

It took an hour of walking for Camille to come upon him. He was sitting quite still, on his own on a narrow strip of grass cut through the willow thicket. He was at the water's edge, his feet touching the surface. He did not appear to be doing anything at all, but for Adamsberg sitting out in the open air was an activity in its own right. Actually, though, Camille saw as she looked at him more attentively that he *was* doing something. He was holding a long branch in the water and he was staring intently at its tip and at the eddies that this minor barrier created in the stream.

239

Unusually, he had kept his leather holster-strap on over his shirt. It was a piece of gear which always made quite an impression, and it stood in stark contrast to Adamsberg's crumpled shirt, his worn trousers, and his bare feet.

Camille was standing at three-quarters angle behind him and saw him almost in profile. He had not changed these past few years, and that did not surprise her. Not that he was exempt from the passing of time, but it left no visible mark on Adamsberg because his face was, so to speak, too eventful. Ageing leaves its signs on faces that are regular and harmonious. But from childhood Adamsberg had had irregular, discordant features, and on the asymmetric muddle of his countenance, the subtle symptoms of advancing years were overwhelmed by the chaotic effect of the ensemble.

For safety's sake, Camille made herself stop to look again at the face she had once put on a pedestal above all others. Basically it was all in his nose and lips. A large and fairly hooked nose, well-defined and dreamy lips. They did not match, they weren't refined, they weren't modest. As for the rest – swarthy complexion, hollow cheeks, receding chin, hastily swept back ordinary dark hair. Brown eyes, which rarely stopped moving and often looked distant, deeply set beneath bushy eyebrows. The face was all wrong. Camille's rigorous intellect had never solved the mystery of its unique seductiveness. Maybe it came from its intensity. Adamsberg's face was, so to speak, overloaded, overdefined, saturated.

Camille saw it all again and ran through the list of details dispassionately. Long ago the glow in Adamsberg's face had been a source of warmth and light. Today she looked on it quite neutrally, as if she was checking the bulb in a lamp. That face wasn't speaking to her any more; and her memory wasn't going to come up with a prompt.

She walked up to him calmly, with almost ponderous indifference. Adamsberg must have heard her, but he did not budge and kept on watching the branch that was holding back the Rhône on its path to the sea. When she was ten paces away from him she stood stock-still. Adamsberg was still looking at the river. But his left hand was holding a pistol, and pointing it straight at her.

'Stay right where you are,' he said softly. 'Freeze.'

Camille did as she was instructed, without a word.

'You know I can pull the trigger much faster than you can draw,' he went on without taking his eyes off the branch in the water. 'How did you find me?'

'Danglard,' Camille replied.

At the sound of this unexpected voice Adamsberg slowly turned to face her. Camille well remembered Adamsberg's slightly graceful, utterly casual low-speed movements. He gazed at her in amazement. Gently, he dropped his guard and rather embarrassedly put the gun down on the grass beside him.

'I'm sorry,' he said. 'I was expecting someone else.'

Camille nodded awkwardly.

'Forget the gun,' he went on. 'It's because of a girl who's obsessed with the idea of killing me.'

'I see,' Camille said politely.

'Please sit down,' said Adamsberg, motioning to a patch of grass.

Camille wavered.

'Come on, sit down,' he insisted. 'You came all this way so you might as well sit down.'

He smiled.

'I killed the girl's partner. A shot from my gun did for him as I was knocked over. Here's where she wants to lodge her bullet,' he said, pointing to his midriff. 'And that's why she won't get off my back. Unlike you, Camille. You've been keeping out of my way. Avoiding me. You made yourself really scarce.'

Camille had ended up sitting down cross-legged fifteen feet from him while he pursued the conversation single-handedly. She was waiting for the questions. Adamsberg knew perfectly well that she had not sought him out for love, but because she needed him.

He looked her over for a moment. No doubt about it: that grey jacket that was too long for her, with its cuffs down to her knuckles, those pale jeans and black boots belonged to the girl he had seen on the television news. Camille had been in the square at Saint-Victor-du-Mont, leaning against the old plane tree. He looked away.

'Made yourself very scarce,' he repeated as he pushed his branch back into the water. 'Something really fearsome must have made you come and find me. In response to some kind of higher authority.'

Camille said nothing.

'So what's happened to you?' he asked gently.

Camille ran her fingers through the dry grass, restrained by her own embarrassment but tempted to run away again.

'I need help.'

Adamsberg lifted his branch out of the water and changed his position so as to be sitting facing her, with his legs crossed. Then carefully, meticulously, he placed the branch horizontally on the ground in front of him, and between the two of them. It wasn't quite straight so with one hand he adjusted its lie. Adamsberg had very fine hands: strong, well-proportioned, and large in relation to his overall size.

'Someone wants to harm you?'

'No.'

Her heart sank at the prospect of having to spew out the whole convoluted story of the sheep and the man without hair, Soliman and his stink-pond, the lorry and their fruitless pursuit. She was trying to find the least outlandish angle.

'But there's the business about the sheep,' said Adamsberg. 'The beast of the Mercantour.'

Camille looked up in surprise.

'Something went wrong,' the *commissaire* continued. 'Something happened that you didn't like. You've plunged into it without telling anyone. Your local *gendarmerie* isn't in the know. You're freelancing, and now you're stuck. You're looking for a *flic* to get you out of trouble – one who's not going to tell you to go jump in a lake. As you're at the end of your tether, and also because you don't really know any other policemen, you've come looking for me, with very mixed feelings. Now you've found me. But all of a sudden you can't remember how you got here. You don't give a damn for the sheep. What you really want to do right now is to be off. To walk away from me. To take flight.'

A smile flitted over Camille's face. Adamsberg had always fathomed things nobody else could work out. Conversely there were masses of things other people knew which remained entirely beyond him.

'How do you know that?'

'Vague smell of the mountains and sheep grease about you.'

Camille looked down at her jacket and started rubbing the sleeves, instinctively.

'Yes,' she said. 'The smell does cling.'

She looked up at him. 'How do you know that?'

'I saw you on the news, when it broadcast a shot of the village square.'

'Do you remember the story about the sheep?'

'Reasonably well. Huge fang-marks found in

thirty-one savaged animals at Ventebrune, Pierrefort, Saint-Victor-du-Mont, Guillos, La Castille and, most recently, at La Tête du Cavalier near the village of Le Plaisse. But the main thing was the woman at Saint-Victor who met the same fate as the sheep. I therefore suppose that you knew the woman, and that's what has been your motive for getting involved.'

Camille stared at him, unbelieving.

'Did the police take any notice of any of it?' she asked.

'The police are totally uninterested in the story,' Adamsberg said. 'Apart from me.'

'Because of the wolves? Your grandfather's wolves?'

'Maybe. Then there's that huge monster, like something out of a time-warp. In the midst of so much darkness. That sparked my interest.'

'What darkness?' Camille did not understand.

'The darkness enveloping the whole story. It has a gloomy, nocturnal feel to it; you can't see through it, but you can think through it. That's what I'd call darkness.'

'What else?'

'I don't know. I wondered if there was someone leading the monster on. It's done a lot of killing, brutally, not out of a need to survive. Like a mad dog, but in fact, more like a man. Then there's Suzanne Rosselin. I don't understand how an animal would have attacked her. Unless the beast was crazy or rabid. What I also don't understand is the failure to capture the animal so far. Much darkness.'

Adamsberg looked at Camille and said nothing for a while. He had never found silence awkward, however long it lasted.

'Tell me what you're up to in all this,' he said softly. 'Tell me what's gone wrong. Tell me what you expect me to do.'

Camille explained the whole story from the beginning: the Ventebrune sheep, then the wolf-hunt, then Massart and his squat figure, smooth skin and twisted legs; then there was the mastiff, the size of the bite-marks, Crassus's disappearance and the murder of Suzanne; Soliman shutting himself in the toilet, Watchee standing stock-still, Massart gone missing; then there was the map, the pencil-marks, the werewolf with his hair inside, the abattoir in Manchester; kitting out the sheep-truck, Woops or whatever the hell the dog was called, Soliman's definitions and the five candles laid out like a M; then the murder of the Sautrey pensioner; then the dead end they'd got into, the brick wall they were up against, and the pond where the soul of Suzanne still lay trapped.

Unlike Adamsberg, Camille had a mind that was fast, sharp and orderly. It took her no more than fifteen minutes to tell the whole tale.

'Did you say Sautrey? I didn't pick that up from the news. Where is it?'

'Not far beyond the Col de la Croix-Haute, downhill from Villard-de-Lans.'

'What did you find out about that murder?'

'That's the thing – we learned nothing. He was

a retired teacher. He was slashed not far from the village, in the night. Nothing is known about his injuries, but there's talk about a stray dog, a runaway Baskerville or something of the sort. Soliman wanted to look inside every church on the route, but then he backed down. He said we'd always be one step behind.'

'And then? What did you do next?'

'We reckoned we'd have to find a policeman.'

'And then?'

'I said that I knew one.'

'Why didn't you go to see the *flics* at Villard-de-Lans?'

'No-one there would have heard us out. We've got nothing tangible.'

'I'm quite fond of intangibles.'

'That's what I thought.'

Adamsberg nodded and said nothing for several minutes. Camille waited. She had explained everything to the best of her abilities. The decision was now no longer in her gift. She had given up trying to persuade other people long ago.

'Was it a big problem to track me down?' Adamsberg asked at long last, looking up at Camille.

'Do I have to tell the truth?'

'If you can.'

'It really pissed me off.'

'Good,' said Adamsberg after another pause. 'That means the case really matters to you. Or else the wolves do, or the Suzanne woman, or your Soliman, or your shepherd fellow.'

'All wrapped up together, I would say.'

'What have you been doing with yourself these last years?' he asked, changing the subject abruptly.

'I repair boilers and leaky pipes.'

'What about your music?'

'I'm composing the soundtrack for a soap.'

'A drama? An adventure?'

'A love story. Major heartaches for M. and Mme Water-Rat.'

'Oh. I see.'

Adamsberg paused again.

'And you're doing all that in this village, in Saint-Victor?'

'Yes.'

'What about the Lawrence Johnstone you mentioned? The wildlife warden who studied the injuries on the first sheep?'

Adamsberg said 'Laurence' as if it was a French girl's name; he never could get his tongue around English pronunciation.

'He's not a warden,' Camille said, on the defensive. 'He's a visiting scientist making a documentary.'

'OK. So let's say this man, this Canadian, then . . .'

'Let's say what?'

'Well, tell me a bit about him.'

'He's from Canada. He's a visiting scientist making a documentary.'

'Yes, you've already said that. Tell me about him.'

'Why do I have to say anything about him?'

'I need to understand the context.'

'He's a Canadian. I've not much more to say about him.'

'Isn't he a tall, fit, strapping fellow? A handsome guy, a good-looker with fair hair down to his shoulders?'

'Yes,' Camille said warily. 'How do you know that as well?'

'All Canadians are like that. Isn't that so?'

'Perhaps.'

'So tell me about him.'

Camille looked at Adamsberg, who, smiling a little smile, was observing her calmly.

'You want to understand the whole context, is that it?' she asked.

'That's right.'

'Including knowing whether I sleep with Johnstone, is that right?'

'That's correct. Including knowing if you go to bed with him.'

'Is that any of your business?'

'No. The wolves aren't any of my business either. Nor are your murderers. Or the police. Nothing and nobody is any of my business. Save for this willow-branch, perhaps,' he said as he touched the piece of wood lying between them. 'And myself, from time to time.'

'All right,' said Camille with a sigh. 'I'm living with the man.'

'That makes it all easier to grasp,' Adamsberg said.

He stood up, took the willow-branch and walked around the clearing.

'Where did you park?'

'Just outside town, at the "Hop Inn" campsite.'

'Are you up to driving all the way to Sautrey this evening?'

Camille said that she was.

Adamsberg walked on again, slowly. At five that morning the Latin Quarter murderer's sea wall had cracked, and confessions had flooded through the breach. He still had to write up the report, call Danglard and the *police judiciaire*. To go back to the hotel, call the prosecution service in Grenoble, ring Villard-de-Lans. He knew the head of the *gendarmerie* at Villard-de-Lans. Adamsberg stopped as he hunted for the name. Montvailland, that was it. Maurice Montvailland. A frightfully logical fellow.

He added it all up on his fingers, went down to the riverbank to pick up his revolver, which he put back in its holster, then put on his shoes.

'Around 8.30 this evening,' he said. 'Can you wait for me?'

Camille nodded and stood up in her turn.

'Will you come with us?' she asked. 'To Sautrey?'

'To Sautrey or wherever. I have to go back to Paris, I've finished what I had to do in Avignon. There's nothing that says I can't go back by way of Sautrey, is there? What's the place like?'

'Misty.'

'OK. We'll cope.'

'Why are you coming?' Camille asked.

'Do I have to tell the truth?'

'If possible.'

'Because I would rather stay under cover at the moment, because of the girl on my tail. I'm waiting for a piece of information.'

Camille nodded.

'Because I'm interested in that wolf,' he added.

Adamsberg paused, audibly.

'And because you asked me to.'

CHAPTER 27

Soliman and Watchee stood at the back of the lorry as soon as it turned eight to look out for the *flic* with special gifts. The sheep-wagon was so out of place amidst the spotless tents and mobile homes that it had barely been allowed in at the 'Hop Inn' campsite. They had parked as far away from other vehicles as possible so that people would not come and grouse about the smell.

Soliman had spent the afternoon showering and shaving and doing the rounds in Avignon on his moped. He had recharged the mobile phone and restocked the lorry with all the neces-saries, and some superfluities too. Watchee did not have the same need for movement and action. Observing ten people was for him as good as seeing ten thousand. He wasn't exactly happy, but he certainly seemed quite content to stand guard by the lorry with his hands on his crook and his dog at his feet, watching the world go by, with a certain disdain. Whereas Soliman was getting more inquisitive and voracious by the hour. He was fascinated by the bustle of a place like

Avignon. Watchee was as alarmed by the boy's interest in something other than Les Écarts as he was by his taste for unexplained absences and for taking off on the moped at all hours of the day and night. The sooner they got hold of the vampire and the sooner they slit him open, the sooner Soliman would get back home to the farm and calm down.

A little further off on a folding canvas stool, Camille was finishing her supper – a helping of rice, moistened with olive oil and downed with a soup spoon. She was also waiting for Adamsberg. Without great relish, on the other hand without dread. Seeing him again had been less stressful than she had feared. And persuading him had been no trouble at all. He had seemed to be willing to take on the wolf case before she even mentioned it. He was a step ahead: as if he had been waiting for her on purpose by the banks of the Rhône, in bare feet. Soliman kept his eyes glued to the campsite entrance as he looked out for the *flic*; Watchee said nothing, but remained on his guard.

Adamsberg turned up at the appointed hour in an unmarked squad car that was close to retirement. With little ado hands were shaken and names exchanged. The *commissaire* did not appear to even notice Watchee's standoffishness. Awkwardness had never much bothered Adamsberg. As he was simply incapable of bowing to social constraints he disregarded pecking orders and their associated rituals;

he coped with human relations in his own blunt way, neither holding back nor pulling rank. He really did not mind who was lording it over whom so long they left him in peace to get on with his job.

The only thing he asked for was Massart's map. He laid it out on the dusty ground and spent a long time poring over it with a vaguely worried look on his face. Everything about Adamsberg was always vague; you could never quite trust his face to tell you what was actually going on in his head.

'That's a pretty odd route,' he said. 'All those minor roads and twists and turns. It's really complicated.'

'He's a complicated guy,' said Soliman. 'Madness is complicated.'

'If he had wanted to hang around and get caught he wouldn't have gone about it any differently. Whereas he could have gone right across the country in a day, and left France in a flash.'

'But he still hasn't been caught,' Soliman pointed out.

'Because he's not being looked for,' said Adamsberg, folding the map.

'But we're looking for him.'

'Maybe *you* are,' Adamsberg smiled. 'But when he's got the whole force on his tail, he won't be able to afford the time to saunter down by-ways and stop off in churches. I don't understand why he's not using the motorway.'

'He spent twenty years of his life traipsing round the back roads of France,' Camille said. 'When he made his living as an itinerant bottomer. He's familiar with all the side roads, he knows quiet places to lay up in, and where to find sheep, too. He wants to be thought dead. And above all he's trying to keep his wolf from being seen.'

'He prowls at night,' Watchee broke in. 'That's when he murders his victims, sheep or human. He sleeps during the daytime. That's why he's making slow progress. He can't show his face, that's instinctive for a man of that sort. And he steers clear of people, that's natural for a man of that kind.'

It was nearly one in the morning before the sheep-wagon reached Sautrey. Adamsberg got there before them, and waited patiently for the other three, parked just outside the fog-bound village. He let his mind wander from the wolf to the map, then to Soliman, the truck, and Camille. He thanked fate for having put his path across Camille's and for having put the big wolf in his way. But he wasn't really surprised. It seemed normal and natural for him to be tackling the beast that had been on his mind ever since its first act of carnage. As natural as having caught up with Camille. Seeing her appear by the river-bank had shaken him a bit, of course, but not so very much. It was as if a tiny but functional fragment of his mind had never stopped watching

255

out for her on the edges of his field of vision. So that when she did enter the field, he turned out to be in some sense already prepared for her to do so.

There was that muscle-man, of course, there had to be, and why not? Adamsberg had nothing against that. Obviously there was a man in the picture. Why shouldn't there be? And handsome, too, from what he had glimpsed. That was fine and all to the good, your life's your own, my friend. Camille had been rather tense to begin with, down by the Rhône, and then she got over it. Now she was calm and neutral. Neither friendly nor hostile, not even evasive. Peaceful and distant. Fine. That was normal. She had erased him. That's how it was. That's how he wanted it to be. And it was OK. And the tall guy, too, why not, there had to be one, why shouldn't it be him? Just as well she had got a good-looking man, she deserved no less. Would Camille take off for Canada, though? That was another question.

He saw the black mass of the sheep-wagon drive past, opened the door of his car and flashed his headlights twice. The lorry pulled in to the side with a clatter of loose metal and its lights went out. Soliman and Watchee were asleep in the cab. Camille shook the young man awake and jumped down to the road. Soliman got out next, all bleary-eyed, and helped the old man negotiate the footholds.

'Bugger that, stop carrying me like a baby,' Watchee growled.

'I don't want you to have a fall, old man,' said Soliman.

'Didn't you have anything more serviceable than that thing?' Adamsberg asked Camille. 'For the journey?'

Camille shook her head. 'I've got used to it.'

'I can see why,' Adamsberg said. 'I like that smell. That's how it smells down my way, in the Pyrenees. It's the wool-fat that does it.'

'I know,' Camille said.

The shepherd screwed up his eyes in the dark, sizing up the *flic*. At last someone, the only one, who did not grouse about the lorry's lanolin smell. Maybe this guy with the rough-cut face would be worth talking to. He went round the lorry and waved Adamsberg over.

'He's summoning you,' Camille explained.

Adamsberg went up to the shepherd, who adjusted his hat and crossed his hands on his crook.

'Listen here, young fella,' said Watchee.

'He's a *commissaire*,' said Soliman. 'You call him "*Commissaire*". No way is he a "young fella".'

'There's one thing about Massart', the old man persevered, 'that the young lady has probably not told you. He's a werewolf. No body hair. You know what I mean?'

'Absolutely.'

'It's all on the inside. Gloves off when you get at him. A werewolf is as strong as twenty men.'

'Sure.'

'And one other thing, young fella. There's a spare bed at the back, on the right. You're welcome to it.'

'Thank you.'

'Watch it,' Watchee went on, with a glance at Soliman. 'We're sharing the lorry with the young lady. Behave respectably, and with respect for her.'

He dismissed Adamsberg with a brief nod and climbed back into the lorry.

'Hospitality,' said Soliman. 'Reception and entertainment of guests with liberality and goodwill.'

Worn out from nine hours' driving, Camille laid stretched out on her bunk, listening to Watchee snoring on the other side of the canvas partition. The side-tarpaulins had been lowered over the latticework and it was almost completely dark inside the lorry. The lorry had heated up on the way to Avignon and it was still at least five degrees warmer inside than out. Adamsberg, too, was asleep beside her. Or perhaps not. She could not hear Soliman either. Watchee's snoring drowned out everyone else's breathing. Adamsberg had not shown the slightest awkwardness about sleeping in the fourth bunk which Watchee had offered with his blessing and warnings. The old man was a bit of a headmaster inside the lorry, he laid down the law about what was and was not to be tolerated, and they all pretended to observe his law. Adamsberg had gone to bed straight away without any fuss. Right now he was lying there next to her, separated by a gap between the bunks of no more than fifty centimetres. That's no great distance. But it was better to have Adamsberg that close than to sleep next to Watchee or Soliman, who had seemed pretty much touch-and-go to Camille ever since they had left Les Écarts.

Adamsberg was preferable, because no flame at all is simpler to manage than a flickering one. Sadder, true, but simpler. She could have touched his shoulder just by stretching out her arm. She had spent hundreds of hours asleep with her head on his chest, in almost perfect oblivion. To the extent that she had once believed she was made for Adamsberg as if by a magic spell which there was no point trying to resist. But now she was not even troubled by his presence. She would have liked Lawrence to sleep here – with Lawrence, the emotional landscape was utterly different from the blatant passion of her old love for Adamsberg. Despite fleeting reservations and common-or-garden hesitations, it was a more tangible landscape altogether. And Camille had lost interest in grand vistas. She had acquired some rather thick skin.

Watchee stopped snoring He must have rolled over. Respite. In the new-found quiet she could make out Adamsberg's regular breathing. He too had fallen easily asleep. Your life's your own, my friend. That's all that's ever left of faith and grandeur when they come to an end: imperturbable respiration.

Kept awake by harsh thoughts of this kind, Camille did not fall asleep until late and so did not wake until nearly nine. She grabbed her boots before putting a foot to the ground, and went through the canvas partition.

Soliman was lying propped up on his elbows reading the dictionary.

'Where have they all gone?' Camille asked as she made her coffee. 'Get out of my way, Threads,' she said as she sat down on Watchee's bunk.

'Woof,' Soliman corrected.

'Yes, sorry, Woof. Where are they?'

'Watchee is phoning the flock. Apparently the lead sheep wasn't in good shape last night, she's got a swollen foot. Psychosomatic. The old man's trying to cheer her up. A limping lead sheep puts the whole flock in a mess.'

'Has she a name?'

'She's called George Gershwin,' said Soliman with a pained expression. 'Watchee wanted to pick at random from the dictionary, but he opened at the proper names part of it. By then it was too late to correct it. What's been said has been said. She's known as George. Anyway, she's got a swollen foot.'

'And Jean-Baptiste?'

'He got up at the crack of dawn to see the *gendarmes* here at Sautrey, then he came back for his car and went to see the police at Villard-de-Lans. He says they've been put in charge of the investigation. He said not to wait lunch for him.'

Adamsberg got back around three. Soliman was washing clothes in a blue plastic bowl, Camille was writing music in the driver's cab, and Watchee was sitting on a stool, scratching the dog, humming. Sitting around like that, the three of them could have been nomads. Adamsberg felt pleased to be back. He was growing fond of the lorry and its crew.

He climbed into the back and came out with one of the canvas folding stools, so rusty you would cut your fingers opening it, and set it up in the middle of the rectangle of mowed grass alongside the lorry. Soliman was the first to join him there. He was in an even greater state of excitement than the day before. He was keen on the *flic* in every respect: he liked his patchwork face, his soothing voice, and his slow-motion movements. He had understood that morning that no person, no rule and no convention would ever be master of the *commissaire*, despite his manifestly gentle and approachable nature. And though the two of them were poles apart, that characteristic reminded him of his mother's elemental independence. He had walked with Adamsberg back to his car and told him a lot about Suzanne.

Soliman put his bowl at Adamsberg's feet.

Watchee, sitting a few feet away, stopped his humming.

'Tell us, young fella, who did Sernot in?'

'A very large dog, or a wolf,' Adamsberg said.

Watchee hit the ground with his crook as if the thump would underscore how clear-sighted they had been.

'I saw Montvailland,' Adamsberg went on. 'I filled him in about Massart and the Mercantour beast. I know that *flic*. He's very good, but he's rational, and that holds him back. He liked the story, but more as a poem than a case. I have to add that Montvailland only puts up with poetry if it's got regular metre and the verses delivered in four-line stanzas. The problem we're lumbered with is that the Massart saga doesn't work with people who think two and two make four. Montvailland buys the idea of a wolf. They had a scare last year south of Grenoble, in the Massif des Écrins. But he does not buy the idea of a man being involved. I told him that made an awful lot of travel and a heap of victims for a lone wolf in a few days, but he thinks a foray like that is possible, for instance, if the wolf has rabies. Or if he's just very disturbed. He's going to ask for authorisation for a hunt and for helicopter surveillance. There's something else.'

Watchee raised his hand for permission to speak.

'You had lunch, young fella?'

'No,' said Adamsberg. 'I forgot.'

'Sol, fetch the mess. Bring some white, too.'

262

Soliman put a crate down next to Adamsberg and handed the bottle to Watchee. He alone was allowed to uncork Saint-Victor white, as Camille had been firmly if politely informed after her vigil at the Col de la Bonette.

'Imperialism,' Soliman said with his eyes on Watchee. 'Collective or individual pursuit of expansion and domination.'

'Watch it,' said Watchee.

He filled a glass and handed it to Adamsberg.

'Fair nose, good legs, and a broad bottom,' he said. 'But be careful, it also has a tail.'

Adamsberg thanked him with a nod.

'Sernot had a head injury, as if he'd been hit with a blunt instrument before having his throat slit. Was anything like that observed with Suzanne Rosselin?'

Nobody said anything.

'We've no idea,' said Soliman, his voice quavering slightly. 'I mean, at that time, we really believed in the wolf. Nobody had then thought of Massart. We didn't examine her head.'

Soliman shut up abruptly.

'I understand,' said Adamsberg. 'I pressed Montvailland on that point. But in his view Sernot hurt himself during the struggle with the beast. It's a rational view. Montvailland doesn't want to take it any further. But at least I got him to examine the body again, to look for hairs.'

'Massart has no hair,' Watchee grunted. 'And the hair that comes out at night on him is not the moulting kind.'

263

'I meant animal hair,' Adamsberg added. 'So we can find out whether it was a dog or a wolf.'

'Do they have a time for the murder?' Soliman asked.

'Around 4 a.m.'

'So he would have had time to cover the distance from La Tête du Cavalier to Sautrey that night. What was Sernot doing up and out at four in the morning? Do they have a clue?'

'That doesn't worry Montvailland. Sernot was a climber and hill walker, he went in for huge and exhausting circuits. What's more, he had insomnia. He sometimes woke up at three and couldn't get back to sleep. When he was fed up staying awake, he would get up and go for a walk. Montvailland thinks he came across the beast when it was out looking for food at night.'

'That makes sense,' Camille said.

'But what made the animal attack him?' Soliman said.

'Very disturbed.'

'Where did it happen?' Camille asked.

'Where two tracks meet, at a place called Calvary Cross. There's a big wooden cross there, on a hillock. The corpse was found lying at the foot of the cross.'

'Candles,' Soliman mumbled.

'Fanatic,' Watchee decided.

'I told Montvailland about that aspect of the case too.'

'Did you tell him about us?'

'That's the only thing I particularly did not mention.'

'We're nothing to be ashamed of,' said Watchee with a flash of hauteur.

Adamsberg looked up at the shepherd. 'Harassment is not allowed,' he said. 'The law forbids acts of harassment.'

'Bugger the law forbids,' Soliman said.

'We're not harassing him,' Watchee said. 'We're hunting the man down. There's no prohibition on that.'

'There is.'

Adamsberg held out his glass for Watchee to fill. 'Montvailland knows I'm under wraps,' he went on. 'He knows my name can't be mentioned by anyone. He thinks I picked up all the info while underground.'

'Are you in hiding, young fella?' asked Watchee.

Adamsberg nodded. 'There's a girl out to nail me, it's a life-and-death affair. If the papers say I'm around, she'll pop up within minutes and put a bullet in my gut. It's all she lives for.'

'What are you going to do?' Watchee asked. 'Are you going to kill her?'

'No.'

The old man frowned. 'So are you going to keep on running all your life?'

'I'm putting a different idea in her mind. I'm building a branch line for her to take.'

'A branch line, now that's crafty,' said Watchee, screwing up his eyes.

'Crafty, but cumbersome. It takes time. And there's a part I still haven't got.'

Adamsberg unhurriedly put the bread and the fruit into the crate, stood up, and stowed it all in the lorry.

'We're going to Grenoble,' he announced. 'I've an unofficial interview with the superintendent of police. I want to let him know that I've planted the Massart business in Montvailland's skull. I want to try to persuade him to steer the investigation in our direction.'

'Which way?' asked Camille, getting up.

'Don't you even know where Grenoble is?' Soliman said.

'Bugger that, Sol. Just stick to showing me the route on the map.'

'She's the driver,' said Watchee, as he tapped Soliman on the shoulder with the tip of his crook.

Ten kilometres short of Grenoble, after the access road onto the motorway, Adamsberg's car let the sheep-wagon overtake. Camille saw it flashing its lights repeatedly in her rear-view mirror.

'We're stopping,' Camille said. 'Something's up.'

'There's a lay-by two kilometres ahead,' said Soliman.

'She saw the sign,' said Watchee.

Camille drew up on the hard shoulder, put on the hazard lights, and walked back to Adamsberg's car.

'Are you breaking down?' she asked, leaning through the open window.

And all of a sudden she found that she was much too close to that face. She pulled away from the window, stepped back.

'I've just had the news on,' Adamsberg shouted through the open window, trying to make himself heard over the roar of motorway traffic. 'Fourteen head of sheep were slaughtered last night north-east of Grenoble.'

'Where exactly?' Camille was shouting too.

Adamsberg shook his head and then got out of the car.

'Fourteen head,' he repeated. 'At Tiennes, north-east of Grenoble. On Massart's itinerary, once again. But this time the wolf has come down from the mountain. We've got him, don't you see?'

'You mean he's left wolf country?'

Adamsberg confirmed this with a nod.

'No *flic* can maintain any longer that we're dealing with a wandering lone wolf. The beast is heading north, following the red pencil line, getting ever further from the wild places. A man is in charge. It has to be a man. I'm calling Montvailland.'

Adamsberg got back into the car, and Camille went to tell Soliman and Watchee.

'Tiennes,' Camille said. 'Show me the map. Fourteen head of sheep.'

'Lord have mercy,' growled Watchee.

Camille put her finger on the place and handed the map to the old man.

'Are there any large sheep farms around there?' she asked.

'Wherever you find decent folk, you'll be finding sheep farms.'

Adamsberg made his way to the lorry.

'Montvailland's beginning to wonder,' he said. 'No animal hairs were found on Sernot's corpse.'

Watchee grunted something inaudible from the rear of the lorry. 'I'll carry on into Grenoble as planned,' Adamsberg said. 'It shouldn't be too hard to persuade the superintendent.'

'Are you going to ask to be put in charge of the case?' Camille said.

'It's outside my bailiwick. And there's the girl – I don't want her to know where I am. Camille, you get down to Tiennes. I'll catch up with you there.'

'Where do we rendezvous?'

'Park wherever you can, by the side of the minor road, or on the way into the village.'

'What if I can't?'

'Well, let's say that if you're not there, it'll be because you're somewhere else.'

'OK. Let's say that.'

'You'll get there in time to look in at the church. Go and see if he's left us a message.'

'Candles?'

'For instance.'

'Do you think he wants to be noticed?'

'Mainly – what I think is that he's leading us a

merry dance. We're going to have to change the music.'

Camille clambered back into the cab. Adamsberg was quite often like that. You could not always be sure you had understood.

CHAPTER 28

Not far beyond Grenoble the mountains shrank to nothing and suddenly gave way to open fields. After spending half a year in the Alps, Camille felt as if walls had come tumbling down all around her, carrying off all her props and compass points. She watched the protective barrier of rock perish in the rear-view mirror; looking ahead, she felt as if she was entering a gaping, unframed world where there was no knowing what the dangers were or what people would do. She had the impression that there was no longer anything solid she could rely on. She would give Lawrence a call as soon as she got to Tiennes. That Canadian voice would remind her of the reassuring cradle of the Alps.

All that musing just because it was flat land. She glanced at Soliman and Watchee. The shepherd was staring glumly at the open vista entirely lacking in grandeur or in boundaries and this seemed to rob him of what had been his lifelong support.

'Talk about flat!' Camille said.

The road was rutted and the lorry rattled from

top to bottom. You had to shout to be heard above the clatter of metal.

'It crushes you,' said Watchee in his low baritone.

'It carries on like that from here to the North Pole. Nothing you can do about it.'

'We're not going that far,' Soliman said.

'If the vampire goes that far, so will we,' said Watchee.

'We'll get him before then. We've got Adamsberg.'

'Nobody's *got* Adamsberg, Sol,' Camille said. 'Do you still not know that?'

'Of course I do,' said Soliman glumly. 'Do you know the story about the man who tried to put his wife's eyes in a tin so he could look at them while he was out hunting?'

'Bugger off, Sol!' said Watchee, banging the side window with his fist.

'This is the place,' Camille said.

Soliman unhooked the moped and zoomed off to inspect the nearest churches. Watchee took his own bottle of white with him to the principal café in Tiennes, a place buzzing with fear and revulsion. Fourteen head, for heaven's sake. There weren't supposed to be any wolves in the lowlands. It's all because of those idiots in the Mercantour Wildlife Reserve, a tinny voice spoke out. They've played around with wolves and now they're breeding and spreading like the plague. Soon enough there'll be wolves all over France and they'll blanket the country in blood. That's what happens when you bring wild things back. A rougher voice climbed above the din. When you don't know what you're talking about you keep your trap shut, the rough voice said. It ain't a plague and it ain't wolves: it's *a* wolf. One single big lone wolf, a bloody monster that's been tracking north for more than three hundred kilometres. A wolf, a solitary wolf, the Beast of the Mercantour. The vet inspected the wounds. It was the Beast, with fangs as big as that. They just said so on the news. So that idiot had better find out about things before opening his gob. Watchee made his way to the bar. He wanted to find out who the sheep farmer was, and whether he had seen a car in the vicinity of his grazing land last night. They would never get Massart until they knew what car he was driving. But they still had not identified the frigging car.

Soliman came back in a state of high excitement. In a chapel very near Tiennes he had come across five candle stubs set out apart from the others, and in the shape of the letter M. The latch was bent so the door couldn't be closed at night. Soliman wanted to collect the candle stubs for finger-printing. After all, you couldn't ask for a better medium than wax!

'Hang on until he comes,' Camille said.

She was reading *The A to Z of Tools for Trade and Craft*; Soliman was stripped to the waist as he got on with the washing in the blue plastic bowl;

272

Watchee was drowsing in the lorry. They were hanging on until the *flic* came.

The best part of an hour went by in silence.

Suddenly a roar of souped-up revs heralded four bikers coming down the road. They cut off towards the lorry and came to a halt a few feet from Soliman. They took off their helmets without a word, smiling intently at the astonished young man. Camille froze.

'What's this about then, nigger boy?' said one of the bikers. 'Having fun with whitie?'

'Not worried about leaving black paw-marks on her, are we?' said another.

Soliman stood up, quivering with anger, holding tight to the linen he had been wringing out over the bowl.

'Quietly does it, monkey man,' the first biker said, dismounting. 'We're going to fix you up. We're going fix you up right and proper so you'll forget about screwing around down to the day you're ripe for retirement benefits.'

Then the second biker, a scrawny ginger-nut, dismounted as well.

'As for you', he said to Camille, 'you're going to get a facial. A right makeover. After that you'll have to make do with niggers 'cos no-one else will want you. That's by way of punishment.'

The four of them drew nearer. They were bare-chested beneath their leather jackets, they were wearing knuckledusters and swinging motorcycle chains. The talkative one was fair and plump.

Soliman crouched ready for the attack and moved over to shield Camille. He had suddenly lost his childish clarity. His upper lip snarled with rage and his eyes narrowed to a slit. Anger made him almost ugly.

'You got a name, monkey boy?' asked the first biker, twirling his chain. 'I like to know what to call things I shunt.'

'Melchior!' Soliman spat at him.

The fat guy grinned and moved closer while the other three circled so as to box the boy in.

'Whoever touches the King of Orient is a dead man,' Watchee's voice boomed through the silence.

The old shepherd was standing bolt upright on the back steps of the lorry aiming his hunting rifle at the bikers. He was rigid, and his eyes shone with loathing.

'A dead man,' Watchee repeated, and he shot a hole in the petrol tank of one of the black bikes. 'These bullets are good enough for wild boar. I don't advise any one of you to move an eyebrow.'

The four bikers stood stock-still, unsure what to do. Watchee raised his chin.

'It is customary to bare your head before royalty,' he said. 'Take off your caps. And your jackets. Drop the chains. Take off your knuckledusters. And your boots.'

The bikers obeyed and dumped all their gear on the ground.

'But keep your pants on,' Watchee continued in a rasping tone. 'There is a lady present. I wouldn't want her to be put off for life.'

The four men stood before the old sheep-hand, bare to the waist, in their stockinged feet, struck dumb with humiliation.

'Now, get down on your knees,' Watchee ordered. 'Like worms. Put your hands flat on the ground, and touch the earth with your forehead. Keep your bums down. Like hyenas. That's right. Good. That is the correct posture for greeting royalty.'

Watchee grinned as he saw them prostrate themselves.

'Now listen to me, you young fellas. I'm past the age for sleep. I stay awake all night long. I stand vigil for young Melchior. It's my job. If you come back I'll shoot you down like mad dogs. Hey, you, fatso, try to keep still,' he said as he took aim with his rifle. 'Or would you rather I start on it now?'

'Don't shoot, Watchee,' said Adamsberg.

The *commissaire* was approaching quietly from behind, his .357 in his hand.

'Unload that rifle,' he said. 'We're not going to lose a single boar-bullet up the arses of these rats. It would take too much time, and we're in a hurry. A great hurry. Camille, come over here, grab my mobile from my jacket pocket and call the local *flics*. Soliman, you drain their tanks, puncture their tyres and smash their headlamps. It'll make us all feel better.'

Camille moved cautiously among these seven warring males. It was the first time she had seen the killer twitch in Soliman's face, or ferociousness in Watchee's expression.

Not a word was said in the minutes that followed. The bikers watched Soliman destroy their machines with measured fury.

The *gendarme*s arrived in a paddy wagon, hand-cuffed the four men and put them aboard. Adamsberg did what was necessary to make the initial statement as succinct as possible and to have the formal procedure put off until a more convenient time. Before they drove off, he put his head through the paddy-wagon window.

'You,' he said to the first biker. 'Soliman will catch up with you. And you', he said as he turned towards the ginger-nut, 'you I'll catch up with myself.' Then he told the *gendarme*s he would follow on behind.

'Since when', Camille asked after the *gendarme*s had driven off, and as Soliman was getting his breath back, leaning on Watchee's shoulder, 'since when has there been a gun on board?'

'Camille, are you not glad there was one on board?' Watchee said.

'As it happens, yes,' Camille said, realising that in all the excitement Watchee had for the first time addressed her by name. 'But we'd said: no guns. That was the deal. We'd said: nobody's going to kill anybody.'

'We're not going to kill anybody,' Watchee said.
Camille shrugged, sceptically.

'Why did you say "Melchior"?' she asked Soliman.

'To let Watchee know I couldn't cope on my own.'

'You knew he had a rifle?'

'Yes.'

'Have you got a weapon as well?'

'No, I promise. You want to go through my things?'

'No, I don't.'

Later that evening Adamsberg gave a summary of his conversation with the superintendent of police in Grenoble. The prosecution service had agreed to launch a criminal investigation for manslaughter. They were looking for a man and an animal trained to kill. Adamsberg had provided a description of Auguste Massart. Inquiries would be re-opened into the death of Suzanne Rosselin, and in all the villages where sheep had been savaged.

'Why don't they put out an appeal for witnesses to come forward?' Soliman said. 'Or publish Massart's photograph in the papers?'

'That would be against the law,' Adamsberg said. 'Until the case against Massart is supported by evidence, we don't have the right to make his name public.'

'I found his bloody candles of penance in a chapel two kilometres away. Shouldn't we take them in for fingerprinting?'

'There won't be any prints.'

'All right,' said Soliman, plainly disappointed. 'If the police are on the case, what use are we?'

'You can't see?'

'No.'

'Our use is to carry on believing in it. We're moving on tonight,' he added. 'We'll not stay here.'

'Because of the bikers? I'm not scared of them.'

'No. We have to get a step ahead of Massart. Or at least get closer to him.'

'Nearer to where? Nearer to what? He puts in at any old place.'

'I'm not so sure of that,' Adamsberg said almost under his breath.

Camille glanced at him. When Adamsberg spoke like that it meant that it was more important than it sounded. The softer he spoke, the more you had to listen.

'Not quite any place,' Soliman concurred. 'He only strikes when he's on his red line, and where sheep are easiest to get at. He chooses his sheep farms.'

'That's not what I meant.'

Soliman looked at him, but did not say a word.

'I'm thinking about Suzanne, and about Sernot,' Adamsberg explained.

'He killed Suzanne because he was afraid,' Soliman said. 'And he slit Sernot's throat because Sernot surprised him.'

'Woe betide him who crosses the vampire's path,' said Watchee, somewhat sententiously.

'I'm not so sure of that,' Adamsberg said a second time.

'Where do you want to go?' Camille asked with a frown.

Adamsberg took the map from his pocket and unfolded it.

'There,' he said. 'To Bourg-en-Bresse. One hundred and twenty kilometres north of here.'

'But for heaven's sake, why?' Soliman said with a shake of his head.

'Because it's the only sizable place he's willing to go through,' said Adamsberg. 'With a wolf and a mastiff in tow, it's no mere detail. Everywhere else the red line keeps away from towns. So if it goes via Bourg-en-Bresse, there must be a reason for it. Seeking whom he may devour.'

'It's a guess,' said Soliman.

'It's instinct,' Adamsberg corrected him.

'He passed through Gap,' Soliman pointed out. 'And nothing happened in Gap.'

'True,' Adamsberg granted. 'Maybe nothing will happen at Bourg-en-Bresse either. But that's where we'll be. Better to be one step ahead than two steps behind.'

It was dark when two and half hours later Camille parked the lorry by the side of the N75, on the outskirts of Bourg-en-Bresse.

She got out on the nearside, towards the open

field that ran alongside the road, with a slice of bread and the one glass of wine allowed her by Watchee. Seeing as the road movie was turning out longer than expected, Watchee said, he had to impose rations on the *blanc de Saint-Victor*. They had to keep some until the very end. That was vital, even if it meant drinking barely a gulp a day. But Camille, as lorry-driver, because she was taking a lot of strain in her shoulders and back, was allowed an extra evening ration, so as to relax her muscles for the night and to ensure they were fit again in the morning. It did not even occur to her to turn down Watchee's offer of liquid embrocation.

She walked along the field to the woods at the end, and then turned back on her steps. A diffuse awareness of danger and vulnerability, the feelings of apprehension and freedom that had arisen on coming out of the Alps, still held her in their sway. Johnstone's voice, a few moments ago, had made her feel much calmer. Hearing him on the telephone had brought back to her Saint-Victor with its high walls, steep inclines, narrow alleys, and the massive mountains that cradled it and blocked all vistas. Back there things all seemed foreseeable and expected. Here everything seemed confused and anything was possible. Camille pursed her lips and stretched out her arms, as if she was trying to shake off fear, physically. She had never been afraid of possibilities before, and she did not like having a reflex that put her on her guard. She downed Watchee's ration in a single swig.

She was the last to go to bed, around one in the morning. She tiptoed past Soliman and Watchee, then carefully drew the canvas curtain and listened for Adamsberg's breathing. She put her boots noiselessly on the floor, undressed without making a sound, and lay down. Adamsberg was not asleep. He did not move, he said not a word, but she could feel that his eyes were wide open. It was not as dark as the night before. If she had turned her head she would have been able to see his face. But she did not turn her head. And lying rigidly still she finally dropped off to sleep.

The mobile woke her a few hours later. By the light seeping through the side-curtains she guessed it was not yet six. She half-closed her eyes again, but not so tight that she could not see Adamsberg sitting up without haste, putting his two bare feet onto the sheep-wagon's filthy floor and getting his mobile phone out of the jacket he had hung on the feeding-trough. He mumbled something and hung up. Camille waited until he was dressed before asking what was going on.

'Another murder,' he said. 'Heavens above. What a mess that man is.'

'Who called you?' asked Camille.

'The Grenoble police.'

'Where did it happen?'

'Where I said. Here, in Bourg-en-Bresse.'

Adamsberg ran his fingers through his hair, raised the curtain, and got down from the lorry.

CHAPTER 29

He caught up with the Bourg-en-Bresse police at Place Du Calvaire. It was at the edge of town, almost in the country, at a three-way junction of minor roads. A stone cross marked the spot. The *flics* were busying themselves over the corpse of a man aged about seventy, who had had his shoulder torn open and his throat slit.

Commissaire Hermel, who was almost as short as Adamsberg, sported a droopy moustache and had his spectacles pushed up over sticking-out ears. He came to shake hands.

'I was told you'd been on this case since the beginning,' he said. 'I'm glad to have your assistance.'

Hermel was a cordial and pliant fellow, who did not care to see Adamsberg as a potential rival. The latter quickly gave him all the information he had. Hermel listened with his head down and rubbed his cheek.

'It all fits,' he said. 'Apart from the wounds, we've got a pretty clear paw-print to the left of the body. It's the size of a saucer. A vet's on his way to look

283

it all over. But everybody is running late on Sunday morning.'

'What time did it happen?'

'Around 2 a.m.'

'Who discovered the body?'

'A nightwatchman on his way home.'

'Have we got an ID yet?'

'Fernand Deguy, former mountain guide. He's been living in retirement in Bourg-en-Bresse for fifteen years or so. His house is round the corner. I've just informed the family. Talk of a disaster. Eaten by a wolf!'

'Does anyone know what he was doing out at that time?'

'We haven't had a proper talk with the wife yet. She's in no condition. But he was often up late. When there was nothing to watch he would go out for a walk in the countryside.'

Hermel waved at the distant hills.

'To watch where?'

'On TV.'

'There wasn't anything worth watching last night,' a *lieutenant* piped up. 'Saturday night. I watched the programme all the same, it's my only quiet evening.'

'He would have done better to follow your example,' said Hermel pensively. 'Instead of which off he went out into the open. And he crossed the path of the man you really don't want to meet.'

'Could you put together everything you can find out about the man?' Adamsberg asked.

'What for?' said Hermel. 'It hit him out of nowhere. It could have been anyone.'

'That's what I'm wondering. Could you do that for me, Hermel? Collect all the facts you can lay your hands on? The Villard-de-Lans people are doing the same on Sernot for me. We'll see if anything matches.'

Hermel shook his head.

'The poor old fellow was in the wrong place at the wrong time,' he said. 'What good will it do to know when he bought his first pair of skis?'

'I don't know. I would like to have that information, though.'

Hermel pondered. He knew Adamsberg by reputation. The man's request seemed inept, but he'd do what was asked. A fellow-officer had told him that Adamsberg often seemed inept. But there was something appealing about the man.

'As you wish, old chap,' Hermel said. 'We'll open a file.'

'*Commissaire*,' the *lieutenant* said as he came back towards them, 'I found this in the grass, beside the body. It's brand-new.'

In the palm of his hand the *lieutenant* held out a crumpled ball of blue tissue. Hermel put on his gloves and unfolded it.

'It's a piece of paper,' he said grumpily. 'Maybe it's a flyer. What do you make of it, old chap?'

Adamsberg picked it up by the tips of his fingernails and looked it over.

'Do you ever stay in hotels, Hermel?' he asked.

'Of course.'

'Do you see all those bits and bobs you usually pocket, off the bathroom shelf?'

'Of course.'

'Mini-bars of soap, mini-shoe polish, mini-toothpaste tubes, and mini-handwipes? You see what I'm talking about?'

'Of course.'

'All that rubbish you stuff in your case when you leave?'

'Of course.'

'Well, that's what it is. It's the envelope that contained complimentary cleansing tissue. It comes from a hotel.'

Hermel took the crumpled paper back, pulled down his spectacles, and looked at it more closely.

'Le Moulin,' he read out. 'There's no hotel called Le Moulin in Bourg-en-Bresse.'

'You'll have to scour further afield,' said Adamsberg. 'And double quick.'

'Why the hurry?'

'Because then we'd have a chance of finding the room where Massart slept last night.'

'The hotel isn't going to fly away.'

'But it would be a whole lot more useful to get there before the cleaning lady.'

'Do you think this thing belonged to the killer?'

'It's possible. It's the sort of thing you stuff in your pocket and which only falls out if you lean right over. And who would have been leaning right over, right here, at the foot of this cross?'

By ten a Hôtel du Moulin had been found at Combes, about sixty kilometres from Bourg-en-Bresse. A car bearing Hermel, Adamsberg, the *lieutenant* and two forensics set off at once from the police station.

'He's crafty,' Adamsberg opined. 'He murders along his marked-out itinerary, but he hides well away from it. You might as well whistle as try to find him on his itinerary. He can be anywhere.'

'If it is him,' said Hermel.

'It is,' said Adamsberg.

They drew up in front of the Hôtel du Moulin, an upmarket two-star, just before eleven.

'Even craftier,' said Adamsberg as he cast an eye over the façade. 'He reckons the *flics* will be looking for him in low dives, and he's not wrong either, so he stays in classy places.'

The young woman at reception was barely able to help them. A man had made a reservation by telephone yesterday and she had not seen him check in. Customers were given the door code. She had come on at six o'clock, and he was gone at dawn, around six-thirty. No, she hadn't seen him, she was laying the tables for breakfast. He had left his key on the counter. No, he had not signed the register yet, and he hadn't settled up. He had said he would be staying three nights. No, she had not seen his car, or anything else. No, he did not have a dog. There was a man, and that's all.

'You won't be seeing him again,' Hermel said.

'Which room?' Adamsberg asked.

'Room 24, second floor.'

'Has the cleaner been in?'

'Not yet. We start with the first floor.'

They worked over the room for two hours.

'He wiped everything,' said the fingerprint specialist. 'He's a wary bugger, and very careful. He's taken off the pillowcase and he's taken the towels with him.'

'Give it all you've got, Juneau,' Hermel told him.

'Yes, sir,' Juneau said. 'They always think they can beat the world, but they always leave something behind.'

Juneau's colleague called from the bathroom.

'He cut his fingernails on the windowsill,' he told them.

'Because he'd got some of the victim's blood stuck under them,' said Hermel.

'Two nail clippings got into the fillister.'

The forensic officer slid his tweezers into the narrow gap and extracted the clippings which he put into a Ziploc. Juneau rescued a fine black hair from disappearing down the shower drain.

'He didn't see everything. They invariably leave something behind.'

Once they got back to the police station at Bourg-en-Bresse, it took them two hours to get the Puygiron police unit to collect samples from Massart's shack and to send the material they'd gathered to the pathology department at Lyon, for comparison.

'What are we supposed to be looking for?' asked the Head Deputy at Puygiron.

'Hair and nail clippings,' said Hermel. 'Every last bit of finger- and toenail you can find. Take fingerprints too, they might be useful.'

'We'll find what we find,' the Head Deputy said. 'We're not paid to manufacture how should I say evidence for you.'

'That's my motto, too,' Hermel said, without losing his temper. 'Collect what's there.'

'Massart is dead. He went missing on Mont Vence.'

'I have someone with me who is not convinced that that's the case.'

'A really tall guy? Athletic? Fair, long hair?'

Hermel looked Adamsberg up and down. 'No,' he said. 'None of the above.'

'I'll say it again, *Commissaire*. Massart fell somewhere up in the how should I say Alps.'

'Perhaps he did. But it would be better to be quite sure, wouldn't it? For your sake as well as for mine. I need those samples pretty damn quickly.'

'Today is Sunday, *Commissaire*.'

'That means you've got ample spare time this afternoon to rake over Massart's place and to have the samples couriered to Lyon no later than this evening. We're dealing with murder, and the murderer is at large. Are you reading me, Head Deputy?'

Hermel rang off a short time later, scowling.

'One of those sorts of people who'll do anything

to put a spanner in the works of the non-military force. I do hope he'll make a thorough job of the search.'

'He's been the spanner in the works from the start,' Adamsberg said.

'I can't risk sending one of my own men down there. That would spark off an unholy row.'

'Do you know anyone in the prosecution service in Nice?'

'Used to, old chap. He moved on two years ago.'

'Try him all the same. We'd be much more comfortable knowing that one of your men was down there.'

Adamsberg got up and shook Hermel by the hand.

'Keep me up to date, Hermel. The lab results and the file of facts. Especially that file.'

'Yes, the file, I know.'

'And about that girl I've got trailing me – warn your men to keep their mouths tight shut. Don't forget.'

'Is she dangerous?'

'Very.'

'Fine by me not to mention your name. Look after yourself, old chap.'

Next morning, Monday, almost all the papers featured the werewolf on the front page. Soliman came back in a sweat from town, laid the moped in the ditch, and threw the fresh bread and an armful of newspapers onto the wooden crate.

'It's all in the fucking papers!' he bawled. 'The whole story! It's a disaster! A monumental leak! Fuck the *flics*, fuck the papers! The werewolf, the sheep, the murder victims, it's all there! Even the map! The route! Only thing not printed is Massart's name. We're done for! We're toast! When he sees that, Massart will run for it. Maybe he's on his way already. He's getting away, bloody sodding hell! They ought to close the borders, close the roads! Stupid tossers, those *flics*! My mother was right! The *flics* are all tossers!'

'Calm down, Soliman,' said Adamsberg. 'Drink your coffee.'

'Haven't you understood?' the young man screamed. 'You've not given him a safety net, you've laid out a bloody red carpet for him to fly away on!'

'Calm down,' Adamsberg said once more. 'Show me.'

Adamsberg unfolded the newspapers, passed one to Camille and one to Watchee. He paused, and then put one in front of Woof as well.

'Come on, dog. Have a read of that.'

'You call this the right time for a joke?' barked Soliman, slitting his eyes, looking murderous. 'You're having a joke and Massart's about to slip out of our grasp and my mother's going to stay stuck in the stink-pond for ever.'

'The pond stuff's not altogether gospel, you know,' said Watchee.

'Sod you, you old duffer!' Soliman shouted. 'Haven't you understood anything either?'

Watchee raised his stick and tapped Soliman lightly on the shoulder.

'Shut up, Sol. Respect.'

Soliman stopped, took a deep breath, and sat down in a bit of a daze with his arms hanging loose at his sides. Watchee gave him a cup of coffee.

Camille was poring over the papers, looking at the headlines.

WEREWOLF HEADING FOR PARIS!!
LYCANTHROPY REVIVED!
MERCANTOUR MONSTER ON HUMAN LEASH
THE WOLF-MAN'S WILD RIDE

Several papers gave details of the route Massart had marked out in red, and showed it on a map with stars for the locations of all the previous murders.

> After ravaging the departments of Alpes-Maritimes, Alpes-de-Haute-Provence, Isère and Ain, where it committed the latest of its murders, the Mercantour Monster is said to be now heading due north, nine days after the start of its rampage. Under the control of a bloodthirsty psychopath suffering bouts of lycanthropy, the beast is believed to be travelling parallel to the A7 autoroute about 30 kilometres east of it, as far as Chaumont, where it is expected to veer west towards

the capital by way of Bar-sur-Aube and Provins.

The man is understood to travel in limited stages of between 60 and 200 kilometres. He moves at night with a wolf and a mastiff, probably in a van with blacked-out windows. He is alleged to have murdered three people so far, as well as more than 40 ewes. All sheep farmers are advised to take precautionary measures to protect their flocks using guard dogs or electrified fences. All persons male or female living along or near the minor roads shown on the map are urged not to go out alone after nightfall. Any persons able to give information likely to be of assistance to the police investigation are re quested to contact their nearest *gendarmerie* or *commissariat*.

Camille put the paper down in disgust.

'The leak comes from the police,' she said. 'They held a press conference. Soliman's not wrong. If Massart has an ounce of sense, he'll vanish before you can say Jack Robinson.'

'The *flics* thought they were doing the right thing,' said Watchee. 'They preferred to warn people so as to prevent more murders. Setting a trap for Massart involves putting lives at risk. You have to see their point of view.'

'Bugger that,' said Soliman. 'It's a massive

cock-up. Just let me get my hands on the dickhead who spewed it all out.'

'Here I am, Soliman,' said Adamsberg.

A ponderous silence ensued in the lorry. Adamsberg leaned over to the dog and tugged the chewed-up paper from his maw.

'Woof liked that a lot,' he said with a smile. 'You should trust the dog. Dogs have got real flair.'

'I don't believe it,' said Soliman, dumbfounded. 'I just don't believe it.'

'You better had believe it, all the same,' Adamsberg said softly.

'Don't make him repeat himself,' said Watchee. 'The man told you.'

'I called AFP yesterday,' said Adamsberg, 'and I told them exactly what I wanted them to know.'

'What's AFP?' Watchee asked.

'It's like a huge leading sheep for journalists to flock after,' Soliman explained. 'All the newspapers repeat what AFP tells them.'

'Good,' said Watchee. 'I do like to understand.'

'But what about the itinerary?' Camille said tensely. 'Why did you pass on the itinerary?'

'That's the point. That's what I wanted most of all to give them. The itinerary.'

'So Massart can scarper?' asked Soliman. 'Is that what you're up to? Is that what the *flic* with no principles is up to?'

'He won't vanish.'

'And why won't he vanish?'

'Because he's not finished what he set out to do.'

'What's that?'

'His job. His murder business.'

'He'll just go and do his business somewhere else!' Soliman shouted as he stood up. 'In Amazonia or Patagonia or Outer Mongolia. There are sheep all over the world!'

'I'm not talking about sheep. I'm talking about people.'

'He'll kill other people in other places.'

'No, he won't. His work is here.'

There was another pause.

'We don't get it,' said Camille, on behalf of all three. 'Are these things that you know, or things that you believe?'

'I've no idea,' said Adamsberg. 'But I would like to know. I already said that Massart's itinerary was precise and contorted. Now his route is known and he's being looked for, he's every reason to change track.'

'And he will!' Soliman said. 'He's changing track right now!'

'Or not, as the case may be,' Adamsberg said. 'That's the crux of the whole story. Everything hangs on it. Will he move away from his itinerary? Or will he stick to it? That is the question.'

'What if he sticks to it?' said Camille.

'It changes everything.'

Soliman pulled a puzzled face. Adamsberg explained:

'He'll only stick to his route if he has no choice. It would mean he has to follow that specific itinerary and that he can't do anything else, irrespective of the risks.'

'And why would that be so?' Soliman asked. 'Because he's mad? Or obsessed?'

'Or because of his needs, and his plans. If that were so, then nothing that's happened could be put down to chance. Neither Sernot's death, nor Deguy's.'

Soliman shook his head in disbelief.

'We're letting our minds wander.'

'Of course we are,' said Adamsberg. 'What else can we do?'

CHAPTER 30

That morning's news brought instant relief to the Wildlife Wardens in the Mercantour. It was decided straight away to drop their efforts to track both packs of wolves.

Johnstone was walking his motorbike, on his way to meet Camille. He had not seen her for days and days. He missed everything about her. Her voice, her face, her body. He had been through a great deal of stress and he needed her. Camille could get him to come out of his shell, out of his silence.

The Canadian was worried. He had not been able to get his visa extended. What he had been sent to do in the Mercantour was well and truly in the bag, and he could not see any way of getting his contract extended beyond its expiry date. He would have to go back, in less than two months' time, by 22 August at the latest. He was expected back in grizzly country. He had never discussed such an eventuality with Camille; neither of them had talked about what might happen between them then. Johnstone could not see himself going back to his old life without her. Tonight, if he could, if he dared, he would ask her to move to Vancouver. But he wouldn't dare. Women struck him dumb.

Late on that afternoon Adamsberg had a call from Hermel.

'It's the same hair, old chap,' Hermel told him. 'Same thickness, same shade, same make-up, same genetic fingerprint. No doubt about it. If it isn't him, it's his twin. You'll have to wait a bit longer for the nails. We've only just spotted some by the bed in his shack. That idiot from Puygiron searched only the bathroom. A man can just as well chew his fingernails and spit them on the floor from his bunk, am I right? I sent one of my own men over there this morning with instructions to comb the bedroom and find nails from each of the man's ten fingers, nothing less would do. So if you hear of a fresh outbreak of hostilities between the police and the *gendarmerie*, you'll know what it's about. In any event, your Massart is the man, almost absolutely certainly. You know what lab people are like. You can never get them to say "yes" without some piddling reservation. Hang on, I haven't told you everything yet. There really were particles of blood on the fingernails we picked up from the groove on the hotel windowsill. And there's not the slightest doubt now – that blood belonged to Fernand Deguy. So the man who stayed in the hotel really did let his beast loose on Deguy. By the way, we did have the body looked at again as you requested, but we didn't find one single unexplained animal hair on

Deguy. There *were* some dog hairs, but they came from his own spaniel. We're working on Deguy, we're scooping up all there is to know about him. Don't expect to be entertained when you read it, Adamsberg. Mountain guide, old chap, then mountain guide. It's all there is. He lived all his life long in Grenoble and retired to Bourg-en-Bresse because Grenoble has ceased to be anything more than the bottom of a bowl filled to the brim with exhaust. Never put a foot wrong either, never did anything exciting, never even had a mistress as far as we know at this point in time. I talked to Montvailland at Villard-de-Lans. He's made progress with his file on Jean-Jacques Sernot. He never put a foot wrong, never did anything exciting, never even had a mistress as far as is known at this point in time. Sernot taught maths in Grenoble for thirty-two years. Grenoble is the only common factor, but it's rather broad, as common factors go. Oh, I'm forgetting, they were both good sportsmen. There are lots of them in this place. The Alps are full of folk determined to walk for hours and hours up and down the rocks. That's not news to you, old chap, seeing as you're from the Pyrenees, or so they tell me. Nothing to indicate that the two men ever met each other. And even less likelihood that either of them ever met Suzanne Rosselin. I'll keep at it all the same and fax the final results wherever you tell me.'

Adamsberg ended the call and went back to the lorry. Soliman had quietened down and had got his blue plastic bowl out again. Camille was in the cab, with the door open, writing music. Watchee was sitting near the back steps, humming. He was delousing the dog: he cut the insects neatly in half with his thumb and the nail of his index finger. Life around the sheep-wagon was settling into its own rituals: each now had his and her own home patch. Camille had the front area, Soliman the side, and Watchee the rear.

Adamsberg went to the front.

'The hair is Massart's,' he told Camille.

Soliman, Watchee and Camille gathered round the *commissaire*. They were silent, serious, almost stupefied. They had known it was Massart from the start, but having it confirmed cast a kind of fright upon them. It was the same kind of difference as between the idea of a knife and the sight of a blade. It gave an extra dose of precision and realism. It made it a certainty that cuts to the quick.

'We're going to light a candle in the lorry,' Adamsberg said, breaking the silence. 'Watchee will make sure it doesn't go out.'

'What's come over you?' asked Camille. 'You think that'll help?'

'It'll help to find out how long it takes to burn down.'

Adamsberg went to his car and scrabbled about in his case and came back with a tall candle. He melted the bottom so that it would stand straight in a saucer. He put it in the lorry and lit the wick.

'There you are,' he said, stepping back with an air of satisfaction.

'Why are we doing this?' Soliman asked.

'Because we've nothing better to do. You're going to come with me on a lazy drive down the side roads so that we can visit all the local churches. If Massart was overcome with contrition after murdering Deguy, then we've got a chance of seeing where he went. We have to check whether he's still following his itinerary or whether he's switched track.'

'Good idea,' said Soliman.

'Camille, if we do come across a trace of Massart, you'll drive the lorry over to where we are.'

'No can do. I'm not planning on driving this evening.'

'Because of the candle?' Soliman exclaimed. 'Watchee will keep it safe in his lap.'

'No,' Camille said. 'I'm staying in Bourg-en-Bresse. Lawrence is coming tonight.'

There was a brief pause.

'Yes, I see,' said Adamsberg. '*Laurence* Johnstone is coming tonight. Fine.'

'The trapper could join up with us further north,' said Soliman. 'What difference does that make to him?'

Camille shook her head. 'He's en route and I can't contact him in the meantime. I made a date with him at Bourg, so I'm staying at Bourg.'

Adamsberg nodded. 'OK,' he said. 'Stay at Bourg. That's quite all right.'

Adamsberg and Soliman looked into nineteen churches. In the twentieth, at Saint-Pierre-de-Cenis, a tiny village about ninety kilometres north of Bourg-en-Bresse, they spotted five candles set apart from the others and laid out more or less in the shape of the letter M.

'That's him!' said Soliman. 'It's as it was at Tiennes.'

Adamsberg took a fresh candle, lit it from one of the others, and stood it in the candleholder.

'What are you doing?' Soliman asked in amazement.

'I'm comparing.'

'Even so. If you light a candle you have to make a prayer. And pay for the candle. Otherwise your wishes won't be met.'

'Are you religious, Sol?'

'I am superstitious.'

'Ah. That must be tiring.'

'It is. Very.'

Adamsberg bent forward to observe the candles more closely.

'They've burned about one third of the way down,' he said. 'We'll measure it against the lorry candle, but Massart was probably here some four hours ago. Between three and four in the afternoon. It's a remote spot. Probably he slipped into the church when there was nobody else here.'

He fell silent and looked smilingly at the candles.

'What good is that to us, really?' asked Soliman. 'He's a long way off by now. And we already knew he lights candles.'

'You still haven't twigged, have you, Sol? This church is on his marked-out route. That means he's not moved off it. He's sticking to the itinerary. That means nothing is happening by chance. If he's been this way it's because he had to be. He won't branch off now.'

Before they left the church Adamsberg put three francs in the silver tray.

'I know you made a wish,' said Soliman.

'I was only paying for the candle.'

'You're lying. You made a wish. I saw it in your eyes.'

Adamsberg drew up twenty metres away from the lorry. He pulled slowly on the handbrake. Neither he nor Soliman got out. Watchee had lit a brazier, which he was poking with the metal-tipped end of his crook. Standing beside him, with his eyes on the fire, stood a tall and handsome man in a white T-shirt. His long fair hair came down to his shoulders, and his arm was around Camille. Adamsberg looked at him for a while without stirring.

'That's the trapper,' Soliman finally vouchsafed.

'I can see that.'

The two of them fell silent again.

'He's the guy who lives with Camille,' Soliman

went on, as if he was telling it to himself over again, just to be sure. 'That's the guy she picked.'

'I can see that.'

'He's good-looking, he's tough, he can hold his own. And he's got ideas up here,' Soliman added, tapping his forehead. 'You can't say Camille picked a dud.'

'No.'

'You can't hold it against her to have picked that guy rather than another one, can you?'

'No.'

'Camille is free. She can pick whomever she wants. Whoever she likes best. If that's the one, well, she goes for him, right?'

'Yes.'

'It's up to her, after all. Not up to us. Not up to anyone else. Up to her. Can't say anything against that, can you?'

'No.'

'And she's not made a bad choice, really. Right? Don't see why it should be any of our business.'

'No. It's none of our business.'

'No, none at all.'

'It's actually got nothing to do with us.'

'Actually, no.'

'No,' Adamsberg repeated.

'What next?' Soliman asked after a pause. 'Shall we get out?'

Watchee put a grill on top of the embers and unceremoniously deposited two columns of chops and tomatoes on it.

304

'Where did you get the grill?' Soliman asked.

'It's chicken-wire. Buteil had left it in the lorry. Heat disinfects everything.'

Watchee kept his eye on the meat as it cooked, then shared it out. He wasn't saying much.

'What about the candles, then?' asked Camille.

'Five at Saint-Pierre-du-Cenis,' Adamsberg said. 'He most likely lit them around three o'clock. He's keeping to his route. We really ought to get moving this evening, Camille. Now that *Laurence* is here we can move on.'

'Do you want to go to Saint-Pierre?'

'He's left there already. He's out ahead. Show us the map, Sol.'

Soliman cleared the glasses out of the way and spread the map out on the crate.

'You see,' said Adamsberg, following the red line with the tip of his knife. 'The route breaks off here and turns due west in the direction of Paris. Even if he doesn't want to cross the autoroute, he could have turned earlier, here, on this minor road, or else there. But instead he's done a thirty-kilometre dogleg. It's crazy, except if he reckons he absolutely has to go through Belcourt.'

'That's not obvious,' said Soliman.

'No, it's not,' said Adamsberg.

'Massart kills at random, when he's disturbed.'

'Maybe so. But I'd still like to get to Belcourt this evening. It doesn't look like a large place. If there's a cross anywhere thereabouts, we'll find it, and stand guard.'

'I don't believe in all that,' Soliman said.

'But I do,' Johnstone said all of a sudden. 'It's not for sure, but it's quite possible. Bugger him, he's done enough killing already.'

'If we get in his way at Belcourt', Soliman said, turning to face the trapper, 'he'll go kill someplace else.'

'Not certain. Fixed ideas.'

'He's looking for sheep,' Soliman said.

'Acquired the taste for humans,' said Johnstone.

'You said he'd go after women,' Camille said.

'Got that wrong. He doesn't go after women to have them, he goes after men for revenge. Comes to the same thing, more or less.'

There wasn't a cross of any kind at Belcourt or anywhere else nearby. Camille parked the lorry on the edge of an esplanade next to the road that went through the village. The open space had been embellished by the commune with a stand of plum trees. Adamsberg had gone on ahead to warn the duty squad at the *gendarmerie*.

Soliman was waiting on his own for the *flic* to come out. He found the *commissaire* disconcerting in the actions he took, and hard to believe in the very partial explanations he offered. But Soliman's doubts did not weaken the loyalty he had felt for Adamsberg from the moment he first met him. Reason and logic set him against Adamsberg. But his natural feelings put him at Adamsberg's side in all his actions, if not in his mental processes, which remained pretty much impenetrable to him.

'What are the *gendarme*s like?' he asked when Adamsberg got back to the lorry around midnight.

'A good lot,' said Adamsberg. 'Co-operative. They'll maintain surveillance in the village until further notice. Where are the others?'

'Watchee's having a glass of white wine under one of the plum trees over there.'

'And the other two?' Adamsberg queried.

'Gone for a walk. The trapper told Camille he needed some time alone with her.'

'Fine.'

'I suppose they've got a right to be alone for a bit, right?'

'Yes, of course they have.'

'Certainly they have,' Soliman parroted.

He unhooked his moped and kick-started the engine.

'I'm going into town. I'll see if there's a café open.'

'There is one, at the back of the town hall.'

Soliman rode down the road. Adamsberg got into the lorry and inspected the candle, which was more than half burned down after seven hours. He blew it out, picked up a folding stool and a glass, and went over to Watchee, sitting fifty metres away, bolt upright, beneath a tree on the other side of the esplanade.

'Have a seat, young fella,' said Watchee as Adamsberg approached.

Adamsberg set up his stool next to Watchee's, sat down, and held out his glass.

'The town's under surveillance,' he said. 'If Massart turns up, he's taking a big risk.'

'So he won't turn up.'

'That's what worries me.'

'Then you shouldn't have blabbed his itinerary, young fella.'

'It was the only way of finding out.'

'Maybe,' said Watchee as he filled Adamsberg's glass. 'I see what you were up to. But the man's a werewolf, young fella. It's quite possible he picks his victims, I'm not saying he doesn't. He's bound to have made enemies when he was a bottomer on the road. But it's the werewolf in him that does the killing. That's the key to it all. You'll see, when he's been collared.'

'I'll see.'

'But there's no saying when he'll get caught. I reckon we've got a while to wait.'

'Well then, we'll wait. We'll wait as long as it takes. Here. Under this plum tree.'

'Exactly, young fella. We'll wait. And if we have to we'll sit here until the end of our days.'

'And why shouldn't we?' Adamsberg asked in a world-weary tone.

'Only thing is, if we do wait for him to show up, we'll have to see about laying in some more juice of the grape.'

'It'll be seen to.'

Watchee took a drink.

'The bikers that came along the other day,' he went on. 'You'll have to have them seen to as well.'

'I've not forgotten.'

'They're scum. If I hadn't had my rifle, they'd have killed my Soliman and disfigured your Camille. Believe you me.'

'I do believe you. Camille, not my Camille.'

'You shouldn't have stopped me firing.'

'Yes I should.'

'I'd have aimed for their legs.'

'I don't think so.'

Watchee shrugged. 'Hey,' he said. 'There they are. The young lady and her trapper have returned.'

Watchee's eyes followed the whitish silhouettes as they walked along the road. Camille got into the lorry first, but Johnstone stopped at the rear footboard, apparently hesitating.

'Why's he messing around?' asked Watchee.

'The smell,' Adamsberg suggested. 'Wool-fat.'

The shepherd muttered something under his breath, and cast a rather disdainful glance at the Canadian wolf-man. Johnstone seemed to be girding himself up, threw his long hair back over his shoulders, and sprang into the lorry in one movement, as if he was diving off a cliff.

'Apparently he's sad because the old wolf he was looking after has died,' Watchee went on. 'That's what they get up to in the Mercantour. They feed old beasts. Seems he's going to go back to Canada, too. Mighty long way off.'

'No.'

'He's going to try to get her to come with him.'

'You mean it's a she-wolf?'

'The wolf is dead, male or female, like I said. He's going to try to get her to come with him. Camille, I mean. And she's going to try to go.'

'I guess so.'

'That's something else you'll have to see to.'

'None of my business, Watchee.'

'Where are you going to sleep tonight?'

'Under this plum tree. Or in my car. It's not cold.'

Watchee made no reply, and filled both glasses again. After several minutes' silence, he asked in his most guttural voice:

'Do you love her?'

Adamsberg shrugged again and said nothing.

'I don't mind if you keep your trap shut,' Watchee said. 'I'm not sleepy. I can ask you the question all night long. When the sun rises, I'll still be here, and I'll ask you again, and I'll go on asking until you answer. And if we're both still here six years from now, still waiting for Massart to make an appearance, I'll still be asking you the same question. I don't mind. I'm not sleepy.'

Adamsberg smiled and drank some more wine.

'Do you love her?' Watchee asked.

'Your question is getting on my nerves.'

'That proves it's a good question.'

'I never said it was a bad question.'

'I don't mind. I've got all night, and I'm not sleepy.'

'Asking a question', said Adamsberg, 'means that you know the answer, otherwise you shut up.'

'That's true,' said Watchee. 'I do know the answer.'

'You see.'

'Why do you let other men have her?'

Adamsberg kept his peace.

'I don't mind,' said Watchee. 'I've got all night.'

'Bugger that, Watchee. She doesn't belong to me. Nobody belongs to anybody.'

'Stop acting all sophisticated. Why do you let other men have her?'

'Ask the wind why it doesn't stay in the leaves of the tree.'

'Who's the wind, then? You? Or her?'

Adamsberg smiled. 'We take turns.'

'That's not bad, young fella.'

'But the wind moves on,' said Adamsberg.

'And the wind comes back,' said Watchee.

'That's the whole problem. The wind always comes back.'

'The last glass,' Watchee warned with a glance at the bottle in the dark. 'Have to ration ourselves.'

'What about you, Watchee? Did you ever love anyone?'

Watchee said nothing.

'I don't mind,' said Adamsberg. 'I'm not drowsy.'

'Do you know the answer?'

'Suzanne, your whole life long. That's why I emptied your ammo case.'

'Fuck you, bloody *flic*,' said Watchee.

★   ★   ★

311

Adamsberg went back to his car, got a blanket out of the boot and settled himself on the back seat with the door open so he could let his legs hang out. Around two in the morning the tail end of a summer storm rumbled over the landscape and a steady drizzle began to fall, so he had to curl up inside the vehicle. It's not that he was tall – 1.71m, the bare minimum required for joining the police force – but it was an uncomfortable position all the same.

When he thought about it, he reckoned he must be the shortest policeman in the whole of France. That was quite something. The Canadian was a whole lot taller. Better-looking, too, no doubt about that. And better-looking than he had expected. Solid and trustworthy. A very good choice, a much better choice than he was. He wasn't worth it. He was wind.

Of course he loved Camille, he had never tried to deny it. Sometimes he realised he did love her and tried to find her, but then he forgot about it. Camille was his natural inclination. Spending these last two nights by her side had been a lot harder than he ever imagined it could be. He had wanted to stretch his hand out to her dozens of times. But Camille did not seem to be asking for anything at all. Your life's your own, my friend.

Yes, of course he was in love with Camille, deep down inside, in the unknown country you hump along inside you like some private but alien submarine world. Yes. And so what? Nothing says that you have to put every one of your thoughts into action. In Adamsberg's case thought did not always result in action. Between the thought and the deed, a whole heap of energy got absorbed in daydreaming.

And then there was that fearsome wind that pushed him ever onwards, even uprooting him from time to time. But on this night he was the tree. He would have liked to stop Camille in his branches. On this night, though, Camille was the wind. She was moving fast and ever upwards, towards the snow-capped mountains. With that bloody Canadian in tow.

CHAPTER 31

Damp and aching though he was, Adamsberg got out and into the driving seat at 7.30, switched on the ignition and drove straight into Belcourt without waiting for the others to be up. He stopped at the public baths and spent twenty minutes under the shower, with his head raised to the tepid stream, his arms hanging loose beside him.

Cleaned up and his mind a blank, he dawdled for thirty minutes in a café and then sought out a quiet spot in the village where he could call Danglard. At last the prolonged inquiry about Sabrina Monge that he had instigated had come up with a tangible lead, one which took them to a village west of Gdańsk.

'Is Gulvain there?' he asked. 'Tell him to leave within the hour and let Interpol know. When he's got the photographs, he should courier them to me from Gdańsk direct to the *gendarmerie* at Belcourt, in the department of Haute-Marne. Danglard, send me the whole of the Polish file too, with the IDs and addresses . . . No, my friend, we're still waiting. I think he'll strike again here,

314

at Belcourt or near here . . . No, old friend, I do not know . . . Let me know if she vanishes.'

Adamsberg went over to the *gendarmerie. Adjudant* Hugues Aimont was just starting his shift. Adamsberg introduced himself.

'So it's you who put the wind up the night shift?'

'I thought it was a good idea.'

'You're welcome,' said Aimont.

The *adjudant* was fair, slim, tall and just a bit wan. Unusually for a *gendarme*, he was a shy, almost stilted man, even occasionally obsequious. He spoke with a kind of cautious elegance, never using abbreviations, never blaspheming, and never resorting to exclamations. Straight away he put half his office at Adamsberg's disposal.

'Aimont,' Adamsberg said, 'your opposite numbers at Villard-de-Lans and Bourg-en-Bresse will be sending us the files on Sernot and Deguy. The Head Deputy at Puygiron should be letting us have what he's got on Auguste Massart, but he might put that off. It would be useful if you called him. The Head Deputy in question doesn't like civilian police officers.'

'Wasn't there a third victim? A woman?'

'I've not forgotten her. But that woman died because she knew something about Massart – at least, that's what I believe. The other two were murdered for some other reason. It's that other reason I'm looking for.'

'Are you', Aimont asked in his tinny voice, 'quite

sure that the third attack will be launched in Belcourt?'

'His itinerary makes a dogleg so as to pass through here. But he could equally well be 200 kilometres away.'

'It does not seem wise to me, sir, to leave chance altogether out of the picture,' Aimont insisted, with embarrassment. 'Those two men who died were in the habit of going out in the dark. Nothing is to say they did not quite simply cross Massart's path.'

'Quite,' said Adamsberg. 'Nothing is to say that.'

Adamsberg spent the whole morning in the *gendarmerie* or hard by, alternating between reading the files and snatches of daydreaming. He read slowly, standing up, and often coming back to the same line of text after his meandering mind had wandered away from it. For some years now he had been trying to impose mental discipline on himself by making notes in a jotter. But this tiresome exercise had not borne the expected fruit.

He lunched with Aimont and then went off to explore the countryside around Belcourt, looking for a hidey-hole. He found one easily enough beside an old mill overgrown with brambles and honeysuckle. He took out his jotter and scribbled in it for over an hour, sketching the trees he could see in front of him. Then he went back to his temporary office. He was completely at ease working alongside the timid *adjudant* and he preferred to settle in at the *gendarmerie* rather than go back to the lorry camp. It wasn't that he felt awkward about Johnstone being around. Adamsberg was almost entirely devoid of jealousy. When he saw it raise its destructive and agonising head in other people, he reckoned he must be missing a part, among the many others that he did not seem to possess. However, he was not at all sure that the Canadian appreciated having him around. Several times Johnstone had looked at him with confident and questioning eyes that seemed to be saying both: 'I'm here' and 'What's your game?' And Adamsberg could not easily answer that question. Johnstone was a prize catch, he had nothing against that. Except that the man wasn't much of a conversationalist, and did not always make his meaning clear. Adamsberg wondered what he meant by the word that to his ears sounded like '*boulechite*', which Johnstone kept using. Maybe it was his mother's name.

Around five, Hermel got through to him.

'Have you read the files, old chap? You could hardly call them page-turners, what? And there's not one single crossover between the two men. They never lived anywhere near each other. I've checked all the membership lists of all the sporting clubs in the Grenoble area for the last thirty years. Not a sausage, old chap. They did not move in the same circles. Now, those fingernails. The ones we got from Massart's dump and the ones we found on the windowsill. Spot on. The grooves make them as near to identical as you can get. What do you say to that, eh? The Head Deputy at Puygiron is still trying to find fingernails in the bathroom. When he gets an idea into his head, it just takes over, like a steamroller. If you want my opinion, old chap, he's dim and muddle-headed. He won't find any. Massart chewed his fingernails in bed, as I said. I told the Head Deputy to drop it, since we've got our samples, but he wants to prove he was right. If you want my opinion, he's going to carry on searching that bathroom until they send him off with a gold watch, no skin off our nose. I reminded him we were expecting information about Massart from him, but I don't think he'll put his back into it. That chap only talks to members of his own force. I'll get the man's photograph direct from his employer, it'll save time. Then, as agreed, I'll have it circulated to all police stations.'

It got progressively hotter through the day. Adamsberg dined alone at the same café, sitting outside on the terrace, then idled around the streets of the little town in the dark. Around eleven he decided to head back to community life.

Soliman and Camille were sitting on the back steps of the lorry, smoking a cigarette. In the dark you could make out Watchee sitting in the plum tree orchard. The motorbike wasn't there.

Soliman leaped to his feet when he saw Adamsberg approaching.

318

'No news,' Adamsberg told him as he waved him back to his seat. 'Just paperwork. Ah, yes, there is,' he added after thinking for a moment. 'The fingernails we found at the hotel do belong to Massart.'

Adamsberg looked around.

'Is M. Johnstone not here?' he asked.

'He went back south,' Camille said. 'He's got visa problems. He'll be back.'

'Apparently his old wolf died,' Adamsberg said.

'Yes,' Camille said in amazement. 'His name was Augustus. He couldn't hunt for himself any more so Lawrence used to trap rabbits for him to eat. But he stopped feeding, and then died. One of the wildlife wardens said: "If you're past it, you're past it." Lawrence was upset by that.'

'I can understand,' said Adamsberg.

Adamsberg went to share a jar with Watchee under the plum tree when Soliman and Camille repaired to bed. He went back to the lorry around one in the morning with his head swimming a little from the tail of the wine. Now that the weather had warmed up the smell of sheep wax had climbed a notch. Adamsberg drew the canvas curtain aside without making a sound. Camille was sleeping on her front, with the bed sheet pushed back and leaving her top half bare. He sat on his bed and looked at her for a long while, trying to think. He had never given up his ambition of learning to think the way Danglard did,

319

that is to say, to some effect. After a few minutes' effort, his mind cut out without warning and drifted off into dreams. A quarter of an hour later, when he was almost fast asleep, he started with a jump. He stretched out his hand, placed it palm down on Camille's back, and said, calmly:

'Don't you love me any more?'

Camille opened her eyes, looked at him in the dark, and went back to sleep.

In the middle of the night another storm, heavier than the previous night, broke over Belcourt. Rain hammered down on the roof of the sheep-wagon. Camille got up, put her boots on over bare feet, and went outside to tie the tarpaulins down over the side-lattices, as they were flapping in the wind and letting in rain. She lay down again noiselessly, alert to Adamsberg's breathing, the way you keep an eye on a sleeping foe. Adamsberg stretched out an arm and took her hand in his. Camille did not flicker an eyelash, as if a single movement from her might suddenly make the situation worse, the way a thoughtless gesture can set off an avalanche. She had the impression that Adamsberg had said something to her earlier that night. Ah yes, she remembered now. She was more troubled than hostile as she tried to work out a scheme for getting her hand out of his without making a fuss, without hurting anyone. But her hand stayed obstinately where it was, entwined in Adamsberg's. It wasn't coming to any harm. Lacking resolution, Camille let it be.

She slept badly, in a state of alertness she was familiar with, and which was always a symptom that something was going off the rails. When morning came, Adamsberg let go of her hand, grabbed his clothes, and left the lorry. Only then did she drop off again, for a good two hours.

Adamsberg drove off at nine to see the diffident Aimont and came back less than thirty minutes later.

'Nine ewes slashed at Champ des Meules,' he reported.

Soliman jumped up and ran to the lorry to fetch the map.

'Don't bother,' Adamsberg told him calmly. 'It's just by Vaucouleurs, due north. He's gone way off his track.'

Soliman stared at Adamsberg, struck dumb.

'You were wrong,' he said at length, in surprise and disappointment.

Without a word Adamsberg poured himself a cup of coffee.

'You were wrong,' Soliman insisted. 'He's changed his route. He's running away. He'll get away.'

Watchee stood up, straight as a staff.

'We'll stick on his tail,' he said. 'On track or off it. We're breaking camp. Go tell Camille, Sol.'

'No,' said Adamsberg.

'What?' said Watchee.

'We're not breaking camp. We're going to stay here. We're not moving.'

'Massart is at Vaucouleurs,' said Soliman, raising his voice. 'And we're going where Massart goes. To Vaucouleurs.'

'We're not going to go to Vaucouleurs', said Adamsberg, 'because that's what he wants us to do. Massart hasn't abandoned his itinerary.'

'Really?' said Soliman.

'No. He just wants us to get out of Belcourt.'

'Why so?'

'So as to have a free hand. He's got someone to kill at Belcourt.'

'I don't agree,' said Soliman with a vigorous shake of his head. 'The more time we waste here, the further away he gets.'

'He's not getting further away. He's watching us. Go to Vaucouleurs if you want to, Soliman. Go on, if it makes you happy. You've got the moped, you can go on your own. You can go too, Watchee, if you want to. Ask Camille, she's the driver. I'm staying here.'

'What's to say you're right, young fella?' asked Watchee, who was quite shaken.

Adamsberg shrugged. 'You know the answer,' he said.

'The dogleg?'

'Among other things.'

'It's not a lot to go on.'

'But it's a something that has no other explanation. There are other things.'

Torn between dissent and devotion, Soliman paced back and forth for an hour by the side of the lorry – his patch – before he came up with a decision. At long last he got out the blue plastic bowl and the dirty washing, signalling that he had given in.

Adamsberg went to his car. He was expected back at the *gendarmerie*, to supervise the investigation at Vaucouleurs. Before opening the car door he got out his pistol and checked that it was loaded.

'Are you armed?' asked Watchee.

'My name's in the papers this morning,' said Adamsberg, wincing. 'Somebody talked. Don't know who. Now she can find me if she wants to.'

'You mean the killer girl?'

Adamsberg nodded.

'Would she shoot?'

'Yes. She'd put a little lump of lead in my gut. Keep an eye open for me, Watchee. Look out for a tall, pale-faced, scrawny redhead, with bags under sunken eyes, long wavy hair, and a small nose. She might have two younger girls in tow, skinny as rakes. Look, here's her picture,' he said, taking a photograph from his pocket.

'What sort of clothes does she wear?' the old man asked gravely, looking at the image.

'Never the same thing twice. She dresses up, like a kid playing games.'

'Do I warn the others?'

'Yes.'

Adamsberg spent the rest of the day with Aimont and the *flics* from Vaucouleurs. It was the first time

Aimont had come face to face with the wolf's work; the carnage wrought on the flock impressed him deeply. Late in the day the Digne police sent over a photograph of Massart and Aimont arranged to have it enlarged and distributed. On the other hand, they were still waiting for the case notes that Puygiron was supposed to be supplying. Adamsberg spent a long while staring at the face of Auguste Massart. Not a nice face. Large, pasty, ill-tempered, angry. Smooth, podgy cheeks, low forehead, black hair in a fringe, close-set dark eyes, sparse eyebrows. A slumbering brute.

Danglard's paperwork got to Belcourt at seven in the evening. Adamsberg folded it carefully, put it away for safe-keeping in his inside pocket, and went back to the lorry.

Before going to bed he took his Magnum .357 out of its holster and placed it by his bed, within easy reach of his right hand. He lay down, took Camille's hand in his own, and fell asleep. Camille stared at her hand for a good while, with her mind empty, and then let it stay where it was.

Instead of keeping Woof curled up on his feet Watchee put the dog on guard duty outside.

'Look out for that girl,' he suggested, scratching Woof behind the ears. 'A tall scrawny redhead. She's a killer. Bark your lungs out. But look on the bright side,' he added, scanning the sky. 'It won't rain tonight.'

Woof gave him a look, as much as to say that

he understood everything, and then lay down on the ground.

On Thursday, 2 July, the heat rose another step. They hung around sweltering. Camille drove the lorry into the village to top up the radiator. Watchee phoned his flock to get news of George's paw. Soliman buried himself in the dictionary. Camille was rather uneasy about her passive right hand, which no longer seemed to respond to mental directives. She dropped composing and took refuge in the *The A to Z of Tools for Trade and Craft*. There must be some gizmo in there designed to cope with the awkward position she found herself in. Perhaps the *earthed single feed thermodecoupler 6-25 amps* would do the trick, she thought. If Adamsberg agreed to let go of her hand, the problem would vanish. The simplest solution would be to ask him.

It was not until nearly five in the afternoon that the *gendarmes* at Poissy-le-Roi informed their colleagues at Vaucouleurs of a sheep savaging that had taken place during the previous night at the Chaumes sheep farm. The Vaucouleurs squad took their time passing on the news onto Belcourt and Adamsberg only heard about it around eight o'clock.

He laid the map out on the wooden crate.

'Fifty kilometres east of Vaucouleurs,' he said. 'Still off his route.'

'He's getting further away from us,' Soliman growled.

'We're not going anywhere,' said Adamsberg.

'He'll give us the slip!' the young man shouted, getting to his feet.

Watchee was poking the fire a few feet away, and he put out his crook and tapped the young man on the shoulder.

'Don't get excited, Sol,' he said. 'Come what may, we'll collar him.'

Soliman slumped back into his seat, looking downcast and exhausted, as he did whenever Watchee brought him to order with his crook. Camille wondered whether he had put something special on the tip.

'Submission,' mumbled Soliman. 'Agreement to abide by a decision or to obey an authority.'

After dinner Camille persevered in her reading of *The A to Z of Tools for Trade and Craft* in the cab until she was ready to drop. She had barely slept a wink the night before, and her eyelids were heavy. Towards two in the morning she crept to her bed as cautiously as a cat burglar. Soliman was still in town with the moped. Watchee was on sentry duty close to the road. He was watching. He was watching for the redhead. He was Adamsberg's guard, and he had Warp at his feet. 'I don't mind,' he had said. 'I'm not sleepy.'

First, Camille sat on the edge of Soliman's bed to take off her boots, even if it meant putting her bare feet on the filthy floor of the sheep-wagon. That

326

way she wouldn't run the risk of waking the *commissaire*. Even a sleeping *commissaire* can't take anyone's hand in his. Slowly, she pulled back the canvas partition, taking things step by step in total silence, then gently pulled it closed behind her. Adamsberg was lying on his back and breathing regularly. She stole her way along the narrow gap between their beds and tried not to trip on the weapon glinting on the floor. Adamsberg raised both his arms towards her.

'Come here,' he said softly.

Camille turned to stone in the dark.

'Come here,' he said again.

Camille's mind was a void and she took one wobbly step. From far beneath the void rose blurry memories and mewling shadows. He put a hand around her and pulled her towards him. Camille caught a glimpse of her old desires, getting nearer but still inaccessible, as if they were sealed off behind a thick pane of glass. Adamsberg touched her cheek and then her hair. Camille had her eyes open in the dark and she was still gripping *The A to Z of Tools for Trade and Craft* in her left hand, but she was more alert to the evanescent images swarming up from the dungeons of memory than to the face that was staring at her. She put a hand out towards the face, anxiously aware that if she touched it something would burst. Maybe that thick pane of glass. Or maybe the deepest storerooms of memory, stuffed to the gills with things that were still functional, hypocritical and deceptive sleepers lying low, defying the passing years. That's more or less what happened. A long slow explosion that was more frightening than pleasant. She looked on as amazing junk spewed up in a great clatter from the bilges of her own boat. She wanted to tidy it up, hold it down, restore order. But as one part of Camille liked disorder, she gave up and lay down beside Adamsberg.

'Do you know the story about the wind and the tree?' he asked, holding her in his arms.

'Is that one of Soliman's stories?' Camille murmured.

'It's one of my stories.'

'I don't much care for your stories.'

'This is not a bad one.'

'I'm still not keen.'

'I don't blame you.'

CHAPTER 32

It was after ten in the morning when Soliman called through the partition.

'Camille!' he shouted. 'For heaven's sake get up. The *flic* has gone.'

'What am I supposed to do about that?' Camille said.

'Come on out!' Soliman yelled.

The young man was in a state of alarm. Camille slipped on her clothes and her boots and joined him at the wooden crate.

'He really did come,' said Soliman. 'But nobody saw him. Or his car. Or anything.'

'Who are you talking about?'

'Massart, for God's sake! Don't you understand?'

'Did he do anything?'

'Camille, he slit a man's throat last night.'

'Fuck,' Camille said under her breath.

'He was right, the young fella was,' said Watchee, banging his crook on the ground. 'Belcourt was where the man struck.'

'And he slaughtered three ewes into the bargain, thirty kilometres down the road.'

'Down his route?'

'Yup, at Châteaurouge. He's striking off westwards towards Paris.'

Camille went to fetch the map, now decidedly dog-eared, and opened it out.

'You mean you don't even know where to find Paris?' Soliman asked, twitchily.

'Calm down, Sol,' Camille said. 'The *flics* didn't catch sight of him in town?'

'He didn't come this way,' said Watchee. 'I had my eye on the road all night long.'

'What happened?' asked Camille.

'What bloody happened?' Soliman repeated. 'What happened was that he came along with his big bad wolf and he set the aforementioned animal on some poor guy! What do you suppose?'

'I don't see why you're getting so steamed up,' said Watchee in a measured tone. 'He had to kill that man, and so he killed him. A werewolf ne'er misses its mark.'

'There were ten *gendarmes* patrolling the town!'

'A werewolf is a match for twice as many. Get that into your skull.'

'Do we know who the victim was?' Camille asked.

'An old fellow, that's all we know. He slashed him outside town, two kilometres off, up in the hills.'

'Whatever has he got against old men?' Camille muttered.

'Folk he knew,' Watchee mumbled. 'He doesn't like folk. Any folk.'

330

Camille poured herself some coffee and cut a slice of bread.

'Sol,' she said. 'You were in town last night. Did you hear nothing?'

Soliman shook his head. 'Adamsberg's asked us to go and wait for him in the main square. In case we have to take off quickly for Châteaurouge. The police will very likely move the whole incident room over there.'

Camille drove slowly into Belcourt and parked the sheep-wagon in a shady spot on the main square, between the *gendarmerie* and the town hall.

'We wait here,' said Soliman.

They were all sitting in the cab and not talking. Camille had her arms stretched out over the steering wheel and looked at the deserted village streets. At eleven o'clock on a Friday the centre of Belcourt seemed virtually uninhabited. Every now and again a woman went by with a shopping basket. A nun in a grey habit glanced up at them from a stone bench opposite the church, then went back to reading a heavy leather-bound tome. Half past struck on the church bell; then a quarter to twelve.

'Nuns must be really hot in summer,' Soliman observed.

Then the cab fell silent once more. The church bell struck noon. A police car came out of a side street and parked in front of the *gendarmerie*. Adamsberg, Aimont and two other *gendarmes* got

331

out. He nodded to the sheep-wagon and followed his fellow-officers into the building. The square was white-hot under the mid-day sun. The nun did not shift from where she sat in the patchy shade of a plane tree.

'Abnegation, self-sacrifice, renunciation,' said Soliman. 'Maybe she's waiting for a date. Or for a visitation.'

'Shut up, Sol,' said Watchee. 'You're disturbing me.'

'And what are you doing that can be disturbed?'

'You can see for yourself. I'm watching.'

A quarter past chimed out on the clock and Adamsberg appeared at the door of the *gendarmerie*. He was alone. He began to walk across the wide cobbled square towards the sheep wagon. When he was halfway across Watchee suddenly shot out of the cab, tripped on the steps, and fell heavily onto the pavement.

'Lie down flat, young fella!' he bellowed for all he was worth.

Adamsberg knew it was meant for him. He flung himself to the ground just as a shot rang out, shattering the quiet of the square. By the time the nun could take aim a second time he had dashed behind the stone bench and got his left arm around her neck in a vice-like half nelson. His right arm was all bloody and hung uselessly at his side. Camille and Soliman were sitting stock-still with their hearts pounding. Camille was the first to react. She jumped down from the lorry and rushed to

Watchee, who was still on the ground, grinning broadly, and muttering, 'Well done, young fella, well done.' Four *gendarme*s were running to Adamsberg.

'If you don't let go', the girl screamed, 'I'll shoot all four of them!'

The *gendarme*s came to a stop five metres off.

'And if they shoot, I'll finish off grandad!' she added, aiming her weapon at Watchee, who remained lying where he had fallen, with Camille trying to help him get his head upright. 'And I shoot straight! This piece of shit here can tell you I shoot straight!'

Silence settled on the square like a cloud of darkness. They all stood or lay where they were, nailed, as it were, to the spot, unable to move a limb. Adamsberg still had the girl's neck in the crook of his elbow. He leaned forward and brought his lips to her ear.

'Listen to me, Sabrina,' he said softly.

'Let go of me, you bastard,' she forced out of her empty lungs. 'Or else I'll finish off grandpa and every last *flic* in this shitty dump.'

'I've found your little boy, Sabrina.'

Adamsberg could feel the girl's muscles tensing.

'He's in Poland,' he went on, his lips almost kissing the cowl. 'One of my men has gone over there.'

'You're lying!' Sabrina hissed viciously.

'He's not far from Gdańsk. Put your gun down.'

'You're lying!' Sabrina was almost gasping, but her arm was still out straight, and trembling.

333

'I've got his picture in my pocket,' Adamsberg went on. 'They took a snap of him the day before yesterday, on his way home from school. I can't reach it as you've injured my right arm. And if I let go with my left arm you'll put more lead in me. So how are we going to manage, Sabrina? Do you want to see your boy? Do you want to get him back? Or do you want to blow everyone's brains out and never see him again?'

'It's a trap,' she hissed back at him.

'Let one of the *gendarme*s come over. He'll get the photograph and show it to you. You'll recognise him. You'll see that I'm not lying.'

'No *flic*'s coming near me.'

'Then someone unarmed.'

Sabrina thought for a few moments. She was still struggling for air in the grip of Adamsberg's arm.

'OK,' she whispered.

'Sol!' Adamsberg called out. 'Come over here, mortal slow, with your arms away from your sides.'

Sol came out of the lorry and walked towards them.

'Come up round behind the bench. In my left inside breast pocket there's an envelope. Lift it out, open it, and take out the photograph. Show it to the lady.'

Sol did as he was told and took from the envelope a black-and-white photograph of an eight-year-old boy. He held it in front of the girl. Sabrina looked down at the picture.

'Now put the photograph on the bench, Sol, and go back to the lorry. So, Sabrina, do you recognise the lad?'

She nodded.

'We'll get him back,' Adamsberg said.

'He'll never let him go,' Sabrina breathed.

'Believe me, he will. He'll give him up. Put your gun down. I'm very fond of the old man lying on the pavement. I'm very fond of the two people in the lorry. I'm very fond of the four *gendarme*s over there, though I don't know them any more than you do. I'm fond of me. And I'm fond of you, Sabrina. If you make a move they'll take a pot-shot at you. Wounding a police officer is not a nice thing to do.'

'They'll put me in clink.'

'They'll put you where I tell them to put you. I'm in charge of you. Lower your gun. Give it to me.'

Sabrina let her arm fall. She was shivering through and through. The gun fell to the ground. Adamsberg slowly released her neck, nodded to the *gendarme*s to stand back, walked round the bench and picked up the weapon. Sabrina hunched up and burst into tears. Adamsberg sat down next to her, carefully took off her grey cowl, and stroked her russet hair.

'Stand up,' he said softly. 'One of my men will come and get you. His name's Danglard. He'll take you back to Paris, and you'll wait for me to get back. I've still got stuff to sort down here.

But you'll wait for me. And we'll go and get the boy.'

Sabrina rose unsteadily to her feet. Adamsberg put his good arm around her waist and led her into the *gendarmerie*. One of the *gendarme*s was attending to Watchee's ankle.

'Help me hoist him into the lorry,' Camille said. 'I'll drive him to a doctor.'

'It stinks in here,' said the *gendarme*, lowering Watchee onto the first bed on the left.

'It doesn't *stink*,' Watchee said. 'It smells of sheep wax.'

'Is this where you *live*?' the *gendarme* asked, rather taken aback by the way the lorry was kitted out.

'Temporarily,' Camille said.

At this point Adamsberg climbed inside. 'How is he?'

'Ankle,' the *gendarme* said. 'I don't think anything's broken. But you'd better have a doctor look at it. You'd better see a medic too, sir,' he added, seeing the *commissaire*'s arm in its first-aid bandage.

'Yes,' said Adamsberg. 'The wound's not deep. I'll take care of it.'

The *gendarme* saluted and climbed down. Adamsberg sat on the side of Watchee's bed.

'How about that for a lark?' the old man said with a broad grin. 'I saved your bacon, young fella.'

'If you hadn't shouted, that bullet would have gone straight through the middle of me. I didn't recognise her. My mind was on Massart.'

'Whereas yours truly', said Watchee, pointing to his eye, 'was watching. You have to admit, I ain't called Watchee for nothing.'

'You've earned your name, old man.'

'I couldn't do anything to help Suzanne,' he said bleakly. 'But you I could help. I saved your skin, young fella.'

Adamsberg nodded.

'If you'd let me keep my rifle', the shepherd added, 'I'd have shot her before she could hurt you.'

'She's just a kid, Watchee. Shouting was quite enough.'

'Well, maybe,' said Watchee sceptically. 'What did you whisper in her ear?'

'I changed the points on the line.'

'Oh, yes,' said Watchee with a smile. 'I remember.'

'I owe you one.'

'Indeed you do. You can get me some *vin blanc*. There's no Saint-Victor left.'

Adamsberg got out of the back of the lorry and went to give Camille a hug, saying not a word.

'Look after yourself,' Camille said.

'Yes. After Watchee's been seen by the doctor, head for Châteaurouge. Pull up on the edge of town, on the D44.'

CHAPTER 33

Wherever they halted they followed the same identical and strict routine for setting up camp, never the smallest variation, so that Camille was beginning to muddle all the town and village outskirts where she had parked the sheep-wagon. Their system, the fruit of Soliman's organised and meticulous mind, had the advantage of allowing them to reconstruct a familiar and soothing environment in places as unhomely as parking lots and lay-bys. Soliman would set up the wooden crate and the rusty folding stools to the rear of the vehicle for meals, see to the washing on the offside, and lay out the reading and relaxation area on the nearside. Camille therefore did her composing in the cab, but came down to the reading corner to study her *A to Z of Tools for Trade and Craft*.

Camille found these stable arrangements gave her a vital prop in their chaotic and hazardous pursuit of Massart. Four folding stools were not very grand things to be attached to, but for the time being they provided essential reassurance. Especially now that her life stretched

338

out before her in complete and radical disarray. She had not dared to phone Johnstone today. She was afraid some part of her disarray would show through. The Canadian was a methodical man, he would be sure to notice something in her voice.

Soliman had spent the rest of that afternoon carrying Watchee around in his arms, getting him out of the lorry, getting him back into the lorry, taking him to pee and to eat, all the while insulting him for being a senile shepherd.

'You really did come a cropper on those steps,' he reminded him.

'But for me', Watchee replied with regal hauteur, 'your young fella wouldn't be around any more.'

'But you really did come a cropper, old man.'

Camille sat down on the red-and-green striped stool, which was hers by right. Soliman carried Watchee to his yellow stool and propped his bad leg on the upturned bowl. His was the blue stool. The fourth, blue-and-green, was Adamsberg's. Soliman did not want folk switching stools.

Adamsberg came back to occupy his stool around nine in the evening. A *gendarme* drove his car back for him, and a second officer walked him over to the lorry without presuming to inquire why he preferred the company of gypsies to the convenience of a hotel in the nearby town of Montdidier.

Adamsberg dropped like a stone onto his rightful seat. His arm was in a sling and his face betrayed stress. With his left hand he speared a sausage and then three baked potatoes and clumsily dumped them onto his plate.

'Handicap,' said Soliman. 'An encumbrance or difficulty that weighs upon effort; disability that puts a person at a disadvantage.'

'In the boot of my car', said Adamsberg, 'there are two cases of wine. Bring them over.'

Soliman uncorked a bottle and filled the four glasses. Seeing as it wasn't *blanc de Saint-Victor*, anyone could serve it. Watchee tasted it suspiciously before expressing acceptance with a nod of his head.

'Tell us, young fella,' he said, turning to face Adamsberg.

'Same story,' said Adamsberg. 'The man was killed by a single bite after being hit on the head. We've got pretty good prints of the beast's two front feet. Like Sernot and Deguy the victim's not a spring chicken. He's a retired commercial traveller. Been round the world twenty times over, selling cosmetics.'

He got out his jotter to jog his memory.

'Paul Hellouin,' he said. 'He was sixty-three.'

He put the jotter back in his pocket.

'This time', he went on, 'we found three hairs near the wound. They've gone off to the IRCG at Rosny. I've asked them to get a move on.'

'What's the IRCG?' Watchee asked.

'It's the *gendarmerie*'s central lab for forensic investigation,' Adamsberg said. 'Where they can get a man a life sentence from a thread of his left sock.'

'Good,' said Watchee. 'I do like to understand.'

He contemplated the bare feet inside his heavy boots.

'I have always said that socks were strictly for the birds,' he added for his own benefit. 'Now I know why. Carry on, young fella.'

'The vet came to look at those three hairs. In his view they're not dog hairs. So they must be wolf hairs.'

Adamsberg rubbed his wounded arm and poured himself a glass of wine with his left hand, spilling drips on the side.

'This time', he said, 'he did the murder on the edge of a meadow, and there wasn't a cross of any kind in the environs. Which tells us that Massart isn't as picky as you think when it comes to getting the job done. And he killed him a long way away from his home, presumably because of all the policeman hanging around town. That presupposes he had a means of enticing him out. Maybe a note, or a phone call.'

'What time did it happen?'

'Around two in the morning.'

'An appointment at 2 a.m.?' Soliman was sceptical.

'Why not?'

'The guy must have suspected something.'

'It all depends on the pretext that was used. Confidential information, family secrets, blackmail, there are all sorts of ways of getting someone to go out at night. I don't think Sernot or Deguy went out just to sniff the night air, either. They were summoned, as was Hellouin.'

'Their wives said there weren't any phone calls.'

'Not that day, no. The meetings must have been arranged earlier.'

Soliman pursed his lips.

'I know, Sol,' said Adamsberg. 'You believe in chance.'

'I do, yes,' Soliman said.

'Give me one good reason why that nice old cosmetics salesman should have gone out for a constitutional at two in the morning. Do you know many people who really do go walking in the dark? People don't like the dark. Do you know how many genuine noctambulists I've come across in my whole life? Just two.'

'Who were they?'

'I am one of them, and the other is a chap called Raymond, from my village in the Pyrenees.'

'So what?' said Watchee, dismissing this Raymond as if he were swatting a fly with his hand.

'So there's no link between Hellouin and Deguy or Sernot, nor is there any reason he should have just bumped into Massart. But', Adamsberg added thoughtfully, 'there *is* something different about Hellouin.'

Watchee rolled three cigarettes in his lap. He licked the papers, stuck them down and handed one each to Soliman and Camille.

'There was at least one man who might have wanted to kill him,' Adamsberg resumed. 'Which is not so common in men's lives.'

'Does it have any connection with Massart?' Soliman asked.

'It's an old story,' Adamsberg continued without answering the young man. 'An ordinary sordid story that I find interesting. It happened twenty-five years ago in the United States.'

'Massart never set foot over there,' said Watchee.

'I find it interesting nonetheless,' said Adamsberg.

He reached into his pocket with his left hand and pulled out some pills that he downed with two gulps of wine.

'For my arm,' he said.

'Does it ache, young fella?' Watchee asked.

'It hurts.'

'Do you know the story about the man who lent his arm to the lion?' asked Soliman. 'The lion found it very useful and a great invention, so he didn't want to give it back. The man didn't know what to do to get his rightful property back.'

'That'll do, Sol,' Watchee cut in. And to Adamsberg he said: 'Tell us that old story about America, young fella.'

'Well,' Soliman went on, 'one day when the man was scooping water from the pond with only one hand, a fish without gills found itself caught in his bowl. "Let me go," begged the fish . . .'

'Put a sock in it, Sol,' Watchee shouted. Turning once more to Adamsberg: 'Tell us that American thing.'

'In the beginning,' Adamsberg said, 'there were two French brothers, Paul and Simon Hellouin. They worked together in a small cosmetics company. Simon set up a branch office in Austin, Texas.'

'This is a crap story,' Soliman said.

'While he was over there', Adamsberg pursued, 'Simon got into a fix by having an affair with a married woman, a French lady with an American husband. Mrs Ariane Padwell, née Germant. Are you following? I often send people to sleep when I tell stories.'

'It's because you speak too slowly,' said Watchee.

'Yes,' said Adamsberg. 'The husband, that's to say the American, John Neil Padwell, got into trouble by allowing jealousy to consume him, and then allowing himself to torture and then to kill his wife's lover.'

'Simon Hellouin,' Watchee said, summing up.

'Yes. Padwell was charged and tried. Simon's brother – Paul, our man – gave evidence and heaped it all on Padwell. He produced letters from his brother describing how cruelly, how brutally Padwell treated his wife. John Neil Padwell was sent down for twenty years, and served eighteen of them. If Paul had not come to the stand, he might have got off much more lightly by pleading temporary insanity.'

'All that's got nothing to do with Massart,' said Soliman.

'As much as your lion has,' Adamsberg retorted. 'Padwell must have come out of jail about seven years ago. If there's anyone he wants to take it out on, it's Paul Hellouin. After the trial Ariane gave up everything and came back to France with the brother, Paul, with whom she lived for a year or two. So it was a double whammy. He'd given evidence against him and then ran off with his wife. I got the story from Paul Hellouin's sister.'

'But what's the point of it all?' Camille asked. 'Hellouin was killed by Massart. We've got the fingernails. The nail results are incontrovertible.'

'I'm well aware of that,' Adamsberg said. 'And the nail business bothers me.'

'So?' said Soliman.

'I don't know,' said Adamsberg.

'Don't stray from Massart,' he said. 'We've don't give a fart for your Texas convict.'

'I'm not straying. I might even be getting closer. Maybe Massart is someone else.'

'Don't make it more complicated, young fella,' said Watchee. 'Sufficient unto the day.'

'Massart only came back to Saint-Victor a few years back,' said Adamsberg, taking his time.

'About six years ago,' Watchee confirmed.

'And nobody had seen him for twenty years.'

'He was doing the rounds of village market days. He reseated rush-bottomed chairs.'

'Is there any evidence? One day a guy turns up and says, "I'm Massart". And everyone chirps back, "Sure, you're Massart, haven't seen you around in a long while." And everyone reckons that the man living all alone up on Mont Vence is Massart. No-one of his family is left, he hasn't got any friends, and his acquaintances haven't seen him since he was barely out of his teens. What evidence is there that Massart really is Massart?'

'Fucking hell,' said Watchee. 'Massart . . . is Massart, sod it. Whatever are you trying to get at?'

Adamsberg looked Watchee in the eye. 'Did you recognise him, then? Could you swear it was the same person as the young man who left the area twenty years before?'

'Good grief. I'm pretty sure it was him. I remember Auguste as a young man. He wasn't a very pretty sight. A bit slow and heavy, like. Raven-black hair. But he had attitude. A hard worker.'

'There are thousands of guys who fit that description. Could you swear it was the same man?'

Watchee scratched his thigh and pondered.

'Not on my mother's head', he said regretfully, after a while. 'And if *I* can't swear to it, then no-one in Saint-Victor can either.'

'That's what I was saying,' said Adamsberg. 'There's no conclusive proof that Massart is Massart.'

'What about the real Massart?' Camille asked, knitting her eyebrows.

'Rubbed out, got rid of, replaced.'

'Why would he have been rubbed out?'

'Because of his likeness.'

'Are you saying that Padwell usurped Massart's identity?' asked Soliman.

'No,' Adamsberg sighed. 'Padwell is now sixty-one. Massart is much younger. How old do you think he is, Watchee?'

'He's forty-four. He was born the same night as young Lucien.'

'I'm not asking you for the real Massart's age. I'm asking you to give a guess as to the age of the man called Massart.'

'Oh,' said Watchee, furrowing his brow. 'Not more than forty-five, and not less than thirty-seven or thirty-eight. Definitely not sixty-one.'

'So we're agreed on that,' said Adamsberg. 'Massart is not John Padwell.'

'Why have you been boring on about that man for the last hour, then?' asked Soliman.

'That's the way my mind works.'

'That's not a mind working. That's flying in the face of common sense.'

'That's right. That's the way my mind works.'

Watchee nudged Soliman with his stick. 'Respect, boy,' he said. 'What are you going to do next, young fella?'

'The *flics* have made up their minds to publish Massart's photograph in an appeal for witnesses.

The magistrate reckons there's a prima facie case for doing so. Tomorrow all the newspapers will print the mug shot.'

'Great,' said Watchee, smiling.

'I've been onto Interpol and asked for the whole file on the Padwell case. I'm expecting it in the morning.'

'But what's it bloody well got to do with you?' said Soliman. 'Even if your Texan has murdered Hellouin, he wouldn't have laid a finger on Sernot or Deguy. Would he? And even less on my mother, right?'

'I know,' Adamsberg said calmly. 'It doesn't fit.'

'So why are you carrying on with it?'

'I don't know.'

Soliman cleared the plates and glasses, put the crate back inside, folded the stools, picked up the blue plastic bowl. Then he picked up Watchee with one arm under his shoulders and the other under his knees and carried him back up into the lorry. Adamsberg stroked Camille's hair.

'Come,' he said after a moment's silence.

'I'll hurt your arm,' she said. 'It would be better to sleep apart.'

'It would not be better.'

'But it would be all right.'

'It would be all right. But it would not be better.'

'If I hurt you?'

'No,' Adamsberg said, shaking his head. 'You've never hurt me.'

Camille wavered, still torn between the attractions of peace and those of chaos.

'I had stopped loving you,' she said.

'Everything comes to an end,' Adamsberg said.

CHAPTER 34

Next morning the same *gendarme* came to collect Adamsberg to get him to the *gendarmerie* at Belcourt for nine o'clock. He spent two hours with Sabrina Monge in the cell where she had spent the night. Danglard and *lieutenant* Gulvain arrived on the 11.07 train, and Adamsberg handed the young woman over to them, together with a great deal of unnecessary advice. He had blind faith in Danglard's psychological insight; and he reckoned his number two was a more qualified practitioner of compassion than he was.

At noon he got himself driven to the *gendarmerie* at Châteaurouge to stand by for the Interpol file on John Neil Padwell. Fromentin, the man in charge at Châteaurouge, was a very different type from Aimont: ruddy and squat, and not exactly eager to lend a hand to the civilian branch. He considered – quite correctly – that Adamsberg, being outside his official area of operation and without official charge of the case, had no standing to give him orders, which Adamsberg refrained from doing anyway. As at Belcourt and at Bourg-en-Bresse, he stuck to asking for information and offering advice.

But since *adjudant* Fromentin was a coward, he did not dare to go head to head with the *commissaire*, whose two-edged reputation had preceded him. Moreover, he turned out to be susceptible to the fog of flattery which Adamsberg could raise when needed, so that in the end the broad-shouldered Fromentin was virtually at the *commissaire*'s beck and call. He too was standing by for the Interpol fax, even though he did not grasp what Adamsberg hoped to get out of a dead case, with no thread of connection to the savagings of the big bad wolf. As far as he knew, that's to say according to the man's sister, Simon Hellouin hadn't had his throat cut by animal fangs. He had simply been taken out *à l'américaine*, that's to say, by a good old bullet to the heart. Before shooting him, Padwell took the time to burn his balls off by way of reprisal. Fromentin winced with dread and horror. Half the population of the United States, he reckoned, had reverted to savagery, and the other half had turned into plastic dolls.

At three thirty the lab results from the IRCG landed on *adjudant* Aimont's desk, and he forwarded them to Fromentin within five minutes. Hairs found on the corpse of Paul Hellouin belonged to the species *Canis lupus*, the common wolf. Straight away Adamsberg sent the information on to Hermel, to Montvailland and to *adjudant-chef* Brévent, at

351

Puygiron. He had nothing against getting up the nose of a man who had still not sent in the long-awaited paperwork on Auguste Massart.

That morning Massart's photograph had been published in the papers, and there was rising pressure in editorials, on television and on radio. The murder of Paul Hellouin and the subsequent slaughter of the Châteaurouge sheep had finally got the press and the police going all-out. The werewolf's bloody progress was mapped out in every daily paper. They showed the route covered so far by the homicidal maniac in bold, and the route he was expected to follow thereafter towards Paris in a dotted line. It was a route he had laid out himself, and which he had followed quite scrupulously throughout, with the exceptions of his side-trips to Vaucouleurs and Poissy-le-Roi. Public interest announcements were being put out all the time, warning the inhabitants of villages and towns on the wolf-man's route to exercise extreme caution and above all to avoid going out after dark. Police stations all over France were now getting floods of calls making denunciations and reporting varied sightings. For the time being they were not following up any of these leads unless they were located on or very near Massart's red-line route. The scale of the case now made it imperative to co-ordinate the various local efforts. The national director of the *police judiciaire* stepped in to put Jean-Baptiste Adamsberg in overall charge of the werewolf affair. He got the news around five in the afternoon, at Châteaurouge. From that moment on *adjudant* Fromentin squirmed at Adamsberg's feet and did his best to foresee and to fulfill the *commissaire*'s every whim. But Adamsberg did not need anything very much. He was waiting for the Interpol file. Unusually for him, he did not go out for a walk in the fields one single time that Saturday evening. Instead he sat around with his ear alert for the chirruping of the fax machine, filling time by doodling in his jotter. He was trying to sketch a likeness of *adjudant* Fromentin.

The documents spewed out of the fax just before six, dispatched to him by Police Lieutenant J. H. G. Lanson, of Austin, TX. Adamsberg swooped on the sheets in impatient expectation and took them over to the window to read. As they were in English he had to ask Fromentin to translate for him.

The marital and criminal history of John N. Padwell seemed to match in all details the story told by the sister of Paul and Simon Hellouin. He was born in Austin, TX and went to work in the metal industry. He married Ariane Germant at the age of twenty-six, and they had a son, Stuart D. Padwell. After eleven years of marriage, he had tortured his wife's lover, Simon Hellouin, and then shot him through the heart. He was sentenced to twenty years in jail, served eighteen of them, and came out seven years and three months ago. Since which time J. N. Padwell had not left the

United States and had had no subsequent criminal record.

Adamsberg spent a long time poring over the pictures of the killer that his American colleagues had forwarded. One was full-face, the other two side-on, from left and from right. He had a square face and a firm look and seemed to be fair-skinned. Rather vacant eyes, thin and slightly cunning lips. There was malice as well as blinkered obstinacy in that face.

He had died of natural causes in Austin, TX, on 13 December, one year and seven months ago.

Adamsberg shook his head, rolled up the fax sheets, and tucked them into his jacket.

'Interesting?' asked Fromentin, who had been waiting with his question until the *commissaire* had finished reading.

'That's the end of that,' said Adamsberg with a look of glum disappointment. 'The man died last year.'

'That's a pity,' said Fromentin, who had taken no interest at all in the Padwell lead.

Adamsberg bade him goodnight with a left-handed handshake and departed the *gendarmerie* at an even slower pace than usual. His temporary equerry fell into step and accompanied him to the small car he had been allocated. Before getting in, Adamsberg took the roll out of his jacket pocket and studied the photograph of J. N. Padwell once again. Then he put the papers back, lost in thought, and slid into the passenger seat.

The *gendarme* dropped him fifty metres from the lorry.

What he saw first was the black motorbike on its kick-stand by the side of the road. Then Johnstone came into view. He was on the lorry's nearside wing, arranging a heap of photographs that he laid out on the ground. Adamsberg did not experience anything unpleasant, only a gnawing regret at not having Camille to hold in his arms tonight, and a fleeting, barely noticeable pang of fear. The Canadian was a much more serious and reliable proposition than he was. Basically, if reason were his sole guide, he would give the man a hearty recommendation. But desire and self-interest went in the other direction and prevented him from just letting go of Camille in favour of the tall chap with the wardrobe chest.

Camille was sitting rather stiffly beside Johnstone and concentrating entirely on the pictures of the wolves of the Mercantour spread out on the scorched grass. The trapper gave a staccato commentary for Adamsberg's benefit: Marcus, Electre, Sibellius, Proserpine, and the snout of the late Augustus. Johnstone was calm and quite welcoming, but he was still giving Adamsberg that quizzical look that said: 'What's your game?'

Soliman laid supper on the wooden crate while Watchee sat stoking the campfire with his bad leg resting on the bowl. With a jut of his jaw Johnstone asked the old man what was wrong with his leg.

'He fell trying to get down from the cab,' Soliman explained.

'Any news from Texas, young fella?' Watchee asked Adamsberg, to change the subject.

'Yes. Austin faxed me the man's *vita*.'

'What's that, then?'

'Your *vita* is the story of your life. Vital, as it were.'

'Good. I do like to understand.'

'But', said Adamsberg, 'our man's vital no longer. Padwell died a year and half ago.'

'You were wrong,' Soliman observed.

'Yes. You've already told me that once.'

With his injured arm Adamsberg gave up the idea of sleeping doubled up in the car. He called the *gendarmerie* and at last had himself driven over to that hotel in Montdidier. He spent all day Sunday in a small, hot and stuffy room listening to the news, keeping abreast of the Sabrina case, and rereading all the files that had amassed over the last week. Now and again he unrolled the faxed photograph of J. N. Padwell and looked at it with a mixture of curiosity and regret, turning the man's image this way and that to catch it in light and in shade. He looked at it the right way round, then the wrong way round. He rotated it every which way. He stared deep into those empty eyes. He got away three times to the hidey-hole he had found in a deserted, overgrown kitchen garden. He made a sketch of Watchee sitting bolt upright with his right leg on the bowl, his be-ribboned hat pulled down over his eyes. He drew a picture of Soliman: bare to the waist, eyes on the horizon, leaning slightly forward in one of the proud and haughty poses he liked to adopt, and every one of which he had copied from Watchee. He did a sketch of Camille seen side-on as she gripped the lorry's steering wheel and stared hard at the road ahead. He drew Johnstone leaning on his motorbike and looking straight at you with that silent, serious question hovering about his blue gaze.

There was a knock on the door around seven thirty in the evening, and Soliman came in, gleaming with sweat. Adamsberg looked up and shook his head, meaning to tell the youngster that there was nothing to report. Massart was having a quiet patch.

'Is *Laurence* still around?' he asked.

'Yes,' Soliman said. 'But that doesn't mean you can't come over, right? Watchee's going to barbecue some beef on the chicken wire. He's expecting you. I came to collect you.'

'Has he had any news of George Gershwin?'

'You don't give a damn for George Gershwin.'

'Maybe I give a bit more than you think.'

'It's the trapper who's keeping you away, isn't it?'

Adamsberg smiled. 'There are four beds. There are now five of us.'

'One man too many.'

'Quite.'

'You're making yourself scarce', said Soliman,

'but it's a ploy. As soon as the trapper's turned his back, you'll move back into his spot. I know what you're up to. Can't fool me.'

Adamsberg said nothing.

'And I'm wondering if that's altogether straight,' Soliman pursued with difficulty, looking up at the ceiling. 'I'm wondering if it's altogether regular.'

'Regular with respect to what, Sol?'

Soliman hesitated.

'With respect to the rules,' he said.

'I thought you didn't give a tinker's fart for rules.'

'True enough,' Soliman said, getting worried.

'So?'

'Even so. You're going behind the trapper's back.'

'He's facing me front-on, Sol. And he's not a new-born babe.'

Soliman shook his head discontentedly.

'You're diverting the current', he said, 'you're re-directing the river, you're taking all the water for yourself and you're jumping into the trapper's bed. That's theft.'

'It's the absolute opposite, Soliman. All Camille's lovers – because we are talking about Camille, aren't we? – draw water from my river, and all my lovers take water from Camille's. At the source of the water there's only her, and me. Downstream there can be quite a crowd. On account of which the head-waters are much less muddy than lower down the stream.'

'Really?' Soliman said, somewhat bewildered.

'I've simplified it somewhat,' said Adamsberg.

'So right now', said Soliman hesitantly, 'you're paddling back upstream?'

Adamsberg nodded.

'Do you mean to say', Soliman went on, 'that if I'd made it over those last bloody fifty metres, if I'd been able to touch her, I'd have ended up at the fag end of your loony drainage system?'

'Something like that,' said Adamsberg.

'Does Camille know that or are you making it up for yourself?'

'She knows.'

'What about the trapper? Does he know?'

'He's wondering.'

'But Watchee's expecting you this evening. He's been bored out of his mind all day with his foot up on the bowl. He's waiting for you. Actually, he gave me an order to bring you back.'

'That's different, then,' said Adamsberg. 'How did you get here?'

'On the moped. Just hang onto me with your left arm.'

Adamsberg rolled up the papers and stuck them in an inside pocket.

'Are you bringing all that stuff with you?' Soliman asked.

'Sometimes I absorb ideas through my skin. I prefer to have them close to me.'

'Do you really hope to make any headway?'

Adamsberg winced as he put on the jacket weighed down with its load of documents.

'Have you got an idea?'

'Only subliminally.'

'Meaning?'

'Meaning that I can't see it. It's hovering on the edge of my field of vision.'

'That's not very practical.'

'No.'

Soliman was telling his third African story of the evening to a tensely silent audience. His floods of words served to submerge the pregnant glances darting about between Camille and Adamsberg, between Adamsberg and Johnstone, between Johnstone and Camille. Adamsberg, unsteadily so to speak, occasionally raised his eyes to look at the trapper. He's giving in, Soliman thought, he's giving in. He's going to walk away from his river. When Johnstone looked back at him, somewhat aggressively, the *commissaire* put his nose in his dinner plate, as if he were mindlessly fascinated by the decorative pattern on the china. Soliman went on with his story, a mightily muddled affair involving a vindictive spider and a terrified bird, a muddle Soliman wasn't quite sure he knew how to untangle.

'When the marsh god saw the brood on the ground', he pursued, 'he was seized with such anger that he went to see the son of Mombo the spider. "Son of Mombo", he said, "it was thee who cut the branches in the trees with thy disgusting mandibles. Henceforth thou shalt never again cut wood with thy mouth, but instead spin thread with your backside. And with that thread, day after day, thou shalt tie the branches back to the trees and leave birds to hatch their eggs in their nests." "Like hell I will," said the spider, son of Mombo . . .'

'For God's sake,' Johnstone interrupted. 'Don't understand.'

'You're not supposed to,' Camille said.

By half past midnight only Adamsberg was left alone with Soliman. He turned down the boy's offer to take him back to the hotel. The one-way trip on the moped had been quite an ordeal for his arm.

'Don't worry,' he said. 'I'll walk back.'

'It's eight kilometres.'

'I need a good walk. I'll take a short cut across the fields.'

Adamsberg's eyes were so distant and lost that Soliman did not insist. The *commissaire* sometimes wandered off into a world of his own, and at such times no-one really felt like keeping him company.

Adamsberg turned off the road to get to the narrow path that had a crop of sprouting maize on one side, and on the other flax. The night was rather dark and windy: cloud cover had come in from the west earlier on that evening. He proceeded slowly, with his right arm held tight in its sling and his head down, following the wavy white line made by the pebbles that marked out the path. He came down to the flatland and took his bearings from the steeple at Montdidier which loomed black in the far distance. He could barely understand what had struck him so forcibly this evening. The river story must have muddied his vision and twisted his mind. But all the same, he *had* seen it. The hazy idea that had been quivering on the edge of his eye earlier on was beginning to acquire shape and consistency. An unacceptable and frightening consistency. But he had seen with his eyes. And all the things that creaked like ill-fitted hinges in the story of the man and the big bad wolf were eased by the hypothesis. The absurd murder of Suzanne Rosselin, the unwavering itinerary, Crassus the Bald, Massart's fingernails, the missing cross, all these clues fitted back into the picture. The hypothesis smoothed off all the awkward corners and left a single, smooth, obvious and well-lit path ahead. And Adamsberg could now see the whole of that path from its beginning to its end, with its diabolical ingenuity, its anguish and cruelty, and its spark of genius.

He stopped walking and sat for a long while with his back propped against a tree-trunk as he sounded out his thoughts. A quarter of an hour later he got up slowly and, turning back on himself, made for the *gendarmerie* at Châteaurouge.

Halfway along, at the head of the path between the maize and the flax, he drew up short. Five or six metres away from him a broad-shouldered, hunched and hulking black shadow barred his way. It was too dark for Adamsberg to be able to make out the face. But he knew instantly that what was standing in front of him was the werewolf. The itinerant killer, the escape artist, the man who had been evading him for two weeks now, had at last come into the open for the bloody duel. Not one of his previous targets had survived. But none of them had been armed. Adamsberg stepped back a few yards, measuring the impressive bulk of his adversary, who came slowly forward, silently, with a sailor's gait. *Bright as a flaming brand, they are, my lad. You can see a wolf's eye a mile off in the dark.* With his left hand Adamsberg got his pistol out of its holster. From the weight of it he could tell that it wasn't loaded.

The man rushed at him and knocked him off his feet with a single heavy body blow. Adamsberg was flat on his back on the ground with the man pinning him down, pressing his knees hard on both his shoulders. He winced from the pain, but tried to push the ton weight off him all the same, with his left arm. To no avail. He gave up the struggle and sought out his adversary's eyes in the dark.

'The man I was looking for,' he said under his breath. 'Stuart Donald Padwell.'

'Shut your trap,' Johnstone said.

'Get off me, Padwell, I've already alerted the *flics*.'

'Not true,' Johnstone replied.

The Canadian reached inside his jerkin and Adamsberg saw what he had got out when it he brought it right up to his face. An immense white jawbone.

'The skull of an Arctic wolf,' Johnstone said with a smirk. 'Won't die without knowing the solution.'

There was a loud bang. Johnstone started and turned, without releasing Adamsberg. Soliman was on him in a flash, pressing the barrel of the rifle into his ribs.

'Don't make a move, trapper!' he yelled, 'or I'll put lead inside you! Lie down! Lie down! Lie down and roll over on your back!'

Johnstone did not lie down. He got to his feet, slowly, with his hands up, and stood in a posture that was not at all submissive. Soliman kept him at gunpoint and made him retreat towards the cornfield. Soliman's long slim body looked pathetically dainty in the dark of the night. With or without a gun the lad wouldn't be able to hold out for long. Adamsberg cast around with his good hand, found a large piece of rock and aimed at the wolf-man's head. Johnstone collapsed. He had taken the stone on his temple. Adamsberg pulled himself off the ground and went over to examine the man.

'That's fine,' he said with relief. 'Give me something to tie him up with. He's not going to stay like that for long.'

'I don't have anything to tie him up,' Soliman said.

'Take off your clothes.'

Soliman obeyed, and Adamsberg undid his holster straps and took off his shirt to use as rope.

'Keep your T-shirt on,' said Adamsberg. 'Give me your jeans.'

In his underpants, Soliman made a good job of securing the arms and legs of the Canadian, who was now groaning as he lay on the ground.

'He's bleeding.'

'He'll recover, Sol. Just look at this, Sol. Look at the beast.'

Holding it carefully by the occipital cavity, Adamsberg showed Soliman the skull of the great white Arctic wolf. In the fitful moonlight Soliman brought his hand up to touch and ran his finger along the row of fangs.

'He's filed the tips,' he said. 'They're as sharp as bayonets.'

'Have you got your mobile with you?'

Soliman felt around in his trousers and took out his phone. Adamsberg called the Châteaurouge *gendarmerie*.

'They're on their way,' he reported, sitting down beside the body of the Canadian. He rested his head on his knees and concentrated on slowing down his breathing.

'How did you know where I was?' he asked.

'After you'd gone I went to bed. Johnstone stole past me and out of the lorry with his clothes under his arms and dressed outside. I lifted the canvas on the side and through the slats I saw him walking off the same way you'd gone. I reckoned he was off to find you to have a proper row over Camille, and I told myself that wasn't any of my business. Right? But Watchee sat bolt upright in bed and said: "Go after him, Sol." He reached under his bed, got the rifle, and shoved it in my hand.'

'Watchee watches over us,' Adamsberg said.

'He surely does. Then I saw the trapper blocking your road and I reckoned you were going to have a right old bust-up. Then it got really rough and I heard you say "Hallo Padwell" or something. Which is when I twigged this wasn't a row over Camille.'

Adamsberg smiled.

'You were going to get yourself murdered.'

Adamsberg frowned. 'We were on the next bus behind him, right from the start. We made up some of the time, but we were still a few hours short of catching up.'

'I thought Padwell was dead.'

'This is his son. Stuart.'

'You mean the son's carrying out his father's wishes?' Soliman said, looking at Johnstone's supine body.

'When Padwell killed Simon Hellouin, his kid was ten years old. Stuart saw the murder happen, and that screwed him up for life. Especially as his mother ran away straight after with Hellouin's brother. For eighteen years, all through his prison sentence, Padwell must have filled his son's head with the idea of taking revenge and eliminating all the men who'd taken the boy's mother away and kept her out of reach.'

'What about the other two guys, Sernot and Deguy?'

'They have to have had affairs with the mother. There's no other explanation.'

'And Suzanne?' asked Soliman in a ghostly voice. 'What's she got to do with the whole story? Did she know all about the trapper?'

'Suzanne didn't know a thing.'

'Did she see him slaughtering the sheep with his bloody wolf's head?'

'She saw nothing, I tell you. He didn't kill her because she spoke out of turn about a werewolf. He killed her because she *had not* said anything about a werewolf and never would. But once she was dead he could have her say anything he wanted, she wouldn't be around to deny it. That's what Suzanne could do for him. Being unable to say she never said it.'

Soliman's voice was all aquiver as he burst out: 'But for heaven's sake, what was the purpose?'

'To get the wolf story going. That's the only reason, Soliman. He wanted to avoid the mistake of starting the rumour himself.'

The young man sighed in the dark. 'I don't get this wolf business. Not one bit.'

'He had to get people believing there was a madman committing random murders out there, and he needed a scapegoat. He certainly managed to get people obsessed with Massart the bloodthirsty werewolf. He had all it took – skills, knowledge, all the tools of the trade. He also had an alibi for being in the Mercantour.'

'What about Massart?'

'Massart's dead. Has been since the beginning of the whole story. Padwell probably buried him somewhere on Mont Vence. Here come the *flics*, Sol.'

With one of them without a shirt and the other in his underpants, Adamsberg and Sol went to meet the *gendarmes*. Fromentin had called in reinforcements from Montdidier as well, since ten men didn't seem too many for getting the big bad wolf-man under control.

'There you are,' Adamsberg said, pointing to Johnstone on the ground. 'Call a doctor in. I wounded him in the head.'

'Who is this?' asked Fromentin, shining his torchlight into the Canadian's face.

'Stuart Donald Padwell, son of John Padwell. He's known here as *Laurence* Donald Johnstone. And this, Fromentin, is the murder weapon.'

'Fuck,' he said. 'So it wasn't a wolf.'

'Just a lupine mandible. You'll find the paws and claws somewhere in the panniers on his motorbike.'

The *adjudant*, fascinated, shone his torch on the skullbone.

'It's an Arctic wolf,' Adamsberg said. 'He set the whole thing up before coming over.'

'I see,' said Fromentin with a nod. 'Arctic wolves are the biggest wolves of all, by a long chalk.'

Adamsberg looked at him, amazed.

'I like animals,' Fromentin explained, abashed. 'So I read up on them when I can.'

He shone his beam onto Adamsberg's arm.

368

'You're bleeding, sir,' he said.

'Yes,' Adamsberg said. 'He reopened the wound when he jumped on me.'

'Whatever made him come out in the open?'

'It was the evening. I gave him a look.'

'And then?'

'I saw John Padwell's features on his face. He knew that I had not let his father's case out of my mind, and he realised I was on the point of coming up with the right answer.'

Adamsberg watched Johnstone being walked to the car by two *gendarme*s. Another *flic* gave him back his shirt and holster-strap, and returned Soliman's trousers to their owner.

'Did you spend the evening with him?' Fromentin asked with a frown as he fell in step behind his *gendarme*s.

'He was never absent,' Adamsberg said as he followed on in turn. 'He created the rumour about a wolf-man, just as he got that threesome to track him down, just in order to keep the story alive. He got daily reports on the progress of the pursuit. We weren't on his tail. He was wagging us.'

Johnstone was taken to the hospital in Montdidier while Fromentin himself drove Adamsberg and Soliman back to the lorry.

'If the Canadian's in a fit state, we'll do the interview tomorrow afternoon at three. Tell the prosecution service, and at the first opportunity tell Montvailland at Villard-de-Lans, Hermel at Bourg-en-Bresse and Aimont at Belcourt. I'll call Brévent myself at Puygiron and get them to spade up the ground around Massart's shack.'

Fromentin made no comment, signalled to one of his men to have Johnstone's motorbike taken in, and drove off.

'Bloody hell!' Soliman suddenly exclaimed as he watched the *gendarme*'s estate car disappearing down the road. 'Good heavens! What about the hair? And the fingernails? How do you account for that?'

'The fingernail issue is now settled.'

'But they were Massart's fingernails! How can you make that fit?'

'They *were* Massart's fingernails', Adamsberg repeated as he paced up and down beside the road, 'and they had been cut with a nail-clipper. Now, Brévent did not find a single piece of fingernail in the bathroom at Massart's place on Mont Vence. Only when Hermel had the bright idea of combing the bedroom did any nail fragments turn up. But they were fragments that had been bitten off, Soliman. That's what really clashed. On the one hand you had a guy who uses clippers, and on the other a guy who bites his nails in bed. Sol, it's always one or the other, not both. With that worked out, I reckoned we'd been really lucky boys to unearth the hotel he was using and to get that hair and those two bits of fingernail. Really lucky, yes indeed. The map made me doubt whether Massart was a random killer. The fingernails made me doubt whether Massart existed.'

'Bloody hell,' Soliman said. 'Explain the finger-nails!'

'Johnstone cut the nails on Massart's corpse, Soliman.'

Soliman winced in disgust.

'It never occurred to him that Massart kept his nails short by biting them. He just couldn't imagine anything like that. He was too clean, too fastidious. That was his first mistake.'

'Did he make any other mistakes?' asked Soliman, his eyes glued to Adamsberg's lips.

'A few. The candle thing, and arranging the murders at the foot of a cross. I don't know if Johnstone found out about Massart's super-stitiousness for himself or if Camille gave him the information unwittingly. He enjoyed making use of it precisely because it seemed to get you interested. But when he had the *flics* breathing down his neck at Belcourt, he did his deed a long way from a Calvary or a cross. Truly superstitious people don't do that. They pursue and persist and get all the more frantic if the challenge is serious. The last thing an obsessive would do in the face of difficulty would be to drop the obsession as if it didn't really matter. Our man murdered Hellouin in an open field, and that told me that the placing of the previous murders beneath religious symbols was just stuff and nonsense, like the candles. Which brought me back to the same thought: that Massart was not Massart. You see, Sol, I was ready for the Padwell line. I was ready and waiting for it.'

371

'But', said Soliman with a trace of anxiety, 'if it hadn't been for the son's physical resemblance to the father, you'd never have put your finger on Lawrence. Not in a million years.'

'Yes I would. It would have taken a bit longer, that's all.'

'How come?'

'If we'd kept on investigating to the bitter end, the link between the Sernot, Deguy and Hellouin cases would eventually have shown up: their common denominator is Ariane Germant. That would have led us back to the Padwell case. Padwell is dead, but he has a son, a son who was present at the original murder. I'd have followed that lead, I'd have got a photograph of the son. And it would have been a photograph of Lawrence Donald Johnstone.'

'And what if you hadn't kept on to the bitter end?'

'I would have.'

'And what if you hadn't followed the lead on the son?'

'But I would have followed it, Sol.'

'But if you hadn't?'

'Well, if I hadn't, the whole thing would have taken even longer. Who knows about wolves? Johnstone does. Who was the first person to mention a werewolf? Johnstone was. Who went to look for Massart? Johnstone did. Who put about the idea that Massart had murdered Suzanne? Johnstone once again. We'd have got him in the end, Sol.'

'And maybe you wouldn't.'

'Maybe, maybe. But there were the wolf hairs, Sol. We wondered why there weren't any – and hey presto, some hairs turn up. Who was in the know? Only the five of us, and the police.'

'I'm going to see Watchee,' said Soliman. 'He has to be told.'

'No,' said Adamsberg, holding the young man back by the arm. 'You'll wake Camille.'

'So what?'

'I don't know how to tell her. Be kind.'

Soliman stopped in his tracks. 'Fuck,' he said.

'Yes,' said Adamsberg.

CHAPTER 35

Adamsberg sat on the side of the bed waiting for Camille to wake up. As soon as she was dressed he took her for a country walk and broke the news to her very, very gently. Camille sat on her haunches in the grass. She was utterly devastated. She sat gripping her boots and staring at the ground while Adamsberg held her shoulder, waiting for the shock to subside. He spoke softly but without interruption so as not to leave Camille all alone in silence with such a sinister revelation.

'I don't understand,' she said, barely audibly. 'I saw nothing, suspected nothing. There was nothing disturbing about him at all.'

'No,' said Adamsberg. 'He was a man in two parts. There was the quiet man, and then there was the agonised child. *Laurence*, and then Stuart. You only saw one of the pair. You shouldn't be sorry about having loved him.'

'He's a murderer.'

'He's a child. He was messed-up.'

'He killed Suzanne.'

'He's a child,' Adamsberg said once again, firmly. 'He wasn't given the remotest chance of having a

374

normal life. That's the truth of it. Think of it that way.'

Watchee learned with stupefaction from the mouth of Soliman that there remained not a chance that the killer would turn out to be a werewolf. That there would be no point at all in slitting Johnstone open from the neck to the crotch, and that harmless Massart had been dead for sixteen days. The old man found it mighty hard to swallow these squalid truths, but paradoxically he seemed to be relieved by knowing the real circumstances of the death of Suzanne, eliminated like a mere pawn in a game of chess. He had been eaten by remorse for not having been at hand when Suzanne was attacked by the wolf. But Suzanne had not been the surprise victim of an unforeseeable act of violence. She had been lured into a trap that all Watchee's vigilance could not have headed off. Johnstone had had the foresight to get Watchee out of the way before calling Suzanne. Neither he nor anyone else would have made any difference. Watchee could breathe easily again.

'You, young fella', he said to Adamsberg, 'you owe your life to me.'

'I should repay you somehow,' Adamsberg said.

'You already have.'

'You mean the wine?'

'Suzanne's murderer. But take care of yourself, young fella. He nearly got you, and so did that red-haired lass.'

Adamsberg said nothing.

'You're too much of a dreamer, young fella',
Watchee went on, 'and you don't look out enough.
Not a good idea, in your line of work. But you
have to admit I ain't called Watchee for nothing.
Fair legs, a broad bottom, and a good eye.'

'What did you see, Watchee?'

'I saw the Canadian going out after you, and I
saw he meant no good. I'm not blind. I thought
it was all about the young lady. And I saw he meant
to have your guts for garters on her account. I saw
it plain as a pikestaff.'

'What made it so clear to you?'

'The way he walked.'

'Where did you get the bullets?'

'I went through your things. Ain't that how you
got them off me in the first place?'

Adamsberg went into the *gendarmerie* at three
o'clock. Fromentin, Hermel, Montvailland, Aimont
and four other *gendarmes* were standing around
Johnstone, who was sitting on the edge of his chair,
in handcuffs, and staring at them with calm confidence. The Canadian kept his eye on Adamsberg
as the *commissaire* shook hands all round.

'Brévent's just called, old chap,' said Hermel,
taking Adamsberg's left hand. 'They've just dug
up Massart, eight metres downhill from his hut.
He was buried with his mastiff, his money and all
his mountaineering gear. His fingernails are cut
right down.'

Adamsberg looked up at Johnstone, who was
still staring at him with a query in his eyes.

'Camille?' Johnstone asked.

'She's not sorry for what she did,' Adamsberg answered, not knowing whether he was telling the truth.

Something seemed to go slack in Johnstone's body.

'There's something only you know,' Adamsberg said as he brought a chair up to sit down next to the killer. 'Did you have any more men to kill, or was Hellouin the last on the list?'

'He's the last,' Johnstone said with a hint of a smile. 'Got the lot.'

Adamsberg nodded and realised that Johnstone would never lose his composure ever again.

Johnstone withstood twenty hours of police questioning without trying to deny anything at all. He was calm, detached, and, in his own way, co-operative. He asked for a clean chair because he found the one he had been given filthy. As was the whole *gendarmerie*.

He replied with truncated and elliptical expressions, but his answers were nonetheless quite precise. He never thought to volunteer help and never expressed any opinions; less out of ill will than out of inherent unforthcomingness, he just waited for questions to be asked. As a result the *flics* took two full days to drag the whole story out of him, bit by bit. Camille, Soliman and Watchee, in their capacity as leading witnesses, were interviewed in the course of the Tuesday.

At the end of the third day Hermel volunteered

to dictate a short draft charge sheet in Adamsberg's place. The *commissaire* did not have the heart for that kind of logical summing up so he accepted the offer with gratitude and went to lean against the office wall. Hermel took a quick look at his notes and those of his colleagues, laid them all out on the table, and switched on the tape recorder.

'What date is it, old chap?' he asked.

'Wednesday, 8 July.'

'Good. We'll get it in the can in a trice and finish it off properly tomorrow. "Date of Wednesday, 8 July, time of 23.45, location Châteaurouge *gendarmerie*, department of Haute-Marne. Follows a report of the questioning of a male person, name of Stuart Donald Padwell, age thirty-five, son of a John Neil Padwell, US national, and of Ariane Germant, French national, accused of a number of murders with malice aforethought. The interviews were conducted on 6, 7 and 8 July by *Commissaire* Jean-Baptiste Adamsberg with the assistance of *Adjudant-chef* Lionel Fromentin, in the presence of *Commissaire* Jacques Hermel and *Capitaine* Maurice Montvailland. John N. Padwell, father of the accused, served a sentence at the corrections facility at Austin, TX, from 19 . . ." – you can fill in the dates for me, old chap – "for the first-degree murder of his wife's lover, Simon Hellouin, a crime committed in the presence of his son, then aged ten."'

Hermel paused the recorder and caught Adamsberg's eye with a nod of his head.

'Can you imagine that, old chap? In front of the boy. Where did he go afterwards?'

'He stayed with his mother until the trial.'

'But after that? When she took off?'

'He was in a home, a sort of state orphanage.'

'Iron discipline?'

'No, it seems to have been a reasonable place, according to Lanson. But if the child ever had a chance of not going psychotic, the father knocked it right on the head.'

'By letter?'

'Yes. He wrote to the boy five or six times in the first year, then it got more intense. A letter a month, then one a week from when the boy was thirteen up to his nineteenth year.'

Hermel drummed his fingers on the table.

'What about the mother?'

'Never sent news. Never saw her son again. She died in France when the boy was twenty-one.'

Hermel shook his head with a pained expression on his face. 'That's a rotten deal if ever there was, old chap.'

He put out his hand and set the tape turning again.

'"Over a period of almost ten years John Neil Padwell prepared his son by means of numerous letters for the sacred task which he intended him to carry out – those are the accused's own words. With this in mind, at the age of twenty-one Stuart changed his identity, with the help of a former convict who had befriended his father, and moved to Canada" – you can fill in the dates, old chap. "While serving his sentence and until the decease of his wife, John Padwell employed a private detective" – I haven't got the name here – "to track down his wife, who had fled to France when the trial was over. That is how father and son kept themselves informed about the love life of Ariane Padwell née Germant, and learned the identities of the two lovers who took the place of Simon and Paul Hellouin, and in turn became guilty of the double crime" – I'm quoting the accused again – "of laying their hands on the wife and of keeping the mother away from her child. There was never any question of killing the woman, since, in the eyes of the father and of the accused, the four men alone were responsible for the shipwreck of the family" – another textual quotation. "With Simon Hellouin dealt with already, Stuart was destined to complete the work of salvation" – the accused's words – "by eliminating Paul Hellouin, with whom Ariane Germant had first fled to France," – you fill in the date, old chap – "and in addition Jacques-Jean Sernot and Fernand Deguy, whom she met when she settled in Grenoble some years later, in 19 . . ." – fill in the blanks, will you. "John Padwell maintained very discreet contact with his son since his change of identity, but he urged him to take all the time he needed to work out a stratagem to keep himself in the clear, since what he wanted above all was for Stuart not to have to serve time as he had. Stuart Padwell, aka Lawrence Donald Johnstone, worked out several successive plans of action in turn, but found none of them entirely satisfactory" – the accused's words again. "In thirteen years working as a warden in the Canadian wilderness areas" – you tell me what places to put down, old chap, I'm a zero at Canadian geography – "the accused became a respected naturalist specialising in caribou."'

'In grizzly bears,' Adamsberg corrected.

'"Correction: in grizzlies. News of the return of wolves to the French Alps reached Canadian naturalists shortly after the sudden death of John Padwell. Stuart saw the conjunction as a sign and also as an opportunity to carry out his task at long last" – that's how he put it himself – "and he spent a year putting all the pieces in place. He got himself seconded to the Mercantour National Park, which was not at all difficult given his own standing in the field. He stopped over in Paris in December" – the dates, old chap, do remember to put in the dates – "to complete his research on French traditions regarding werewolves, and he also met Camille Forestier. He encouraged the young lady to come with him both because he had grown fond of her" – his words – "and because a single man attracts comments and curiosity in small villages" – the accused again. "Once he got to Valberg in the Alpes-Maritimes, where he took up temporary residence, he started looking for a patsy. He identified three possible subjects and" – I quote – "picked Auguste

Massart as the best of the bunch. Massart resided at Saint-Victor-du-Mont in the Alpes-Maritimes, and the accused moved there in . . ." sometime around January, check the date. "He lived in Saint-Victor for six months, taking all necessary time to research Massart and to establish his own reputation as well as to complete his specialist mission. He launched the operation on Tuesday, 16 June by savaging several sheep during the night, at a sheep farm at Ventebrune, then over the following nights" – put in the dates, Adamsberg – "committing further massacres at Pierrefort and Saint-Victor. He used the skull of an Arctic wolf with filed teeth. On Saturday, 20 June he fomented the rumour of a werewolf at large, whom he identified as Auguste Massart, on the alleged authority of Suzanne Rosselin, a sheep breeder at Saint-Victor-du-Mont. On the night of Saturday to Sunday 21 June, he gave his partner Camille Forestier a sleeping draught, left his residence and murdered Auguste Massart, whom he buried with his dog and his climbing gear, then killed Suzanne Rosselin. He left a road map with an itinerary marked on it at Massart's house, so as to make an obvious apparent link between Massart and the slaughtered animals. After successive attacks on sheep farms at Guillos and . . ." What's the other place called, old chap?'

'La Castille.'

'". . . La Castille, he went to see *Adjudant-chef* Brévent, and also set in pursuit of the alleged wolf-man a group consisting of Soliman Diawara, ward of Suzanne Rosselin, and Philibert Fougeray, known as Watchee, a shepherd resident at Saint-Victor. The accused's partner, Camille Forestier, being also part of the group. The accused then murdered in succession Jean Sernot, at Sautrey, department of Isère, on the night of 24 to 25 June, and Fernand Deguy, at Bourg-en-Bresse, department of Ain, on the night of 27 to 28 June. He lured the police investigating the case to a hotel at Combes, where he placed two fingernail clippings and a hair coming from the body of the deceased . . . Massart. Subsequently he murdered Paul Hellouin, at Belcourt, department of Haute-Marne, on the night of 2 to 3 July, while also savaging a number of sheep at farms lying on his route at . . ." – you'll provide the list, old chap, won't you? I get them all in a muddle, I do – "with the aim of substantiating the belief that a were-wolf was responsible. An identical modus operandi was employed for all the murders. The accused used his motorbike to get to the scene of the crime, while his work in the Mercantour National Park provided him with an alibi – an area so vast and remote that his presence there could never be checked. Nonetheless he did make a few short trips to the area for safety's sake" – *dixit* the accused – "and on his final visit obtained the three strands of wolf coat which were found on the body of Paul Hellouin. In the night of Sunday to Monday, 5 to 6 July, at Châteaurouge, department of

Haute-Marne, with the investigation led by *Commissaire* Adamsberg on the Padwell affair hanging over him, he attacked the *commissaire* at the place known as Camp du Tondu. The attack was repulsed thanks to action taken by Soliman Diawara. *Commissaire* Adamsberg admits having thrown a projectile at Stuart D. Padwell, aiming at his head, and causing an injury which Dr Vian certified as minor at Montdidier Hospital on Monday, 6 July at 01.50 hours. Accused arrested by *Adjudant-chef* Lionel Fromentin the same day at 01.10 hours."'

Hermel switched off the tape recorder.

'Did I forget anything?'

'Crassus the Bald and Augustus.'

'Who are they?'

'Two wolves. Johnstone must have disposed of the first one as soon as he got to the Mercantour. Unless Crassus just disappeared of his own accord, and that's not impossible. It was the largest wolf in the pack. Augustus was an old wolf he took under his wing. When he was on his campaign he wasn't there to give Augustus his food, so the old wolf died. Johnstone was very sad about that.'

'He murdered five people and cried for a wolf?'

'It was his wolf.'

CHAPTER 36

It was after one in the morning when Adamsberg got back to the lorry. Camille was squatting on her bed reading her *A to Z of Tools for Trade and Craft* by the light of a torch. Adamsberg sat down next to her and looked at the page displaying drills and sanders.

'What do you see in all of that?' he asked.

'Comfort.'

'Is it that bad?'

'Everything is haphazard, confused and precarious, outside the *A to Z*.'

'Are you sure of that?'

Camille shrugged her shoulders and smiled fleetingly.

'Johnstone is being transferred to Paris tomorrow,' Adamsberg said. 'I'll be taking him up.'

'How is he?'

'As ever. At peace. He finds that the *gendarmes* smell of sweat.'

'Is he right?'

'Of course he's right.'

'I'll write to him. When I'm back in the Alps.'

'Are you going back to Saint-Victor?'

'I'm driving them back to Les Écarts. And I'm going home too.'

'Yes.'

'I'm the driver.'

'Yes, of course.'

'They can't drive.'

'Yes. Be careful on that road.'

'Yes.'

'Do be careful.'

'I will be.'

Adamsberg put his good arm around Camille's shoulder and looked at her by the light of the torch.

'Will you come back?' he asked.

'I'll stay down there for a few days.'

'And then leave?'

'Yes. I'll miss them.'

'Will you come back?'

'Where to?'

'Well, I don't know. Paris?'

'I don't know.'

'Oh sod that, Camille, stop talking like I do. We'll never get anywhere if you speak like me.'

'Good,' Camille said. 'That's fine by me. Things are fine as they are.'

'But tomorrow or the day after they won't be the same. No more lay-by, no more lorry, no more just for the time being, no more just making do for now. No more riverbanks, either.'

'I'll make some more of those.'

'Riverbanks?'

'Yes.'

'What with?'

'With the *A to Z of Tools for Trade and Craft.* You can make anything with an *A to Z.*'

'If you say so. What will you do with a spare riverbank?'

'Go and see if you're around.'

'I'll be around.'

'Maybe,' Camille said.

Next morning Camille slid into position behind the steering wheel, switched on the engine, and reversed the lorry into a three-point turn amid the clatter and rattle of old iron. Watchee, as straight-backed as ever though supporting himself on his crook, Soliman and Adamsberg stood in line to one side, solemnly watching the lorry perform this manoeuvre. Camille went forward onto the road, then reversed again with the opposite lock, and then eased the lorry forward into position with its nose to the east on the opposite side of the road, and switched off.

Adamsberg slowly crossed the road, climbed up to the cab, kissed Camille and stroked her hair, and then returned to the field where the other two and Woof stood waiting. He shook Watchee's hand.

'You look after yourself, young fella,' Watchee said. 'I won't be there to watch out for you.'

'Not everybody needs to have you under their feet,' said Soliman.

Soliman glanced at Camille then shook Adamsberg by the hand.

'Separation,' he said. 'The action or an act of withdrawing oneself or leaving the company of others.'

He went over to the lorry, clambered into the cab through the nearside door, hauled Watchee up after him into his seat, and pulled the door shut. Adamsberg raised his hand, and off the livestock transporter rumbled in a clatter of wood and steel. He watched it go, and then halt eighty metres down the road. Soliman fell out of the cab and came running back towards him.

'The bowl, sod it.'

He went straight past Adamsberg and onto the lorry's parking spot to collect the bowl that had got lost in the grass flattened by the vehicle and trampled by its crew. He walked back with long strides, quite out of breath. When he got as far as Adamsberg he held out his hand once more.

'Fate,' he said. 'A person's appointed lot. A fortuitous encounter. Circumstances which cause a person or thing, by chance or otherwise, to cross your path.'

He smiled and went back to the lorry, graciously swinging the blue plastic bowl up and down. The lorry started up and disappeared around the bend in the road.

Adamsberg got out his jotter and noted down Soliman's last definition before he forgot it.